Louis Figuier, Abby Langdon Alger

Joys Beyond the Threshold

A Sequel to The To-morrow of Death

Louis Figuier, Abby Langdon Alger

Joys Beyond the Threshold
A Sequel to The To-morrow of Death

ISBN/EAN: 9783337404727

Printed in Europe, USA, Canada, Australia, Japan

Cover: Foto ©Andreas Hilbeck / pixelio.de

More available books at **www.hansebooks.com**

Joys Beyond the Threshold:

A SEQUEL TO

𝔗𝔥𝔢 𝔗𝔬-𝔪𝔬𝔯𝔯𝔬𝔴 𝔬𝔣 𝔇𝔢𝔞𝔱𝔥.

BY

LOUIS FIGUIER.

TRANSLATED BY

ABBY LANGDON ALGER.

BOSTON:
ROBERTS BROTHERS.
1893.

TABLE OF CONTENTS.

	PAGE
INTRODUCTION	1

CHAPTER I.

Transformations of Man after Death. — Solar Divinities 5

CHAPTER II.

Sad Conditions of Earthly Humanity 25

CHAPTER III.

Let us not fear Death 44

CHAPTER IV.

Inhabitants of the Ethereal Medium : their Attributes. — Vast Development of their Intellect. — New Senses and New Faculties. — Celestial Hierarchies. — Angels in Christian Dogma. — Travels of the Soul through the Universe 60

CHAPTER V.

The Intelligence of Superhuman Beings belonging to the Highest Celestial Hierarchies, reveals to them the Essence and Abode of the Supreme God of the Universe 81

CHAPTER VI.

Joys beyond the Threshold. — We shall meet in Heaven . . . 89

CHAPTER VII.

Joys beyond the Threshold (*continued*). — Studies and Tasks inter-
rupted on Earth will be continued in the Abode of the Blest.
— Vocations missed here will find Full Scope after Death. —
Schemes cut short will be carried out in Higher Worlds . . 108

PAGE

CHAPTER VIII.

The Idea of Justice and Truth innate in us, will be realized in our
Second Life 127

CHAPTER IX.

Intercourse of Arisen Souls with the Great Men of History. —
Dialogues with the Dead 130

CHAPTER X.

Comparison of our System with that of the Religions actually
existing on the Earth: Buddhism, Brahminism, Christianity,
Islamism, Judaism 210

CHAPTER XI.

Scientific Proofs in Support of the Theories set forth in this Book 292

CHAPTER XII.

Summary and Conclusions 314

JOYS BEYOND THE THRESHOLD.

INTRODUCTION.

SOME twenty years ago I published "The To-morrow of Death; or, The Future Life according to Science," — a work which made a great impression upon the philosophic world, if I may judge by the many editions which have been published,[1] by the translations which have appeared in English, German, Italian, Spanish, Portuguese, Russian, and Dutch, and by similar publications which it called forth from writers in various countries. Ever since the appearance of this work, philosophers of all enlightened nations have seriously considered the idea developed in it; that is to say, the principle of the permanence of the human soul after death, and its reincarnation in a chain of new beings, whose successive links are unrolled in the bosom of ethereal space.

Like every work which has made its mark in the history of literature or of morals, "The To-morrow of Death" has been greatly discussed. In France

---

[1] Ninth edition, 1889, 1 vol., 18mo, Hachette, publisher.

1

and Germany materialists and positivists accused
it of exalting the doctrine of the immortality of the
soul, of carrying spiritualism to its intensest degree,
of strangely enlarging the manner of conceiving of
divinity, and of recommending the practice of religious worship according to the rites peculiar to
each nation. It was criticised by L. Büchner, the
leader of German materialists. On the other hand,
religious writers assailed it, as attacking Catholic
dogmas ; they gave various refutations of it in their
reviews and journals, while one priest took up his
pen to rewrite my work from the Roman Catholic
standpoint.[1]

These contradictory opinions have, however,
moved me but little. Writers are far less sensitive to criticism than is thought. Time is the only
judge of mental productions ; and the true philosopher, indifferent to praise as to blame, pursues his
meditations, solely occupied in perfecting his work
by his own reflections.

But there are other testimonies which the writer
should heed. These are the private communications
which he receives from his readers. No one can
form any idea of the number of letters which I
have received from persons whose imagination was
touched, in various ways, by reading " The To-

---

[1] "The Life after Death ; or, The Future Life according to
Christianity, Science, and above all the Splendid Discoveries of
Modern Astronomy." By Abbé L. M. Pioger, of the diocese of
Paris. A work honored by a brief from the Pope.

morrow of Death." I might make up a volume
of this correspondence alone.

Of all the impressions thus conveyed to me, the
one which has struck me most forcibly is that my
work is eminently consoling, — that it lifts up and
comforts the hearts of people terrified by the fear
of death, by showing them in the resurrection of
the human being a blissful and rapid change from
mundane destinies, by giving them a hope of again
meeting beyond the tomb the loved ones whom they
have lost, and thus aiding them to await with courage the critical instant of the separation of soul
and body.

How many disconsolate mothers, how many de-
spairing sons, how many weeping parents, how
many wretched victims to the fatalities of life, how
many sick persons trembling at the phantom of approaching death, how many unfortunates a prey to
moral or physical pangs, have found a cure for their
agony, and serenity of mind, from reading the " To-
morrow of Death " ! If I am to believe some of my
correspondents, more than one hand already armed
for suicide has dropped on reading my book, peace
being restored to that desperate soul.

It is these considerations which lead me to give
to the public, under the title of " Joys beyond the
Threshold," the development of, and comment on
the consoling idea resulting from the system contained in " The To-morrow of Death." I desire to
give the practical sanction of this principle, that

the certainty of our new birth after our earthly
end is the best means of arming ourselves against
all weakness in the presence of death, and that the
help offered by science and philosophy to take that
tremendous step bravely is far superior to that presented by any of the existing religions.

CHAPTER I.

ALTHOUGH this new work is merely the development of a chapter in the "To-morrow of Death," we must sum up, before beginning, the system of the transmigration of souls and celestial resurrections set forth in that book.

Lonely wanderer on the plain or through the wood, have you ever noted, on the bark of trees, on herbaceous plants, or in furrows freshly drawn by the laborer's ploughshare, the grub of the oak or the chestnut, the cockchafer or the moth? If so, you saw a black hairy being, crawling along the bark of the tree, hidden beneath a tuft of grass, or clinging to a leafy stem. If your walk again led you, some days later, through the wood or the fields, you found that the grub had disappeared, or rather that it had been replaced by a new being. To the living, active, moving insect had succeeded an insensible, motionless, frozen body; a sort of corpse, a *caput mortuum*, enclosed on every side in

a tomb, a tissue of fibrous substance. This is the
larva, or *chrysalis.* "The worm is dead," you say.
No, it is not dead; it has undergone a natural
change; it has become a larva, or chrysalis; it has
changed its outward form, but it still lives.

Return once more to the same spot after a
certain space of time, and you will seek the larva
in vain. It has vanished; it has pierced its mem-
branous shell; and through the opening, still gaping,
we might have seen a being wholly new, absolutely
different from that which slept in its temporary
tomb, soar forth. It is a butterfly, with variegated
wings, which flies through space and feeds on the
sap of trees and the pollen of flowers. The counter-
feit corpse has become a charming inhabitant of the
air; it hails the light, and gluts itself with the per-
fume of plants. This is the final result of the
transformation of the worm into the larva, and of
the larva into the butterfly.

To our thinking, the human being undergoes a
natural change of a similar kind.

After all, what is man but a sort of grub? Like
the caterpillar in our woods, it is impossible for him
to lift himself to any height above the ground, without being compelled to fall back instantly. His eyes
have scarcely greater range than those of the
worm; and if we consider the immaterial world,
man is, like the insect, surrounded by mysteries
which his understanding cannot penetrate. His
pride, doubtless, leads him to believe in the omnipo-

tence of his intellect ; but go to the root of things, and you will recognize that man knows nothing about the first cause of the phenomena which surround him. He can, undoubtedly, calculate the effects and the laws of the physical actions which rule the universe ; but it is forbidden him to know the first reason of the phenomena taking place before his eyes. If he sees a stone fall, it is impossible, despite the genius which he grants to himself, for him to know why that stone falls. " It is," he says, " their *weight* which produces the fall of bodies ; and weight is caused by the mutual attraction of bodies one for another, — an attraction exerted in direct ratio to their masses, and in inverse ratio to the square of the distance. If the stone falls to the earth, it is because the stone is smaller than the earth, and because they are but a short distance apart from each other. If the earth revolves around the sun, it is because it is a million times smaller than the sun, and it is therefore attracted toward the central star."

This is why your daughter is dumb!

Do you not indeed see, dear reader, that what we call *attraction* is merely a word put in place of an explanation ? You say that bodies *attract each other ;* but this expression is not to be taken literally, for it is nothing but an expedient, an artifice of language, intended to mask our ignorance. When Newton likened the universal gravitation of the stars around the sun to weight, he did not claim to grasp the true cause of weight, — that is, the force which impels bodies one towards the other in proportion to their masses. He recommends us, on the contrary, to take the word *weight* or *gravitation* as an hypothesis only, permitting us to set forth phenomena more clearly, and to search out their laws; and he is careful to add that we must leave among the secrets of Nature the cause of what he called *attraction*.[1]

This is so true that in our day certain physicists explain the fall of bodies and universal gravitation by electricity. The body most powerfully electrified, they say, attracts that which is less so; and this in inverse ratio to the quantity of electricity which each contains. The solution of the phenomena is in no wise changed by this new hypothesis; and one hypothesis is as good as another, as far as ease of demonstration and study go.

Before Newton, Kepler, the founder of modern astronomy, had a name for the hypothetical cause of the revolution of the planets around the sun. It was *love* which made the larger stars revolve around

---

[1] "What I call attraction," says Newton in the preface to his "Principia," "may possibly be caused by some impulse or in some other way unknown to us. I merely use the word 'attraction' to designate the force by which bodies tend one towards the other, be the cause of that force what it may. For it is requisite that we should learn, from the phenomena of Nature, which bodies are mutually attracted one towards the other, and what are the laws and the properties of that attraction, before it is fitting for us to seek out the efficient cause of the attraction."

the smaller ones ; the earth, Mars, Venus, etc.,
around the sun, and the moon around the earth.

Thus we are left in the deepest obscurity when
we would pierce to the real essence of the most
important phenomena of the universe.

Besides weight, we are surrounded by natural
forces which give the external world power and
activity. These forces are heat, motion, mechanical
energy, electricity, magnetism, and light. Ask
any physicist what a force is, he will be compelled
to silence. In fact, we are absolutely ignorant
what forces are. We are perfectly familiar with
the laws which govern them, but we know nothing
of their origin and first cause.

Modern physics has discovered that forces may
be transformed one into the other, as heat, developed by the combustion of coal, by means of the
oxygen of the air, is changed in our steam-engines
to mechanical energy, that is to say, motion ; as
motion and mechanical energy, when they are
destroyed, are transformed into electricity ; and as
electricity, when it disappears, is converted into
light. And furthermore, taken inversely, light may
produce heat, heat give rise to electricity, and
electricity be changed to motion.

Every one knows that this beautiful discovery of
our century finds daily application in the theories of
physics, and that, in practice, it has given us electric
lighting and the transferrence, from long distances,
of mechanical energy by means of electricity.

But what do we learn from all this as to the nature of the force, either natural or transformed? It is impossible for us to venture upon any explanation here; and the wisest physicist of our academies knows no more about it than the humble worm of the fields.

What is thought? In what does it consist? Where does it reside? Has it a special organ? How do we explain the fact that it travels from one end of the world to the other with incalculable speed? No physiologist would be daring enough to answer these questions. The so-called nervous fluid, the vital fluid, electricity, have been invoked by bold theorists, who reaped nothing but derision. It is certain that the phenomena of thought — which is the cause of our actions, our activity, our will, our relations with the external world as well as with the moral world — defy all explanation, and that it is no more possible for man than for the insect to solve this insoluble mystery.

A seed is sowed in the earth, and by the mere influence of heat and moisture that miracle of organization known as a plant is formed. An egg is subjected to the simple action of heat, either natural or artificial, and a bird appears. Who can ever explain such amazing marvels? Thou hast imparted thy secret to none, O impenetrable Nature!

A child comes into the world: place your hand on its heart; it beats from the instant of its birth.

And it goes on for twenty years, for thirty years, for sixty years, for a hundred years, perhaps! That tireless organ throbs on, throughout that long space of time, without rest or repose, without a second's pause, under penalty of death. How do you explain this miracle of living mechanism, ye most learned humans? Why does that heart beat? Why does it stop some day? It is as impossible for you to find out the reason, you physiologist *emeritus*, as it is for the poor caterpillar, who feels his heart palpitate even as do you.

Ask a botanist how and why a tree grows in height. He will answer you, "I do not know." Ask him why the tree only grows up to a certain limit, and why it does not go on growing indefinitely, but stops, on the contrary, at a height which is the same for all species of the same genus. He will again say, "I do not know." No theory of vegetable physiology can explain the mode of increase in height of trees, stopping at a level which is always the same. This is one of Nature's secrets; so that in regard to one of the fundamental phenomena of organic life, since arboreal vegetation covers a great part of the soil of our globe, man knows no more than the insect that lives upon that vegetable sphinx.

Let us continue, strange as it may appear, this parallel between man and the worm.

We may say that man undergoes the same metamorphoses as the insect of our woods and fields.

When man dies, he becomes, like the worm which gives birth to the larva, a senseless, cold, and motionless being. His material elements are slowly dissociated, and are lost in the air, the earth, or the water in the shape of solid, liquid, and gaseous products. But while his material elements are dissolved, the soul, which is immaterial, escapes from that body deprived of life ; and like the larva which, giving over to putrid fermentation a part of its substance, the remnant of its former apparel, is itself changed into an airy butterfly, the human corpse sets free the immaterial and indestructible soul, which is to animate and compose the new being, — which we called in " The To-morrow of Death " *the superhuman being*, and which the Christian religion has baptized by the name of *angel*. As the butterfly which, overcoming the resistance of its temporary tomb, soars joyous and free through the fields of air, so the superhuman being soars through infinite space.

To our thinking, then, man is a sort of caterpillar; a corpse is the chrysalis of the human worm; and the butterfly set free from the corpse-like cocoon is the superhuman being.

Toussenel called the dog *a candidate for humanity ;* we might say that man is a *candidate for the angelic state.*

But, you may say, we do not see, no one has ever seen, this new being whom you regard as man transfigured, after death.

Do you see the countless animalculæ that swarm in every puddle? Do you see the minute beings that live in such vast numbers in the matter resulting from the decomposition of bread, milk, vinegar, flour, paste, etc.? To-day your eye equipped with a microscope beholds them; but the microscope is a recent invention, — it is but two centuries old. If Leuwenhoek had not created the composite microscope in the seventeenth century, you would still be ignorant of the fact that the water of rivers and pools, and all organic substances in a state of decomposition, contain billions of animalculæ. Their existence would be hidden from us, if we were reduced to the mere evidence of our senses.

The air is full of floating particles, invisible under ordinary conditions. Yet they exist; for if you admit a sunbeam into a dark room through a hole cut in an outside shutter, you will at once see these foreign bodies appear and move about. If you shut out the ray of light, the particles disappear, to reappear if you restore the outside light.

Did you ever see microbes, or virus? They can be seen with a microscope, you may answer. But if the composite microscope did not exist, how could you assert their existence? And had not a man of genius, Pasteur, the honor of his age, taught you their destination in the living economy, would you have guessed the part played by these tiny creatures in the production of contagious diseases?

The discovery of microbes has revolutionized contemporary surgery. It has permitted us to save the lives of thousands of wounded, by means of what are called *antiseptic* dressings, and to attempt with success the most marvellous surgical operations. It has thus prolonged human life. Medicine, in its turn, has profited by this fresh conquest of science; and the most dreaded, the most frightful of contagious diseases, hydrophobia, thanks to Pasteur, has found a sure cure. You never saw these microbes, the cause of so many of the ills to which flesh is heir; and yet you believe in their existence, since you have recourse, for the treatment of your ailments, to the modes of healing and treatment based upon microbiology.

Did you ever see the air? No; for it is colorless. Yet you admit its existence, not because you have seen it, but because you have felt its effects. The winds, the tempestuous motions of the ethereal medium wherein you are plunged, the obstacles overthrown by its violence, the sails of ships swollen and borne along by its breath, suffice to prove to you that air exists; but if you lived in an absolutely calm medium, you could have no suspicion of its reality.

There are stars so lost in the depths of the sky that no human eye has ever been able to see them. Yet their existence is certain; for photography reveals to you that which your eyes, even aided by optical instruments, are incapable of beholding.

This is made startlingly apparent in the composition of the chart of the heavens, which, at the suggestion of the Director of the Paris Observatory, is now occupying the thoughts of the astronomers of both worlds. Every instant, photographic machines reveal stars which the astronomer's glass has never pointed out, and which take their places in new stellar catalogues.

We may add, taking another point of view, that our eyes are not such faithful witnesses as we may think. They sometimes lead us to see the very opposite of the truth.

Is it not true that the sun is motionless and that the earth revolves? Now, what do our eyes tell us? Exactly the opposite; for they show us the sun in motion, making the circuit of the sky, and the earth motionless. This error has even passed into our speech; for we say that the sun *rises*, that it is *up*, that it *is setting*, which is absolutely false; for it is the earth that revolves, and the sun does not budge, whatever may be the testimony of our eyes.

When we gaze at the heavens, they appear to us like a blue vault, stretching its graceful curves from one edge of the horizon to the other, and the earth seems to us a flat surface, bounded by that vault. The truth is just the contrary. The earth is round, and the sky is not in the least like a vault or a half sphere.

When a stick is plunged into the water, it looks to us as if it were broken. That is the effect of refraction, you say.

" Reason straightens the stick which the water bends,"

says the poet.

This is all very well; but it is none the less true that under certain physical conditions your eye leads you to look upon an object which is straight as if it were bent.

If you stand at the head of a long avenue of trees and look straight before you, five hundred paces away the trees seem to you to meet; and yet the width of the avenue is everywhere the same. That is due to perspective, you say. To be sure; but here, again, your eyes give you an idea which is contrary to reality.

Thus your eyes are not irreproachable witnesses, which can be invoked with perfect assurance.

Therefore, friendly reader, do not conclude that an object does not exist merely because it is not visible to you; and do not declare that the *super-human being* sprung from man cannot exist merely because you never saw it issue from the tomb. Suppose it should escape from the human corpse in the form of a colorless and translucid substance, like air, you could not see it.

Whither goes this new being set free from the human *caput mortuum?* What is its residence? I felt empowered to advance, in " The To-morrow of Death," that its *habitat*, as naturalists say, is the space which divides the planets from the stars; that is to say, the *ethereal medium*.

All the natural media — earth, air, water — being peopled with inhabitants, we cannot admit that the vast space which stretches from one star to another can be void of animate beings. In this space, to our thinking, is passed the existence of the higher beings sprung from humanity. There the cycle of their transformations is accomplished ; that is, their successive deaths, followed by as many new births, with the continual improvements which refine their qualities more and more, and lead them to an increasing state of intellectual power and moral purity, until they have at last attained the height of perfection which permits them to enter the central star of our world, where they form a part of the solar divinity.

But beings coming from the earth are not the only ones, in our opinion, to inhabit the ethereal plains. We have largely abandoned the idea, antique and superannuated to-day, that the earth is the centre of the universe, or rather the entire universe itself. We now know that the earth is but one member of the immense family of stars ; that it is only a simple planet gravitating around the sun, in harmony with its sisters, the planets Venus, Mars, Mercury, etc.

The earth being inhabited, the planets which form a part of the same celestial procession must be peopled with human beings similar to ourselves.

The idea of the inhabitability of the planets is very ancient. Its origin may be traced back as far as Plutarch ; but dating from the fifteenth century, this idea arose in many minds. Giordano Bruno, one of the first partisans of the idea of the rotation of the earth, was the first to utter this opinion, in his book " The Universe and the Worlds ; " and let us note, in passing, that his philosophic boldness cost him dear, for he was burned at Rome, Feb. 1, 1600, by order of the Inquisition. The illustrious Kepler, among other sublime flights of his imagination, foresaw the aspect of the inhabited worlds, in his " Astronomic Dream." Cyrano, of Bergerac, in his " Travels in the Moon, in the States and Empires of the Sun," gave free vent to well-known eccentricities. Kircher, the Jesuit scholar, set forth the same ideas in his " Ecstatic Journey." Fontenelle wrote that masterpiece of mind and imagination entitled " The Plurality of Inhabited Worlds," and forever impressed this theory upon all minds, by the double privilege of reason and grace.

From Fontenelle on, the cause was won ; and throughout the eighteenth century appeared countless writings to defend the theory of the inhabitability of the planets.

In our own day, Camille Flammarion has displayed true genius in setting forth the same idea. In his " Imaginary Worlds and Real Worlds," and later on, in his " Kingdoms of the Sky," he has considered the question in all its aspects. We may say that he has exhausted it, and established beyond a doubt the fact that the planets which form part of the solar procession are inhabited, like the earth, by beings similar to terrestrial man.

We must only add, to render the fact generally acceptable, that the human beings living in each planet of our solar system must differ, in structure and intellectual faculties, from the inhabitants of the earth. The temperature varies in each planet according to the distance from the sun. Gravity also varies according to the same distance; and as the structure of organic bodies depends upon the atmospheric and climatic conditions of the external medium, the weight, size, density of tissues, duration of life, quantity of air breathed, kind of nourishment, and intellectual force cannot be the same for the inhabitant of burning Venus as for the inhabitant of the earth or of cold Jupiter.

With this reserve, we must declare, with Flammarion, that the planets Venus, Mercury, Mars, Jupiter, Saturn, Uranus, etc., afford shelter to human beings similar to ourselves.

We believe that the various *planetary humanities* are subject to the same order of organic changes which we imagine peculiar to man; that is to say, they pass successively through the states of *human being* on their respective planet, and *superhuman being* by soaring after death into ethereal space.

Universal ether, therefore, is the general domain whither tend not only risen earthlings, but also the dwellers in Mars, Venus, Jupiter, Neptune, etc. It is, in our opinion, this general battalion of superior beings that inhabits planetary ether, and constitutes the population, which we may, without any play on words, call floating, since it flies like the bird through the ethereal medium.

To our thinking, therefore, all the inhabitants of ether traverse together the phases of their successive metamorphoses and progressions, which end with their final entry into the sun.

In brief, we admit that interplanetary space is occupied by beings superior in intelligence and faculties to the inhabitants of the earth. We can assert the contrary only by asserting that man ranks first after God, — which is impossible. The space dividing the worlds one from the other cannot be empty, for there can be no void in the universe; and if this space be occupied, by what can it be, if not by creatures intermediary between man and divinity? Were it otherwise, the plan of the universe would be imperfect. Its inferior part would be peopled by an endless number of living creatures, while its superior part would be but a vast desert, and beyond that, without any intermediary, would shine, above and in the depths of space, the person of God.

The ether which divides the planets one from the other must therefore be occupied; and, to our thinking, it serves as the dwelling of higher beings proceeding from earthly humanity, conjoined with other planetary humanities.

But, you may say, there are other suns than that which warms and lights our globe.   The sun, with the planets Mercury, Venus, the earth, Mars, Jupiter, etc., make up our astronomic system; but there exist other stars, which, surrounded by their planets, form other solar systems, separated from us by distances so great that we can scarce imagine them, but of which we may gain some idea when we learn that it takes their light endless years to reach us.   These distant suns are what we call *fixed stars*.

If these fixed stars or distant suns are stars surrounded by their train of planets, those planets, reasoning by analogy, must be inhabited, as the planets of our solar system are.   Around fixed stars, like Cassiopeia, Sirius, Arcturus, etc., revolve planets, too far distant for us to see them, but none the less existing.   There must be inhabitants in the planets belonging to distant suns; and if these planets have their inhabitants, like the earth, like Mars, Venus, etc., those inhabitants must, in our opinion, undergo the same organic evolutions which are peculiar to earthly humanity, — that is to say, they die upon their planetary earth, are born again, and are diffused through universal ether in the form of superhuman beings.   Then, just as superhuman beings, perfected in aptitudes and moral faculties, are at last reunited in our sun, so too the superhuman beings of other solar systems must end in their particular sun, and enter into the substance of their particular star, to compose portions of the solar divinity.

There would thus be as many divinities as fixed stars in the sky.

And as, according to astronomical catalogues, a thousand million fixed stars are known, the number of solar gods would be the same.

This strangely enlarges our idea of God!

Fontenelle proved the "Plurality of Inhabited Worlds;" modern science tends to make us accept the "plurality of gods."

Greek and Roman antiquity peopled Olympus with gods and demigods; our system extends the plurality of gods to the entire universe, and somewhat upsets the notions which have hitherto prevailed in regard to the destiny of the stars which spangle the firmament. The fixed stars which shine through the serenity of night, shedding their mild, soft lustre upon our globe, are not a mere decorative spectacle, designed to delight our eyes and to plunge our soul in vague reveries; they are divine lights, which reveal to us the existence, in the immensity of the heavens, of an innumerable quantity of higher powers, watching over the immutable order of Nature, as well as the perfecting of immortal souls issuing from various planetary humanities.

To the scourge of atheism, which now threatens to destroy the foundations of social order, we oppose *astronomic polytheism*, its direct antagonist.

We must, however, follow out our theories to the end.

We have supposed that the sun, as well as other stars of the same order, is fixed. The truth is that they move, and that they move with a speed ten times, twenty times, a hundred times greater than the speed of a cannon-ball shot from a gun. If they seem to us motionless, it is merely because the distance which divides them from our solar system is so vast that their motion is imperceptible to us, and that long calculations and multiplex observations were required to ascertain the fact. And yet this motion is a certainty, and we know that all the fixed stars, all distant suns, revolve, like our sun, around a central point, situated so deep in space that we can only conceive of it in imagination.

In our system it is at this central point that the supreme god, *Jehovah*, may be found, hidden, to use Pliny's expression, " in the majesty of worlds," — *latet in majestate naturæ.*

Did the English poet Young foresee this astronomic theogony, when he wrote in his " Night Thoughts," —

> " Not the God alone :
> I see his ministers ; I see, diffus'd
> In radiant orders, essences sublime,
> Of various offices, of various plume,
> In heavenly liveries, distinctly clad,
> Azure, green, purple, pearl, or downy gold,
> Or all commix'd."

" Think'st thou my scheme, Lorenzo, spreads too wide ?
Is this extravagant ? — No ; this is just;
Just in conjecture, though 't were false in fact.
If 't is an error, 't is an error sprung
From noble root, high thought of the Most High.
But wherefore error ?   Who can prove it such ? "

Thus we may sum up the cosmogonic theosophy developed in " The To-morrow of Death."

With this statement we will take up the chief subject of our new work ; that is, in conformity with its title, we will give a sketch of the various joys awaiting man in the new existence opening for him beyond the tomb.

CHAPTER II.

AN Arab proverb says: "It is better to sit than to stand; it is better to lie down than to sit; it is better to die than to live."

Homer regarded man as the most miserable being in the world.

The Greek poet Theognis (570 B. C.) in his "Elegiac Sentences," composed after misfortunes overtook Megara, his country, and stamped with the impress of his sorrows, says: "The happiest fate for mortals is never to have seen the light of day; and if they be forced to see it, to cross the portals of death as soon as may be."

So too the Thracians hailed new-born babes with groans of despair, while they celebrated funeral rites with shouts of enthusiasm and joy.

"Since you seem not to know how we mourn the dead," says Lucian, "I will tell you: —

"'Ah! poor child, nevermore shalt thou thirst; nevermore shalt thou be hungry or cold. Thou art forever lost to me. Thou art forever safe from fever,

tyrants, and foes ; nevermore shalt thou be tormented
by the pangs of love ; nevermore shall pleasure sap thy
strength ; never shalt thou be an old man despised by
all.' " [1]

To love, to regret the earth, human existence
should abound in satisfactions and joys. Now, on
the contrary, life upon our globe is but a long succession of physical sufferings and moral agonies.
The inequalities of the seasons or the inclemencies
of climates, resulting from the peculiar inclination
of the earth on its axis, expose us to diseases which
we can only ward off or combat by dint of ingenuity
and care, by wonders of art and industry. Now
blistered by a burning sky, now subject to icy cold,
man, of whatever age and condition, is attacked by
physical infirmities due as much to outward influences as to causes of organic disorder inherent in
himself ; and the constant dread of suffering and
sickness makes his life almost perpetually painful.

But it is on the moral side particularly that the
majority of mankind is miserable. In modern society an honest, simple-hearted man exhausts his
strength in superfluous efforts, and takes infinite
pains to obtain the smallest results ; while the violent, bold, and unscrupulous attain everything.

And what a contrast there is in the destinies
of men ! Here flaunt the happy and the favored, —
happy and favored because they are bold and unscrupulous, or because they inherit from a wealthy

---

[1] Lucian " On Mourning."

parent. There cower the famished, the dejected, the dying, — famished, dejected, dying because they choose to be honest and simple, or because they belong to a poor family. The father without work, the wife ill, the children pale, ragged, and crying for bread, see from the window of their wretched garret the millionaire deaf to the sufferings of others and solely occupied in gratifying his caprices. For the one, the pallet on the damp ground, hunger his constant companion ; for the other, palaces, luxurious apartments, adorned with all the most precious things that art and industry can offer, and gold lavished with open hands for idle whims. For the one, mean array, a humble, sad, and submissive attitude ; for the other, a haughty mien, costly horses, rich equipages, and grand hunting-parties amid forests whose maintenance would suffice to feed the inhabitants of an entire town.

Hear this story : it happened but yesterday.

It was early in the month of June, 1892. Paris was in all its glory ; luxury and pleasure on every hand. The King of Sweden visited the capital, which delighted in dazzling its royal guest by the splendor of its feasts. The first performance of "Salambo" was given at the Opera, with Madame Caron ; and at the Théâtre Français, "Athalie," with Mounet-Sully. The double exhibition of painting and sculpture at the Champ de Mars and the Champs Élysées attracted lovers of art. As it was the eve of the great races, the *grand prix de Paris*, rich equipages displayed their brilliant trappings in advance, their reins glittering with flashes of steel, and rosettes of ribbon at the horses' heads. The flower festival drew a throng of fashionable ladies, in their most ravishing toilets, to the avenues of the Bois de Boulogne. Their carriages, opened wide, were nests of flowers; the wheels, the seats, the horses were hidden beneath perfumed wreaths, and from one carriage to another were thrown nosegays, every one of which cost a louis. The earth was strewed with blossoms, which were trodden underfoot by the horses and the crowd. All was joy and rapture in that throng of happy idlers, drinking in long draughts of the pleasures of high life.

Meantime at the top of a poor house in the Rue Monge, a young sculptor — a pupil of the École des Beaux Arts, named Peyre — lay dying in his bare room.

His province had sent him to Paris to continue his studies in sculpture at the School of Fine Arts. But his scanty allowance was exhausted soon after his arrival; and while he waited for the next month's instalment, he was daily forced to reduce his portion of food. Knowing no one and too proud to ask help, the poor young man saw his strength ebb day by day for want of nourishment, and the moment came when he was too weak to leave his bed.

The porter, surprised that he did not see his ten-ant going in and out for several days, went to his room. The door was open; he entered.

The young man was dead.

The police commissioner was summoned, and came with a doctor, whose office it was to certify to the death.

"What was the cause of his death?" asked the commissioner.

The doctor tore a slip of paper from his note-book, wrote three words on it, and handed it to his companion, who read, —

" Died of hunger."

The doctor readily recognized that death was caused by starvation, from the emaciation of the victim, and the very evident contraction in the region of the stomach.

That same evening, in the Faubourg St. Ger-main, the Chaussée d'Antin, and in the Quartier de l'Étoile, there were splendid balls, where the most fashionable ladies displayed their freshest gowns, while on their naked bosoms glittered diamonds and jewels worth millions.

A single stone from the necklace which adorned your fair shoulders, Countess, would have prevented the poor sculptor from dying of hunger in his wretched garret!

Peyre was but seventeen years old. That slen-der body, so wasted, so bloodless, — that childish body, which was borne to the grave next day, per-haps contained the soul of an artist. His pride, which forbade him to sue for aid, leads us to think so. If that noble heart had continued to beat, if it had not been silenced by the fierce grasp of hunger, who knows if this pupil of the École des Beaux Arts, who was allowed to die on a pallet, alone, without a relation, without a friend, might not have become a Michael Angelo, or less great, — a Houdon or a Carpeaux ?

Not to confine ourselves, however, to individual cases, let us pass in review the conditions of men in different parts of the world.

What sad pictures meet the eye of the philosopher who studies European society in our day! Entire nations bowed beneath the hand of a despot, by virtue of the adage, " Might makes right," or in obedience to century-old traditions; generous people given over to interminable slavery, and the oppressor laughing at the tortures of the oppressed ; war periodically letting loose its furies, and carrying devastation and death to country and town, harvesting in an instant thousands of existences, sowing mourning and funeral rites, leaving widows and orphans, making people who know not even the cause of these murderous conflicts the victims of the ambition and caprice of sovereigns.

Individual misfortunes are added to public calamities. What do we see in many European families ? Young girls worn out by suffering and toil, and unable even to earn their daily bread ; youths and grown men forced to submit to the will of a capricious master ; children given over from their birth to vice and corruption, and to whom evil is second nature ; the public mind corrupted by licentious literature, which delights in setting forth all that is low, discouraging, and debasing in human nature, in place of great virtues, noble examples, and consoling truths.

The fate of workers in Europe to-day is the most miserable imaginable, whether we take them from the rural districts or the cities.

Every one knows the striking sketch which La Bruyère drew of the French peasant in the time of Louis XIV. : —

" We see certain wild beasts, male and female, scattered through country regions, black, livid, and burned by the sun, bowed to the soil which they dig and on which they labor with stubborn persistence. They have articulate speech, and when they rise to their feet they reveal a human face. And, indeed, they are men. They retire at night to dens, where they live on black bread, water, and roots. They save other men the trouble of sowing, ploughing, and reaping to live, and hence do not deserve to lack the bread which they have sowed."

Has this picture changed much since La Bruyère's day ? Doubtless the French peasant is better fed, better lodged, and better dressed than he was in the time of Louis XIV. ; but his wages are absurd. For forty or forty-five cents a day, from sunrise to sunset, in rain or frost or beneath the heat of a burning sun, he digs or ploughs the earth, he weeds, harrows, or performs the exhausting tasks of the harvest. The peasant class, which forms more than a third of the whole French population, is in a profoundly melancholy state of intellectual inferiority in consequence of the necessity under which it lies of laboring from morning till night, with no rest save on Sunday.

Upon ships, fishing-smacks, and coasting-vessels the sailor is exposed to incessant dangers, the greatness and frequency of which we do not fully realize. But spend some time at any seaport, and you will learn to how many accidents the toilers of the sea fall victims. Question the annual reports of the French office whose duty it is to point out the number and importance of shipwrecks among all seafaring nations, and you will be amazed at the quantity of human lives which the gulfs of ocean swallow up every year. Question the families of sailors on our shores, and you will learn with pain how many unhappy fishers set forth from port never to return. And in return for the roughest work, upon icy waters beneath the howl of the tempest or the gale, these wretched sailors scarcely earn the price of a scanty livelihood.

The same may be said of the toiler in great cities and in factories scattered in various centres. Forced to perform the most fatiguing tasks, either in the vitiated atmosphere of a workroom or in the open air, now under the blazing sun, now beneath the wintry blast, the workman is exposed to everything likely to produce disease, if he would ward off misery from himself, his children, and his wife.

In my youth, in the pursuit of my scientific studies, I went to the bottom of a coal-pit, a thousand feet below the surface of the earth, and I shall never forget the sad spectacle presented by the miners at work with their picks, often in the most painful positions possible, lying on their backs to detach the coal from the course overhead, compelled to crawl on all fours in order to pass from one low passage-way to another lower still, which they were just beginning to work; their faces and hands blackened by coal-dust; scarcely able to breathe, where there was little ventilation, the current of air striking against a blank wall in the gallery; or elsewhere, on the contrary, exposed to inflammation of the lungs when, streaming with perspiration, they receive the furious gusts of a neighboring blast-engine full in the face.

And I say nothing here of the fearful dangers of fire-damp; for, thank God! all coal-mines are not infected with fire-damp. But in those liable to the escape of this fatal gas, what can be more frightful for the miner than to work in the bowels of the earth, in a narrow space, where he is well aware that he has no guarantee against an awful catastrophe, and that he may at any moment be crushed against the walls of the gallery by the explosion of the inflammable gas?

The accidents which occurred in the coal-pits of St. Etienne in 1891 and 1892, and at Anderlues in Belgium, are still too recent to allow of our dwelling on this melancholy picture. I can understand a man's working in a coal-pit not acknowledged to be liable to fire-damp, if pressed by necessity; but I ask myself how it is that men can be found to work in certain pits notoriously filled with it.

Not to confine ourselves to agricultural laborers, to the toilers in factories and great towns, to sailors and miners, let us say, in general, that workers in the various professions do not receive sufficient wages in any country of Europe. Considering the general increase in the price of everything, French, English, and German workmen are not paid enough to meet their necessary expenses; and as want gives rise to corrupt morals, it is in London, where working-people's wages are lowest, that we find the saddest instances of human degradation.

In the capital of England, at the approach of night, four or five hundred thousand people come forth from foul lairs and filthy dens, men and women of wretched aspect, to seek their horrible subsistence in the mire of the gutter or in the offal thrown out from kitchens.

Side by side with the awful misery to be seen in the city of London, we should place in opposition the scandalous fortunes of certain lords who, heedless of the suffering of the poor, devote their fabulous incomes solely to the purchase of luxurious equipages for riding, driving, and hunting, to keeping up their parks and castles, and providing for their splendid entertainments. One seventh of the population of Great Britain belongs to ninety proprietors, while the working-classes are given over to black misery.

The scanty wages paid in France as well as in other countries to women employed in working with the needle, is a subject of painful surprise to the philanthropist. It is a well-known fact that the wages of women in our large cities cannot suffice for their material wants. The workwomen of Paris, Lyons, Lisle, etc., earning but fifty cents a day, periodically stopped by slack seasons, are forced to endure constant privations, if they would remain honest.

How can all these workers, men or women, cultivate their minds, preserve their moral faculties, think of God, of their immortal soul, their future destiny, when they are obliged from morning till night to turn up the earth with their ploughshare, to hew granite or cut stone twelve hours a day, to handle the rigging or the sails of boats and vessels, to shunt cars on railways, etc., to provide for their daily wants ; while their wives wear themselves out at needlework or at shopwork, which shortens their days by incessant fatigue ?

Are you surprised after this that the claims of the laborer all over the earth become daily more urgent, and that workmen in cities and manufacturing populations demand the share of happiness and ease to which they have a right? Are you surprised that workmen in every land cry out for an eight-hour law, — which does not mean that they want to work only eight hours a day, but it means that they demand an increase of pay; for they would continue to work ten and twelve hours a day, with extra wages, based on the pay for a day of eight hours.

And yet it has not hitherto seemed possible to satisfy the claims of the worker; so that manufacturer and citizen are reduced, in every land, to live in constant terror, always dreading some crisis or social catastrophe.

Nor are the European middle classes much better off than the workers. Crushed by taxes, forced to submit to a steady rise in the price of food, dress, and rent, they are often as poor as the day-laborer, although they preserve an outward show of comfort.

And on the other hand, the military servitude to which every man is now subject in almost every country of Europe interferes with his occupations and studies throughout the best years of his life, the same forced servitude continuing during his mature age.

Thus the fate of the European is miserable indeed. In Asia, which has a population much larger than that of Europe, it is no better. There the imperfect religions to which the people are given over — Buddhism, Brahminism, and Islamism — forbid all intellectual and moral progress, and cause them to cling to their ancient customs. Oriental nations, moreover, are oppressed by autocratic governments, and stripped of everything by corrupt officials. Others are subject to English rule, which makes it a law to change no jot or tittle of the ancient religious or political customs of the Oriental and other nations which have become their vassals.

The Asiatic, therefore, is always poor, oppressed, and plunged in deep apathy, resulting from his acknowledged inability to accomplish anything for himself.

Thus the people of the Orient place little value on life, which they regard as of no worth, and readily sacrifice it, whether voluntarily or by force. The Indian, the Japanese, the Chinese, the Persian, throws away his life on the most futile pretext, or submits without flinching to the most fearful torture.

In Africa slavery, that hideous plague-spot of modern society, afflicts thousands of unhappy wretches, whose only crime is that they were born beneath a tropical sky and have a black skin and woolly hair.

The continent of Africa long held aloof from the social movement; but now Europeans, finding themselves pinched for room at home, their limited territory no longer sufficing to feed an exuberant population, covet those vast regions which they scarcely know, but where they hope to find the outlets which they lack, or to create productive industries whose products they may transport to other parts of the world. It is greatly to be feared that this calculation will be belied by facts, and that Africa with its sandy deserts and its scattered tribes who have a hatred for servitude of any sort, can never become a commercial market. Be this as it may, European governments, in their common impatience, have hastened to divide the African continent, in advance, into a certain number of shares, which they have distributed among themselves without exploring them, hoping some day to conquer them. We may therefore expect sooner or later to hear of African massacres.

We have now spoken of civilized man; if we consider man in a savage state, as he still occupies vast portions of the inhabited earth, we shall find the conditions of his existence still more wretched. The savage people of both worlds, deprived of any true religion, are, moreover, decimated by diseases of every sort which soon become mortal for lack of care. Without agriculture, without trade or manufactures, they are forced to seek their subsistence by hunting and fishing, or from the natural products of the country which they inhabit.

Add to this that their native ferocity provokes incessant wars between tribe and tribe, whose special object is to reduce the vanquished to slavery ; for this horrid scourge still exists in spite of the efforts, more or less sincere, of other nations, and condemns a portion of the non-civilized peoples to the most abominable oppression to which man or woman can be subjected.

Savage nations are still the victims of bloody wars on the part of civilized peoples. When the Spanish found a fresh field on the American continent for their martial and commercial activity, they began by exterminating the native races. Pizarro, Cortez, and their lieutenants were pitiless slaughterers. By order of the kings of Spain, who hoped to find in those virgin lands inexhaustible mines of gold, silver, and precious stones, they gave these new domains over to fire and the sword. The people who had until then lived quietly and happily in the empire of the Incas, in Mexico, Peru, or Chili, were butchered by wholesale.

Later on, the English followed the example of the Spanish conquerors in North America. They rid the American forests of their peaceful inhabitants with gun-shots ; and it was by this barbarous method that they substituted the Anglo-Saxon for the native races. The few savage tribes still existing in certain regions of the United States and Brazil are even now the object of the same homicidal wars ; and the time is not far distant when not a single Indian will remain in the New World.

Thus, in whatever direction we look throughout

the inhabited world, we see man, civilized or savage, given over to the saddest fate.

And it is to endure these sufferings, moral or physical, that we are on the earth! It is to be the meek servants of countless masters; to stretch forth a hand into which nothing falls; to abdicate personal dignity; to wear away by the friction of life the illusions and hopes cherished in youthful days; to bow beneath the unending labor of an ungrateful profession, which exhausts our powers and scarce suffices to keep us alive; to have children whom we adore and who are torn from us by death, leaving an incurable wound in our hearts; it is, finally, to grow old without shelter and without food, that we are here below! Ah! to how hard a trial Providence subjects us in ordering us to sojourn thus on earth!

"This world is a vale of misery," says Voltaire. And Chateaubriand writes: "In our vale of tears." Indeed, what smallest of our joys is not expiated by our tears? Love and paternity are the greatest and perhaps the only sources of human happiness; but how many trials and pangs must they not endure? Love, even the purest, most honest, most completely shared, is poisoned by constant and mutual suspicions, by vague alarms, by the pursuit on both sides of an ideal forever dreamed and never found.

> "The joys of love in a moment are past,
> The sorrows of love a lifetime last,

as the enchanting song by J. Martini says, — the song which we all sang in our youth.

As for paternity, the most enviable of our privileges, since it gives us the satisfaction of seeing ourselves live again in our children, by how many torments is it not purchased? Childhood is a long succession of diseases which agonize the parent and keep him in continual terror. When my little son was ill or in pain, I felt an actual physical pang, my very heart seemed to be wrung; and when I lost him, at the age of fifteen and a half, in all the flower of his intellect, strength, and apparent health, it was like the rending, the giving way of my entire being. It is twenty-five years since he left me, and even now in my lonely nights I wake, my eyes wet with tears, crying out, " My poor child! my poor child!"

On reaching manhood, our sons are taken from us by a profession or by military service, and we become as it were strangers to them. If we have a daughter, a husband soon leads her to forget her parents, and she has no thought or interest for any but her new family. Why, moreover, should we wonder, why complain at this, since such is the law of Nature, which requires the husband to replace the father and mother, to create descendants? Nature's law is obeyed; but by their solitary hearth the parents silently weep at the filial ingratitude.

Chateaubriand was therefore right when he called the earth " a vale of tears."

"On earth we never know entire joy,
  A price we pay for every pleasure here ;
There is no rapture without some alloy,
  And each delight is followed by a tear." [1]

The sole happiness which we can hope for here below, is not to suffer; and we must not ask for more.

Then why should we regret to leave the earth? Why should we wish to prolong the brief sojourn which we are compelled to make? Is it to grow old, sad and alone by our deserted fireside; to see the companions of our labors depart before us; to see our friends, our relations, all whom we have loved and respected, disappear in turn? Is it still to endure the inclemencies of climates and seasons, — to dread in turn the winter's cold and the summer's heat? Is it to bear a series of infirmities, the inevitable companions of old age; to feel ourselves slowly wither away; to see our powers and our intellect decline from day to day, thereby warning us of the imminence of our end? Would you suffer yet again from love betrayed, friendship unappreciated, your rights trampled under foot by iniquitous judges? Would you again take up in old age your schemes so often cut short by disloyal rivalry or by envy? Have you not heard enough of those commonplaces, insincere speeches, and truisms about the weather, the table, and the chase, which are the eternal and insipid

[1] Reboul: The Angel and the Child.

basis of ordinary conversation?   Are you not tired of listening to the sullen and malignant imprecations that swell the breast of the proletary when, yielding to excess of toil or of privation, he sees flaunted before his eyes vast riches acquired without labor by bold speculators or doubtful financiers?   Do not selfishness and indifference prevail in this world, and is it not, as Voltaire says, " The wise who go bare, and the geniuses who starve in the mire "? How many virtues hold firm against the plea of interest or of passion?   What hand is extended to aid silent poverty or undeserved misfortune ?

Why, then, we repeat, should we regret the earth, and why should we wish to prolong our sojourn on a planet so unevenly divided ?

CHAPTER III.

IT is of deep purpose — that is to say, for the preservation and perpetuity of the species — that Nature inspired the heart of man with a terror of death, even as she made the desire for reproduction from the pleasure of the senses ; but science and philosophy can dispel the fears which man feels at the mere idea of death.

It is an error to believe that the instant of the separation of soul and body is accompanied by acute sufferings. The anatomist Bichat, in his "Researches concerning Life and Death," clearly establishes that at the approach of our final moment the brain is the first organ affected, and that hence the dying are spared all pain. At that supreme moment moral terror is therefore the only impression against which we have to contend in the dying, as there certainly is no physical pain. The bystanders and the relations suffer far more than those about to expire.

The sleep which every night takes possession of our being steals over us without our being conscious of it, and the transition from a waking to a sleeping state is imperceptible to us. Here we have a faint image of death. The dying have no more sense of the passage from life to death than the living have of the passing from waking to sleeping.

It is unfortunate that painting and sculpture should represent death in the form of a hideous skeleton armed with a scythe mowing down mankind, or of a spectre wrapped in the melancholy winding-sheet of the tomb. They should have shown him to us with the features of a messenger of joy, who comes not to destroy, but to bear us away to another and a happier sphere. Death should be pictured as a beneficent spirit, who aids us to cross the bounds set by nature between the earthly and the celestial voyage, and who introduces us to ethereal spheres beyond which rises the mysterious throne of the God of the Universe.

Instead of adorning cemeteries, as we do, with dark-leaved cypress, the symbol of mourning and affliction, the Orientals were quite right to plant them with varied trees, to fill them with groves and flowers, — to make them smiling gardens, places for promenade, recreation, and pleasure.

Lamartine ("Death of Socrates") most perfectly expresses the idea which we should have of death in the following lines : —

" To die is not to die, my friends : it is to change.
While he lives burdened by his body here below,

Man towards his God but languidly doth go ;
Forced his vile wants to feed, no progress makes,
Moves with a tottering step, or truth forsakes.
But he who, verging on the end which he doth pray,
Sees glorious glimpses of the eternal day
Like sunset rays ascending towards the skies,
An exile thence, in God's own arms he lies,
And quaffing eagerly the nectar which doth rapture give,
That day on which he dies he first begins to live."

The Queen of England, Victoria, after the death
of her husband, Prince Albert, as we all know,
wrote a very eloquent book, entitled " Meditations
upon Death and Eternity." In this work, filled
with most profound and touching thoughts, may be
found many pages which we would gladly quote,
for they uphold the ideas which we developed in
the " To-morrow of Death." We will merely cite
what the august writer says to dispel the terrors
with which death inspires most men.

" The terrors with which we clothe death," says
Queen Victoria, " come largely from the erroneous and
revolting descriptions of it given to us. Thus, it is
sometimes styled decomposition or corruption ; but we
do not, speaking exactly, fall into either one or the other
of these states.

" Some say that to die is to leave the world ; but we
never do leave the world, that being in itself impossible.

" Others again claim that death is synonymous with
destruction ; but we cannot be destroyed. No ; to die is
to return unto our Father. Our souls merely cast off gar-
ments which do not become them, to put on others more
worthy of them. The shudder caused by the usual de-

scriptions of death is due to the fact that these descriptions are largely borrowed from the state of the inanimate
body. Every false conception is justly repulsive to us.
So soon as the reason is wounded, everything in us is
wounded, and the imagination strives in vain to make
that which is irrational seem becoming. The state of
the corpse in the tomb is not our state, but simply that
of the covering which we have stripped off. And what
is our earthly covering if it be not the worn-out or dam-
aged garment of the immortal spirit?"[1]

And now let us hear Young, the poet of " Night
Thoughts." Says the English writer : —

> " But were death frightful, what has age to fear ?
> If prudent, age should meet the friendly foe,
> And shelter in his hospitable gloom.
> I scarce can meet a monument but holds
> My younger ; ev'ry date cries, 'Come away ! '
> And what recalls me ? Look the world around,
> And tell me what. The wisest cannot tell.
> Should any born of woman give his thought
> Full range, on just dislike's unbounded field :
> Of things the vanity ; of men the flaws, —
> Flaws in the best; the many, flaws all o'er ;
> As leopards spotted, or as Ethiops dark ;
> Vivacious ill; good dying immature
> (How immature, Narcissa's marble tells !)
> And at his death bequeathing endless pain.
> His heart, tho' bold, would sicken at the sight,
> And spend itself in sighs for future scenes." [2]

> ". . . Why cling to this rude rock,
> Barren to us of good, and sharp with ills,
> And hourly blackened with impending storms,

[1] First Meditation, — Interpretation of Eternity.
[2] Night IV.

And infamous for wrecks of human hope, —
Scar'd at the gloomy gulf that yawns beneath."

"   .   .   .   The thought of death indulge ;
Give it its wholesome empire ! let it reign,
That kind chastiser of thy soul, in joy !

.   .   .   .   .   .

And why not think on death ?   Is life the theme
Of ev'ry thought, and wish of ev'ry hour,
And song of ev'ry joy ?   Surprising truth !
The beaten spaniel's fondness not so strange.
To waive the num'rous ills that seize on life
As their own property, their lawful prey.
Ere man has measured half his weary stage,
His luxuries have left him no reserve,
No maiden relishes, unbroacht delights ;
On cold-serv'd repetitions he subsists,
And in the tasteless present chews the past, —
Disgusted chews, and scarce can swallow down.

.   .   .   .   .   .

"Live ever here, Lorenzo ?— shocking thought !
So shocking, they who wish disown it too ;
Disown from shame what they from folly crave.

.   .   .   .   .   .

A truth it is few doubt, but fewer trust :
"He sins against this life who slights the next."
What is this life ?   How few their fav'rite know !
Life has no value as an end, but means, —
An end deplorable ! a means divine !"[1]

Death, far from being a scarecrow, since we all
must inevitably yield to it, should be regarded as a
supreme benefactor, who comes to remove us from
the misfortunes, deceptions, and despair peculiar to
life, to lead us to the splendor of realms above,
where all is happiness, power, and peace.

Queen Victoria, in the work already quoted, thus
expresses herself : —

[1] Night III.

" What is death? Nothing but the separation of the soul from its earthly case. . What becomes of the case when it is cast aside? Does it vanish from God's creation? No; it falls to dust and ashes, and is mingled with the rest of earth, whose nutritive elements formed it in the beginning. It does not leave creation, but remains there, awaiting another destiny.

" But what becomes of the soul stripped of its veil? Does it vanish from God's creation? Oh, no! How could it be possible for the nobler element to cease to exist when the viler is imperishable ?

" Must we believe that it has been removed from the infinite multitude of created beings, because it has thrown off the veil through which alone it could reveal its presence to our senses? No, it lives; for its very dust, which once served to enwrap it, still exists. It lives ; for God creates and does not annihilate. It lives ; for in his sovereign wisdom, he could not repent, in any sort, of the high destiny for which he gave it being.

" Is it, then, so painful to cast off this earthly veil? In truth, the natural love of life which the Creator has so deeply implanted within us, inspires us with fear at the idea of parting from our mortal form ; but the power of the human mind can triumph over the terrors of nature. How many generous men have faced death for their God, their country, their faith, and their friends! Death had no terrors for them. How many poor, weak, degenerate beings, driven by despair, have voluntarily laid down the life which had become a burden to them !

"Dying men do not dissimulate, and we can judge by their features what is going on in their mind. From such study it would seem almost as if the soul must

4

experience an agreeable sensation at the moment that it lays aside its mortal spoil; for it has been often observed that the features of persons dying of painful maladies, assume at the final instant an expression of calm serenity, while a peaceful smile quivers on the lips of the lifeless body, left there by the departing soul, — a smile which seems to say, 'Ah! what relief!'"

Victor Hugo has aptly translated this idea in the following verses in his "Contemplations":—

"O death! O moment grand! O mortuary rays!
    Hast thou ne'er turned the sheet from dear dead face,
    While others wept and stood beside the bed, —
    Friends, brothers, children, mother with down-hanging head,
    Distracted, sobbing, of wild grief the prey, —
    Hast seen a smile across the dead man's features stray?
    He groaned, he choked, he died just now;
    And yet he smiles.   Dread gulf, oh, whence and how
    Cometh that light seen on the face of death's unwilling slave?
    What is the tomb?   Whence cometh, O thinker grave,
    The awful calmness on each dead face we see?
    It is that the secret is out, it is that the spirit is free;
    It is that the soul — all seeing, all shining, all burning so bright —
    Laughs aloud, and the body itself takes part in its fearful
        delight."[1]

Farther on, the poet reflects as follows, in the cemetery at Villequier, where his daughter lies buried:—

AT VILLEQUIER.

Now, O my God! I have the calmer woe;
    Able, the while I weep,
To see the stone where in night well I know
    She does forever sleep.

[1] Contemplations, book vi.: On the Brink of Infinity, xiii.

Now that, made softer by these sights divine, —
  Plain, forest, valley, river, rocks, and sky, —
Viewing myself by these vast works of thine,
  Reason returns before immensity.

Father and Lord, in whom we must believe,
  I come, perverse no more ;
Shreds of the heart thy glory fills, receive,
  Shattered by thee of yore.

I come to thee, O Lord, who art, I know,
  O living God ! good, merciful, and kind.
I own that you alone know what you do,
  That men are reeds that tremble in the wind.

I say the tomb in which the dead is shut
  Opens the heavenly hall ;
And what we here for end of all things put,
  Is the first step of all.

Now on my knees I own, O Lord august !
  The real, the absolute belong to thee ;
I own that it is good, I own it just,
  My heart should bleed, since such is God's decree.

Whate'er may happen, I resist no more,
  But in thy will comply.
The soul from loss to loss, from shore to shore,
  Rolls to eternity.

We never see more than a single side, —
  The other plunged in night's dread mystery.
Man feels the yoke : thou dost the causes hide, —
  Brief, useless, fleeting, all that meets his eye.

Thou makest a perpetual solitude
  Wrap all his steps around ;
Thou hast not seen it fit that certitude
  Or joy should here be found.

Whatever good he has fate takes away;
  Naught can he call his own in life's quick flight,
So that he here can make a home or say,
  " Here is my house, my field, or my delight."

All sights he may but for a moment see, —
  Must age, unhelped, alone,
Since things are thus; 't is that they so must be;
  I own it, — yes, I own.

Dark is the world ! The changeless harmony,
  O God ! of cries as well as songs is made.
Man but a speck in dread infinity ;
  Night where the good mount up, and sink the bad.

He asserts still more clearly his belief in the resurrection of the human being, the *individual,* in the
following passages, which we quote, concluding
with them these thoughts from great authors :

" Some day, soon perhaps, the same hour which
struck for the son will strike for the father. His turn
will come. He will wear the look of one sleeping ; he
will be laid between four boards ; he will be that unknown quantity called a dead man, and he will be carried
to the great, gloomy opening. There the new-comer is
awaited by those who went before. The new-comer is
welcome. What seems the exit is to him the entrance.
The eye of the flesh closes, the eye of the spirit opens,
and the invisible becomes visible, While shovelsful of
earth fall on the dark and echoing bier, the mysterious
soul forsakes that garment, the body, and rises in light,
from the gathering shadows. Then, for that soul those
who have vanished reappear, and those truly living,
whom in earthly darkness we call the dead, softly call

to the new-comer, and bending over his dazzled face, wear that radiant smile worn amid the stars. Thus shall the laborer depart, leaving, if he has played his part well, some regrets behind him, and at the same time received with joy in eternal day." [1]

"*Everything ends under six feet of earth?* No, everything begins. No, everything germinates. No, everything blossoms, and grows, and springs up, and bursts forth.

" I believe in immortality, — not in the immortality of the name, which is but smoke ; but in the enduring life of the *individual*. I believe in it, I feel myself immortal.

" Yes, I believe in God and in another life. . . .

" If I face death with a calm smile, it is because I believe in a future life. And note that I am on my guard against the caresses which we bestow on our ideas to the end that they may become opinions. But here it is an absolute conviction. I believe — I say more, I am sure — that we do not utterly and wholly die, and that our *ego* survives." [2]

" Yes, I believe profoundly in this better world ; it is far more real to me than this wretched chimera which we devour and which we call life. I believe in it with all the strength of my conviction ; and after many struggles, much study, and many trials, it is the supreme certainty of my reason, as it is the supreme consolation of my soul." [3]

---

[1] My Sons (Mes Fils), p. 38.
[2] Victor Hugo at Home, by Gustave Rivet, pp. 245, 246.
[3] Literature and Philosophy, vol. iii. p. 291.

Therefore let us have no fear of death. What is laid in the tomb is not ourselves, but simply the material wrapping of our souls. This wrapping perishes in obedience to the laws of chemical decomposition; but the soul, which is our true individuality, does not disappear: it goes on to pursue a fresh career in the skies. The body is the cloak of the soul; the body is changed to dust, the soul is changed to light.

Sometimes during stormy nights which cover the abode of the dead with darkness, light flames escaping from the soil flicker in the heavy air. Naturalists call them *will-o'-the-wisps;* chemists, carburetted hydrogen gas; spiritual philosophers and poets, as well as the common people, regard them as the souls of the dead rising from the tomb.

We do not shudder when we see various parts of our bodies perish. If we cut our hair or our nails, or if we lose a limb by a surgical operation, we do not distress ourselves about those lopped-off portions of our personality which are left to decay. Why, then, dread its total destruction?

Our bodily substance is perpetually changing; and physiologists, such as Buffon and Flourens, have ascertained that the human body is renewed in all its parts once in every seven years. These are so many bodily deaths which do not alarm us in the least.

If you dread death, it is because you have at some

time gazed on a human corpse with terror, and told yourself that you would some day enter the same state. But if your eyes had never beheld this sad sight, you would be free from the agonies that you feel at the idea of death. For, we repeat, that which is laid in the tomb is not you, but only your earthly garment; and you have too often renewed that fleshly garb, without suspecting it, to dread its final destruction.

When the worm, become a butterfly, leaves on the ground or on a branch the frail shell which once contained it, does it trouble itself about the worthless remnant which it abandons to the wind?

It is important, besides, fully to take in the idea that the instant of the separation of soul and body is inappreciable. Just as we pass from a waking to a sleeping state without any knowledge of the precise moment when the change is effected, so too we pass without knowing it and without pain from life to death. The sort of pleasant prostration which we feel when we fall asleep gives us some idea of the vague and happy sensation which must prevail at the supreme moment when the torch of our existence is extinguished.

Our last moments are so far from painful that many persons have been able coldly to describe the successive symptoms proclaiming their speedy death. We may quote the case of Professor Richet (of the Institute), who died in January, 1892, of an inflammation of the chest, and described to those around

him with the greatest precision the successive
phenomena which revealed the effusion of the
lungs and the growth of the disease, and who pre-
dicted with assured and peaceful look the instant
when he should draw his last breath.

Dr. Trousseau's death was most singular; for up
o the last he described the progressive phases of his
disease, and ceased to give a sort of clinical lecture
upon himself only when he ceased to live.

Haller, the famous physiologist of the eighteenth
century, felt his own pulse as he lay dying, and
said quietly : " The pulse still beats, — the pulse
still beats, — it has ceased to beat!" and he expired without another word, without a groan.

Chirac, a physician of Montpellier, in the eighteenth century, fancying on his death-bed that he
was himself called to a patient, seized his own arm,
felt his pulse, and exclaimed: " You sent for me
too late! You should not have bled this man; you
should have purged him; now he is a dead man!"
and he closed his eyes never again to open them.

Dr. Baillarger, a member of the Academy of Medicine at Paris, who died in 1891, faded away gently
and almost without pain. He retained complete
possession of all his faculties up to the last moment. A few instants before he died, having talked
with Professor Potain, who, together with Desnos
and Guyon, had charge of his case, he asked one of
his daughters to read him an article from the medical dictionary upon a certain morbid symptom

which he felt at the moment. The reading over, he made a brief remark about the symptom in question, and turned on his pillow. A few seconds later he was no more.

" I feel the approach of death, and I feel it with joy," said Berthollet to his friend Chaptal, who was trying to reassure him. " Why should I fear it? I have never done any evil, and in my last hour I have the comforting thought that the friendship which has united us for more than forty years, and of which you have given so many proofs to me and mine, has never been troubled for a single instant. It is given to few men to pay such homage to themselves! That is enough for me; I desire no other."

This fine funeral oration, uttered by dying lips, far outweighs the words repeated by the physiologist Claude Bernard in his last agony: "The game's up!"

Here is a touching anecdote of the last moments of the celebrated surgeon Philip Ricord, who died in 1889.

Sinking beneath an inflammation of the chest, Ricord woke suddenly towards midnight, half rose in bed, and moved his hands in cadence, as if playing on the piano. The doctors, Horteloup and Pigrot, who were watching beside his bed, were greatly amazed, and took this gesture for an outbreak of delirium. Ricord, after repeating it several times without the power to pronounce a sound, fell back exhausted, the doctors being unable to divine what he wanted. Soon he died.

Next day his granddaughter, a child of ten, reached Paris with her mother, who had hastened from Algiers at the first news of his illness. " What a pity," said the child, " I could not keep the promise which I made to poor grandpapa ! " And she told how she had learned to play on the piano " Mary Stuart's Farewell," by Niedermeyer, because her grandfather had made her and also Batta, the famous violinist, promise that they would play for him, when he came to die, this piece which he loved above all others.

This was the idea which haunted Ricord's mind at his last hour. The family obtained permission to have the much desired melody played at his funeral.

Death may come during a fit of hilarity. We are told that the Stoic philosopher Chrysippus died of irrepressible laughter caused by seeing a monkey eat figs.

Reydellet, in the article on " Laughter " in the " Great Dictionary of the Medical Sciences," relates that a nun seized in the refectory with forced laughter all at once became as motionless as a statue. This was thought to be some new jest ; on approaching her, she was found to be dead.

Set aside, therefore, all these hideous images of death which arise solely from the sight of a motionless and icy human body. Let those who surround the dead shed no tears; for they may see on the colorless lips and in the dim eyes a vague smile at the delights perceived by those who have left them only to enter into a better world.

CHAPTER IV.

Inhabitants of the Ethereal Medium: their Attributes. — Vast Development of their Intellect. — New Senses and New Faculties. — Celestial Hierarchies. — Angels in Christian Dogma. — Travels of the Soul through the Universe.

"NATURA non fecit saltus" ("Nature makes no sudden leaps"), says Linnæus, by which he means that in the living creation everything moves by insensible gradations. The organism is perfected, in an ascending scale, from plants to animals and from animals to man. But there is a vast interval, in intellectual respects, between the animals and man : the animal is endowed, not with *instinct*, — a word meaning nothing, — but with a certain degree of intelligence limited by the imperfection of his organs and the slight development of his brain. Between man and God, in respect to morals, there is a yawning gulf. It is, therefore, impossible that there should not exist between God and man a series of creatures forming a progressive chain of intellectual potencies to fill up this huge hiatus.

These intermediary beings between God and man, whose necessity is most apparent, if Nature is to remain true to her general plan, are what the Christian religion calls *angels*, and what we call in the " To-morrow of Death " *superhuman beings*, who in our opinion inhabit interplanetary space.

Let us add that among these superhuman beings, regarded as a whole, there must exist consecutive degrees of perfection, progressive generations, in respect to intellect and morals.

There is nothing to hinder our believing that these successive generations of superior beings inhabit superimposed levels of planetary ether, — that, dying after a longer or shorter lease of life in a primary region of celestial geography, they pass after that death to the level immediately above, where they assume a new form ; and thus moving from district to district, from one celestial station to another, growing ever more perfect and acquiring fresh faculties more and more exquisite, in proportion to their successive deaths and reincarnations, they end by attaining to the supreme goal of their sublime journey, — that is to say, by penetrating to the central star of our world, the sun, where they become incorporated with the Divinity.

Is it not rash to try to particularize the degree of intelligence, the new senses and special faculties, vested in the inhabitants of ether, and to hazard somewhat in regard to the physical structure of those same beings ? We ventured this, in treating of the attributes of the superhuman being, in the

"To-morrow of Death." We will now carry that study, or rather those conjectures, further yet. Our readers will pardon us for trying to lift the veil which hides from us mysteries which death alone can reveal. Our boldness is explained by the title and object of the present work.

It seems to us most evident that superhuman beings must be, in both intellectual and moral respects, infinitely superior to man; that they must be as far superior to humanity as humanity itself is to animals.

The vast increase of intelligence in risen man results from two causes, — the perfecting of the senses which he possessed on earth; and the acquisition of new senses, which will lead him to enrich himself with faculties other than attention, judgment, comparison, memory, etc.

The acquisition of more subtle senses and new faculties will come to us from our knowledge of other planets than the earth, of other prospects than those upon which our eyes have gazed here below.

We know that our intellectual riches are increased by the comparisons which we draw from the various sights which we see. Our intelligence is developed in proportion as our comparisons are extended, multiplied, and diversified. What an advance, therefore, must our mind make when, instead of confining ourselves to a knowledge of earthly geographical localities, of the continents, islands, seas, and oceans of our globe, we can compare whole worlds one with another; when, instead of comparing the animal and vegetable species, we can compare the organic creations peculiar to the different regions of space?

It cannot be doubted, indeed, that the different zones of ether as well as the planets of our solar system have each their natural products, their individual economy, their special physical laws, and that there is nothing exactly the same in the various localities of heaven or in each planet. To believe, in fact, that all must be exactly alike in the infinite extent of celestial space would be to attribute to the Creator a sterility not of his essence; for fertility, in the realization of the forms of beings, is the peculiar attribute of the divine potentiality. If there be not on the earth two leaves, two insect wings, absolutely similar, what must not be the variety of types in the creatures peopling the ethereal medium? What varying aspects, temperatures, atmospheric pressures, and physical states the numerous interplanetary regions must present! Each celestial world must form an individual system, a distinct totality of things, not to be found in any other point of space.

What new forms of knowledge the superhuman being will gain, when he flies from planet to planet, or traverses the entire extent of the ethereal plains peopled with varied populations! How perfect will his intelligence become when he can com-

pare each with the other the inhabitants, natural
products, and peculiar economy of so many different regions! What a splendid cosmology will
result from an acquaintance with this transcendent
geography! What light it will throw upon physics, geometry, astronomy, and the natural sciences,
the means for observing which are so limited on
our globe! If we penetrate but a slight distance
into the domain of physics, we are stopped short
by the imperfection of our knowledge. The superhuman being will meet with no obstacle in the explanation of the physical action which bodies exert
one upon the other, because he will be acquainted
with all the phenomena and all the laws of Nature
in the various planets composing our solar world.
Chemistry will cease to have a secret for him, because, instead of laboriously combining, as we do,
the atomic formulas representing the chemical
molecule of composite bodies, he will distinctly
see the internal arrangement from which the interior structure of the molecule results. Instead
of reasoning, he will see that mysterious secret
architecture of composite substances which we
strive to fathom by every sort of comparison and
effort, usually in vain. The domain of astronomy
will be singularly enlarged in its turn, since the
inhabitant of celestial regions will have within his
reach the stars, which our optical instruments
find it so hard to show us, the majority of them
actually evading our telescopes.

It is therefore natural to conclude that new senses
will be added to those which man possesses on
earth, and that those already his will become
strangely perfect; finally and consequently, that
new faculties will be added to those which were
his upon earth.

We can form some idea of the development to be
attained by the superhuman being's faculties, by
considering the rare examples afforded by certain
individuals of the vast increase of memory.

Morphy, the famous chess-player, carried on ten
games at once, on as many boards, with his back
turned to them; and we have heard of several
amateurs at the present day who can perform the
same feat. The teacher of chess at my club played
ten games in this fashion in May, 1892; to be sure,
he lost half of them.

Paris, in 1892, saw the calculator Jacques Inaudi
renew the marvels of Henri Mondheux and Vito
Mangiamelo, stupefying, astounding the public as
well as scientists by his mnemonic power applied
to numbers. The young Piedmontese performed
instantaneous sums in arithmetic, addition, sub-
traction, division, multiplication, the extraction of
square or cube roots, etc., dealing with numbers
composed of some twenty figures at least; and this
without the least hesitation in a very few minutes.
He gave almost instantly the result of compound
interest embracing hundreds of years. He also
recited from memory all the figures written on the

blackboard for the sums that he had performed, and that without once glancing at the board.

All these feats of memory are plainly beyond the scope of human ability; and the case of Inaudi may be cited to show the great increase which our powers of memory may attain after death.

What then may not be the intellectual power of arisen man in celestial regions, when new senses and new faculties are added to its original senses, themselves singularly perfected? He will be infinitely superior to earthly man in the extraordinary activity of his intellectual life. Endowed with more organs and with new faculties, he will bring them into play according to circumstances. He can handle and work at his will living or inanimate matter, and act upon beings inferior to him with more energy, precision, and rapidity than we do here below. He can even act upon human beings without their knowledge, since we ourselves act upon animals, who are unconscious of the influence that we exert over them.

Can we form any idea of the form of the structure of the superhuman being? If we admit that the human soul set free from the perishable body is to take up its abode in a new body, we must acknowledge that the superhuman being must be composed of an immaterial substance, of a spirit, contained in a material envelope. But how slight must be the proportion of inorganic substances contained in that new body! The body of the superhuman being is semi-spiritualized, and the slight proportion of mineral matter which it contains gives it the privilege of floating in planetary ether as a bird flies in the air.

In addition to this, the superhuman being must be set free from all need of food, the absorption of the ethereal medium sufficing to replace those functions which in man constitute nutrition, respiration, and the circulation of the blood. The earth-dweller cannot exist without abundant daily food, without uninterrupted respiration, without an incessant circulation of the blood through internal canals. He maintains his life only by watering with the sweat of his brow the earth which supports him. It is only at the cost of excessive labor and fatigue that he provides for his nourishment, his locomotion, his clothing, and his lodging. The superhuman being freed from the necessity of providing for his nourishment, and locomotion costing him no effort, what vast happiness must fall to his lot !

Let us not forget, moreover, that in ethereal space there is neither day nor night. The inhabitant of interplanetary regions always sees the sun, since he is not confined as we are to a planet whose rotation upon its axis, hiding the radiant star from his sight for half the space of its revolution upon itself, produces the succession, the alternation of day and night. He is perpetually bathed in light ; no cloud, no interposition of any star, ever coming to deprive him of the sight of the sun.

In celestial space no seasons are known, — that is, those periodical variations of temperature and moisture which result from the earth's periodic course about the sun, and which provoke on our globe heat and cold according to its distance from the sun. Placed outside the range of all planets in motion, the superhuman being is exempt from the vicissitudes of the seasons, and is, consequently, sheltered from the diseases which afflict the human race and which result from climatic causes.

In brief, in arisen man there will be found, in our opinion, the same elements as in terrestrial man ; only they are metamorphosed, and made worthy of the destiny of the higher being to whom they belong. Spirit predominates in enormous proportions over matter. All that was destructible and ephemeral in man disappears. All principles of fragility, inferiority, and corruption are eliminated. The physiological functions being reduced to their extremest simplicity, the new being has neither any effort to produce, nor any disease to dread. His life is a uniform and constant state of serenity and happiness. No more hate, no more jealousy, either between individuals or between nations. A general affection unites groups as well as persons. All desires, all pleasures, assume a similar character, — inward happiness and adoration of God. Love, so selfish, so restless, so tyrannical on earth, changes its nature and is turned to continual admiration of the Creator's works and to divine affection. Reproduction, generation, are no longer necessary; the fresh legions destined to replace those elevated to higher levels being replaced by arrivals from the various planets. The multiplication of beings takes place below; their reunion and sojourn, above.

And yet, let us clearly state, it is the same individual, it is the same *personality*, that endures. In passing from earth to heaven, it retains its memory, judgment, and freedom. It has merely acquired organic and spiritual perfection. In taking possession of his new and blest domain, the individual loses nothing of the integrity of his being, and the remembrance of his past existence makes him appreciate yet more the joys of his present life. None of the imperfections of his earthly body are to be found in him; none of the vices which may have degraded his original soul. All corruption has vanished in the brilliant flame of his moral regeneration. During his earthly life his intellect was often depressed by disease; the imperfections of his organs caused him sufferings which arrested his activity. All is now changed. If death surprised him in his youth, resurrection gives him the experience which time brings to old men; if he dies full of days, the resurrection restores to him the vigor and energy of youth. In heaven there is neither old age nor youth; all possess integrality in perfection, as well as equal power of physical constitution and morals.

It is, of course, impossible to know what form the inhabitants of planetary space wear. We only know that often in earthly man the soul fashions the body, that a good and upright soul stamps upon the features of the face and the forms of the body a character in harmony with its qualities; that a fine body is usually the dwelling of a pure spirit, and that a noble countenance proclaims a beautiful soul. It is, therefore, to be presumed that beauty of form, grace of feature, limpid gaze, charm and sweetness of physiognomy, harmonious proportions between the different parts of the body are the privilege of the happy beings whom we dimly perceive by a bold glance through the veil cast over the great mystery of the resurrection.

Among the privileges granted to the angel of space, we must note the ease with which he travels from one part of the world to the other. If we ourselves can journey in thought from one end of the earth to the other, the superhuman being, who is essentially composed of spirit, must possess the same advantage, and be able to traverse any distance almost instantaneously. The journeys which our mean human condition surrounds with so many obstacles are but child's play to him. He visits at will all points of our globe; and he traverses not only the earth, but the other planets of our solar system. What treasures of knowledge he will glean in these excursions from one world to another, these bold flights from planet to planet, these marvellous peregrinations in the depths of space which divide one star from another! It is probably through these distant journeys that the spirit of the inhabitants of ether is made perfect, and that they acquire the progressive perfection of their intelligence, while by a succession of deaths and resurrections, resurrections and deaths, they cast aside their material elements more and more wholly, to end at last by becoming pure spirits; for the superhuman being must become absolutely spiritual before his existence is finally ended, — that is to say, before he enters the sun, and is incorporated with its substance, to constitute a part of the divinity.

By admitting the existence of beings superior to humanity, a sort of intermediaries between man and God, we do but revive a dogma peculiar to many ancient religions and to Christianity. China, India, Chaldea, Persia, and Egypt were early imbued with this idea. The religion of Buddha establishes a long hierarchy of angels, or demi-gods, now dwelling on earth and now residing in heaven; and the books of Zoroaster contain numerous details in regard to the angels recognized by the Persian religion.

This dogma, which prevailed throughout the East, was introduced after their captivity in Babylon by the Jews, who learned it of the Chaldean Magi. The Bible often speaks of angels acting as messengers and agents of the divine will. In the New Testament stories, the appearance of angels is connected with all the great facts of Jewish history.

The prophet Isaiah tells us that God is upborne by a cloud of cherubim who sing his praises. An angel named Michael overcomes a fallen angel known as Asmodeus.

The number of angels, according to the Hebrews, is incalculable. " Thousand thousands ministered unto Him," says the prophet Daniel, " and ten thousand times ten thousand stood before Him."

Jesus Christ, addressing the apostle Saint Peter, who has drawn his sword to defend him, says: " Thinkest thou that I cannot now pray to my Father, and he shall presently give me more than twelve legions of angels ?"

In addition to the missions intrusted to the angels Gabriel and Raphael, we find in sacred history other angels holding back the arm of Abraham who is about to sacrifice his son ; predicting to Sarah that she is to become a mother ; consoling Hagar in the desert and showing her a spring, to restore her dying son ; struggling with Jacob to test his strength ; saving Lot from the destruction of Sodom ; succouring the Maccabees in the heat of battle ; delivering Saint Peter from his cell ; bearing the prophet Habakkuk upon their wings to Daniel in the lions' den ; teaching Tobias the secret of the fish's liver, which he is to roast upon hot coals to cure his blind father.

Sacred Scripture, which speaks of the existence of these ethereal natures, says nothing of their essence or their attributes. It limits itself to glorifying their felicity, purer than ours, and to saying that they are the ministers of the will of God. Jesus Christ says nothing of their prerogatives. He represents them to us merely as intermediary beings, much nearer than ourselves to the throne of the Most High, taking a tender interest in the happiness of humanity ; just as charitable mortals constitute themselves the friends and protectors of inferior beings.[1]

The following are the attributes of these various beings, according to the book of Saint Denis the Areopagite, entitled *De cœlesti hierarchia.*

The *seraphim* preside over love ; the *cherubim* are vowed to silence ; the *thrones* possess divine majesty ; the *dominations* have power over men ; the *virtues* possess the gift of working miracles ; the *powers* are opposed to demons ; the *principalities* watch over empires ; the *archangels* and the *angels* are the messengers of God.

Each of these *hierarchies* inhabits a different part of heaven, higher in proportion as they approach more nearly to God.

In the religion of Buddha, of which we shall have occasion to speak in the course of this volume, we find the same distribution of beings superior to humanity in different regions of the sky, superim-

[1] Matthew xviii. 10.

posed one upon the other according as they are nearer to the divine essence through their merits and their virtues.

In the Catholic doctrine, which here again approaches Buddhist ideas, the angels are not absolutely perfect. They were created, no doubt, in a state of happiness and grace; but they are free to choose between good and evil. Hence come *good angels* and *bad angels*, a dogma which is one of the fundamental points of Roman Catholic doctrine in regard to the angelic state.

It was pride which brought about the decline and fall of certain angels, who became demons. Satan is the leader of these degenerate legions.

Mysterious relations exist between good angels and humanity. These good angels guide and sustain men in the right path, while bad angels are the instigators of evil.

An opinion which is very prevalent, although not an article of faith, holds that every man has his good angel, who is known as his *guardian angel*.

The guardian angel allotted to each one of us at birth or baptism upholds us in moments of temptation; he leads us to choose what is right instead of what is evil; he offers our prayers to God, and himself prays for us.

Another very general opinion is that each nation, each country, each church, each community, and even each star in the firmament has its special angel who watches over its preservation. In virtue of this, the archangel Michael is considered the protector of France.

Let us hasten to say that all which relates to the angels is not an article of faith in the Roman Catholic doctrine. No ecclesiastical decision authorizes the accusal of heresy of those who reject them. Certain councils have even combated all these views *in toto ;* but they finally triumphed, however, and the fact of the existence of angels and of the homage which is due to them has become canonical. We know that the Catholic Church celebrates the feast of the Holy Guardian Angels on the 2d of October each year. Nor do we really see why angels should be shut off from worship when saints are admitted. There is a forced correlation between dogma and worship. It was impossible to attribute to angels a direct and close action on man, and to prevent the faithful from soliciting their aid by prayers and religious homage. The worship of angels and the periodic celebration of their feast-days were introduced into the Catholic rite by the force of things.

During the Middle Ages much difficulty was felt as to the proper way of representing the angels of the various hierarchies in pictures. According to a Byzantine work, the " Guide to Painting," the *thrones* should be represented by a wheel of fire, surrounded by wings, the middle of the wings being sprinkled with eyes, and the whole simulating a throne. Several hierarchies of angels are provided with wings: the *cherubim* have two, the *seraphim* six. The *dominations, virtues,* and *powers* should wear ample white robes, with gold sash and green stole.

The wings and white vestments given to good angels by artists of the Middle Ages express their immaterial essence and the purity of their nature.

The angel, as represented by mediæval artists, with his regular features, long hair held in place by a fillet, his white robes and hieratic attitude, made a deep impression on the minds of religious persons. Thus conceived, the image of the Christian angel has come down to our day.

Mediæval theologians asked an endless number of questions in regard to the angelic nature. How far, they inquired, does the knowledge of these pure spirits extend? Do they penetrate the thoughts of man? Do they know the essence of God? Can they foretell the future? What is their language? What is the form of their body? What are their abiding-places?

Casuists gave very varied answers to these questions; but the Church has never declared herself upon these particular points.

We now venture to take up, in our turn, the bold problems which Christian scholastics put to one another. We have ventured some ideas as to the physical and moral conditions proper to the being higher than humanity whose type we have conceived. Our rashness is not without excuse, since in striving to lift the veil which hides so great a secret of

Nature, we have but followed in the path traced by ecclesiastical authors.

A final consideration will close this chapter.

In spite of the perfection of astronomy, there is a class of stars whose origin it has never been able to explain ; we refer to comets.

Not all the stars in our solar system obey the laws of gravitation ; that is, not all are subject to describe ellipses, in variable orbits, around the sun. There are those that are detached from our solar system, which deviate from it, as if to bear to remote globes news from our solar world. Thus Laplace called comets *the vagabonds of space.* If comets enter a region where there is considerable solar attraction, they diverge towards the sun, and at last plunge into its fiery heart. But if a chance encounter with a nearer star turns them aside from this road, they pass into another solar system, and we see them no more.

Comets are, in brief, absolutely irregular stars, which are sometimes destroyed in the body of our sun, sometimes depart from it, never again to re-appear, at least to our eyes.

No astronomer has yet been able to explain the nature of comets, to estimate their size or their weight, or even to prove that they have any weight whatsoever. Some of them are seen to reappear, if any one is able to observe them long enough to trace their orbit ; but even if they reappear, they are changed in form, disjointed, and fragmentary. They often break to pieces, on meeting other stars, which explains their deformities. They are, generally, furnished with a luminous train, always directed away from the sun, and known as their *tail;* but this train is frequently missing or disappears, without affecting their motion.

What is the matter which constitutes comets? What is the cause of their strange and variable forms? The changes which they undergo during the period of their appearance, and which sometimes follow one another with amazing rapidity, clearly denote a very peculiar physical constitution, but throw no light whatever on the nature of the matter which constitutes them.

We know, it is true, that their nucleus is a physical body, but there is nothing to prove that the rest of the comet — the tail, for instance — is a body. We cannot attribute either mass or density to the tails of comets; the form and motion which they affect are contrary to the laws of gravitation.

Thus we know nothing of the nature of cometary substance. Scientists disagree as to the chemical elements composing it. "To establish our knowledge of these points," says M. Amédée Guillemin, in his work on "Comets," "one of those events so dreaded by timid and superstitious people must occur: our globe must encounter a comet in its journey, or rather, to make the matter more harmless, even taken hypothetically, we will say a mere fragment of a comet. The penetration of the material of that fragment into the atmosphere, its fall to the ground, permitting scientific men to see with their eyes and touch with their hands the cometary substance, would cut short all uncertainty."

However, as no comet has hitherto come in contact with the earth, astronomers have lacked opportunity to become acquainted with the composition of these vagabond stars.

And yet their number is so considerable that it is surprising that none of them has dashed against our globe. Kepler writes : "There are as many comets in the sky as there are fishes in the ocean." And according to Amédée Guillemin, there exist some *seventy-four thousand billions* of these stars subject to the dominion of the sun !

Since science fails us, evades us, when we ask an explanation of the nature of comets and the part that they play in the universe, it is lawful for imagination to put in its word. Shall I, dear reader, venture an opinion here, connected with the system of interplanetary existence worked out in this book ? I have already suggested that the happy inhabitants of ether have the privilege of travelling through the depths of heaven, before they attain the final goal of their existence, — that is to say, before they enter the sun. Is it forbidden us to believe that certain comets, those which re-enter our solar system, are *agglomerations of the souls of superhuman beings,* who have just accomplished a journey through the deeps of heaven, and are completing their voyage by hastening into the fiery furnace of the sun ? According to this hypothesis, comets would be the *excursion trains of the population of ethereal space!*

I travelled in my youth; but it was for my scientific instruction. Since acquiring my novel ideas, I have led a sedentary life. And when my friends express surprise at this, I answer : " I shall have plenty of time for travelling after I die ; and I shall see countries whose existence you do not even suspect." This makes them laugh ; but I do not waste my time in explanations.

CHAPTER V.

THERE is in the human mind an immense desire to know and to learn, which can never be fully satisfied on this earth, by reason of the inefficacy of our means of observation and comparison, and the absence of instruments giving us the means to pierce to the secret heart of matter. We cannot unravel the reason or the end and aim of the great natural phenomena occurring all about us. We must rest content with admiring them and profiting by them when we can. Heat, light, electricity, magnetism, are manifested on our globe by effects which we clearly observe, without being able to estimate either their object or their cause. The earth is an inexhaustible field of study to the philosopher; but he can only admire the pictures which it spreads before him, without the ability to explain them.

In the air and in the bosom of the waters live innumerable legions of animal and vegetable species,

6

whose types are infinitely varied by the inexhaustible fertility of the Creator.   At the bottom of the deepest seas, and beneath vast pressure, live animal species, fishes, mollusks, and crustacea, differing notably from those dwelling in the upper regions of the selfsame waters.

On the other hand, the invisible world, the beings of microscopic dimensions, which we can only appreciate by using magnifying-glasses, are quite as rich in animal and vegetable species; and their types vary in extraordinary fashion.   The population of the kingdom of the invisible, whether peculiar to normal organic liquids, or to organic substances in a state of decomposition, lives and is reproduced with a rapidity akin to the miraculous, and which the naturalist can never cease to admire. Under the eye armed with a microscope, whole generations of animalculæ are born and die; and yet it is impossible for us to understand the exact part which these infinitely little creatures play in the economy of Nature.

After the infinitely little, the infinitely great. The innumerable stars which shine in the firmament reveal to us wonders of another order. Thousands of suns, surrounded by their train of planets and satellites, are borne along by the movement of universal gravitation.   There are, as we have already stated, stars which we cannot see, because it would take their light thousands of years to reach us.   The depths of space, therefore, are filled with stars like those which we see. And all these systems of stars, moving in harmony with unchanging laws, compose regular whirlpools, which become intertangled, and extend to the uttermost depths of the heavens. The mind pauses in amaze, when it strives to understand the cause of this vortex of motions.

Thus the invisible world with its smallness, and the visible world with its immensity, exceed the bounds of comprehension of our intelligence.

Well, — we have not a moment's doubt of it, — the superhuman being, endowed with senses and faculties appropriate to his sublime essence, is in a state to grasp the reason and cause of all these mysteries. He knows why the infinitely little exists, and why the infinitely great was created. He pursues the treasures of universal Nature, living or lifeless, into yawning gulfs where the thought of man could never penetrate. Raised to an incalculable degree of comprehension, he embraces all that is, and knows the final causes of all the creations of God.

Let us add that, higher yet than all these creations, is that which contemplates them, admires and judges them : our mind, which is a no less amazing marvel. During our earthly life our own intellect is an enigma to us. We know neither the origin nor the mechanism of our faculties. We cannot explain the mode of the union of the soul with the body. We cannot tell what

thought is, the principle of intellect; nor what
speech is, the means of expression and special
relation to our species; nor what life is, the addition of which to soul and body composes the *human
aggregate*. Embarrassed in our study of ourselves
by paucity of time, lack of means of observation,
and by other causes, hardly suspected, we can
explain nothing in regard to our individuality, and
we live in complete ignorance of our own nature.
No doubt, after death the obstacles which hin-
dered the study of our thinking personality will
disappear, and we shall be in possession of the
happiness of knowing ourselves, — that is to say, of
knowing wherein our own thought consists.

For after death our faculties are transformed,
extended, multiplied. Memory ceases to be a fugi-
tive, feeble, intermittent faculty; it embraces all
that ever existed. Intelligence is no longer that
laborious effort so rarely crowned with success; it
is an instantaneous intuition, by which we understand everything suddenly and without fatigue.
The will is no longer that prolonged hesitation,
that painful deliberation, that vacillation between
opposite decisions, moving from one extreme to
the other; it is a firm and prompt choice, going
straight to the mark, without pause, without
uncertainty, without distraction, which strikes
and acts at once. On quitting earthly life, we
are in possession of a personality always fully lord
of itself, and ruling its thoughts and actions with

a firm hand. True moral light guides its conscience, illuminates its thought, concentrates its
actions, as a crystal lens reunites and concentrates
the rays of the sun upon a single point, which it
ends by setting on fire.

But it is not enough to know and explain the
phenomena peculiar to earth, to astronomic worlds,
and to ourselves. We must also strive to understand the sublime Creator of all these entities; we
must conceive God, that supreme potentiality, whom
science recognizes, whom philosophy proclaims, and
whom religion points out for the adoration of men.

We have already stated how, in our astronomic
theosophy, we conceive of divinity. We place it in
the geometric centre of the universe, at that unknown focus towards which the orbits of all systems
of stars converge, around which stellar worlds revolve, with a slow but continuous motion. This
general focus is placed somewhere in the depths of
the heavens: we cannot point out the place where it
lies, save in imagination; but it exists, since all the
stars, apparently fixed, revolve around His radiant
throne.

This unknown focus, the cause of all the movements of the universe; that JEHOVAH, who beholds
all the stars which make up the universe revolve
about this burning mass; that supreme God, who
compels the secondary gods (that is, the stars) to
march obediently past his sublime rays; that Cre-

ator, whose essence no human philosophy has ever
been able to penetrate, — is probably not unknown
to the superhuman being, when he reaches the highest spiritual hierarchies of the celestial battalions.

The spiritualized being, ready to enter into the
substance of the sun, and already himself a portion
of divinity, will probably be privileged to understand JEHOVAH and to grasp His supreme attributes.
He will see that JEHOVAH is infinite in extent, since
He is greater, in Himself alone, than all the solar
systems combined. He will understand that He is
infinite in duration; that is to say, that He had no
beginning and can have no end. He will know why
He is infinite in perfections and in power, why
everything emanates from Him, everything proceeds
from Him, everything derives its life from His
radiant bosom, everything finds its source in His
inexhaustible and sublime fertility.

And having once understood the essence of the
secondary divinities and the residence of the supreme divinity, the ruler and master of the universe, the superhuman being wholly spiritualized
will have the key to every event in the history of
earthly humanity and planetary humanities. He
will know why Providence permitted certain events,
apparently inexplicable, or seemingly contrary to
providential wisdom and goodness. He will know
why on our earth the just man is persecuted and
vice triumphant. What astonished us in the history of nations or in the destiny of individuals will

strike him as just, and he will admire it. What once distressed him will be his consolation ; what filled him with fear will be his joy. The magnificent sum total of the general plan of the universe will appear to him clearly, and will light up for him the history of the past and the apparent injustices of human society towards its most deserving members. Everything will be explained in the destiny of nations and the fate of empires. We shall understand the formation, the progress in power, and the decline of nations, in harmony with the decrees of the divine will, which shall be made known to us. The struggles, passions, and various actions of men belonging to other planets than our own will likewise be explained by the general plan of Providence, which will appear to us in all its distinctness. Spectators of God's dominion over his creatures, we shall be made acquainted with the motives for his decrees, and shall proclaim their universal grandeur.

If we pass from these cosmologic grandeurs to that which is personal to us, we shall also comprehend God's action in regard to ourselves ; the part which He assigned us during our earthly life, His reasons for afflicting us during that period with misfortunes, grief, and tears, and the compensations which He reserved for us during our succeeding lives. We shall understand that our misfortunes on this earth were merely the preparations by which God paved the way for our future happiness, and we shall even perceive, in spite of our humbleness and the small space which we occupy in the infinity of worlds, what part has fallen to our lot in the harmony of the universe.

In the presence of such prospects, how can any one fear death? Death is only a natural incident in the continuity of our existences, and it is destined to open to us a career of eternal happiness. Let us become thoroughly imbued with this thought, in order that we may endure the critical moment of the separation of soul and body, and banish the apprehension which that dreaded moment arouses in the heart of all men.

In the following chapters we shall enumerate the *joys to be found beyond the threshold,* the chief subject of this work.

CHAPTER VI.

Joys beyond the Threshold. — We shall meet in Heaven.

OF all the joys which await us after death, the first which is assured to us is that we shall again find upon the threshold of our new life those whom we have loved and lost.

To establish this fact I start from the following train of reasoning : —

Whatever may be the evolutions, the transformations through which we must pass after death, they are the same for all men. Thus we are subject to the self-same metamorphoses, on leaving this earth, we traverse the same road traversed by those who preceded us to the tomb. Hence we must meet them in the new abiding-place which is their lot. How many consolations lie in this one thought, — that death, far from severing the ties which bound us to loved ones, to parents and friends, does but reunite us to them for eternity !

The friend of my childhood, the companion of my youth, was named Henry Barre. He was the son of a glover and haberdasher, whose shop was situ-

ated in the Rue du Cardinal at Montpellier, just opposite the apothecary-shop kept by my father, Jean
Figuier. We were sent together, as mere children,
to the dame school of Mother Grand-Jean, in the
Place du Petit-Scel. Mother Grand-Jean was a tall,
thin woman, who sat in a high arm-chair, with a
rod as long as the room, within easy reach, which
she used to correct from a distance, with a tap on
the head or shoulders, any child who fell asleep or
rebelled. We went together later on to M. Crozal's
boarding-school, on the ground floor of a fine house
in the Rue Embouque-d'or, whose second story was
occupied by the Faculty of Sciences, then including
Professors Gergonne, Lentheric, Balard, and other
distinguished men. Finally, we were both sent to
the grammar-school as day scholars.

Henry Barre was a studious and attentive scholar,
but I was heedless enough. I never studied between the morning and afternoon sessions. I
devoted the entire interval to furious and endless
games with comrades as hot-headed as myself, —
hide-and-seek, leap-frog, ball. Our games were
renewed at five o'clock, when school closed, and
lasted until nightfall. There were mad races and
hand-to-hand contests, that left us exhausted and
panting with fatigue ; which did not however prevent us from beginning anew next day.

By these endless sports I lost the instruction
which I might have gained ; but I gained the
robust constitution which has never left me.

It was only in rhetoric and philosophy that Father Flottes, our teacher, afterward professor of the Faculty of Letters, seeing in me some literary aptitudes, succeeded in inspiring me with a taste for study. I made sufficient progress to win the prize for rhetoric and for a philosophical essay.

Father Flottes liked to read my compositions to the other pupils. He considered my style " too redundant ; " but he added that Quintilian did not object to this fault in youth, as it disappears with age. And when Quintilian is on your side, you may hold yourself to be a fair classical scholar.

But I never acquired any idea of mathematics at school, for want of good teachers. Still I had to know how to cipher in order to pass the examinations which precede any university degree. Henry Barre, who was all-accomplished, constituted himself my teacher in mathematics. Thanks to him, at eighteen I took the degree of Bachelor of Arts, for which an extensive knowledge of mathematics was requisite, since it embraced the half of algebra and rectilinear trigonometry.

I shall never forget the agitation and singular emotion which I felt one evening on hearing my young friend, who was also my master, explain the physical theory of the rainbow to me.

Is there any phenomenon at once more majestic, more impressive, and more beautiful than the splendid appearance known under the name, both exact and poetic, of rainbow ? Whenever we witness the wondrous spectacle of this sort of gigantic bridge spanning the horizon across the celestial arch, where the richest colors play in regular bands, we feel a longing desire to know the real cause of this magnificent piece of stage scenery in the open air.

Newton gave us the physico-mathematical explanation of the rainbow.

Every one knows that light, white light, is the result of the union of the seven primary colors, — violet, indigo, blue, green, yellow, red, and orange. In fact, a ray of solar light passing through a prism made of transparent glass or clear water gives us a colored band, reproducing the seven colors above named. It is an experiment which has now become commonplace.

The rainbow is the result of the decomposition of the light of the sun, produced by means of the drops of water suspended in the air. We know that this phenomenon occurs only after a rain which, owing to peculiar meteorological circumstances, allows tiny globules of water to float in the air while the sun is shining at the opposite extreme of the horizon. The drops of water in suspension play the part of small liquid prisms which decompose the light into its primary colors.

The rainbow resulting from the decomposition of light by globules of water floating in the atmosphere, we must turn our back to the sun in order to see it; so that the rays of light, once decomposed, are reflected in the interior of the drop of water, and meet the eye of the spectator. If he turn in the direction of the sun, the effect vanishes.

There is thus a double cause for the rainbow : the decomposition of light into its seven elementary colors, effected inside the drops of water; and the reflection of these decomposed rays which takes place inside the same drop of water.

The rainbow appears in full splendor only in the morning and at sunset. This is because the nearer the sun is to the horizon, the greater is the visible portion of the arch. In proportion as the sun rises in the heavens the arch decreases, and it completely disappears when the sun is forty-two degrees above the horizon.

Newton summed up in an algebraic formula all the conditions on which this phenomenon depends; namely, the width of each band of color, the exact proportions of each of them, the shape of the arch according to the height in the sky, etc.

This theory my young friend developed for me on the blackboard. As he traced the series of corollaries of the Newtonian law, each phase and each condition of the phenomenon appeared, one after the other, with its clear, rational, and perfect explanation ; and the most minute secondary pecu- liarities were explained with the most amazing precision.

As all these deductions were thus drawn, one by

one, master and pupil were both overcome by deep emotion; and when the calculation ended, tears flowed from their eyes.

Laugh who will at this outburst of sensibility in two young students before the solution of a problem in mathematics; but we were working at the time in my little room on a summer night. The open window showed us the moonlight reflected, on the horizon, in a long silvery ribbon, in the Mediterranean. The stars shone in the sky, and the poetry of that sight combined with the marvels of science to throw our souls into a state of emotion readily understood by those who love both science and Nature.

To rest us after our studies we had music, dear to all Southerners. The Catholic Society of Montpellier had arranged organ masses in the Church of the White Penitents, sung in the gallery by amateurs of the town, and in his leisure moments directed by Laurens, secretary of the Faculty of Medicine, but an artist to his very marrow. Laurens, who died director of the Montpellier Museum of Painting and Sculpture, made engravings and lithographs for illustrated papers of Paris, representing the most interesting points in the scenery of Lower Languedoc and Provence, as well as the costumes and types of beauty of Arles and Provence. He was also passionately addicted to ancient music. The masses which he gave at the Church of the White Penitents were by Cherubini, Sebastian Bach, and earlier masters.

One had to be able to read music at sight to gain admission to the masses of Laurens. We took as teacher, at ten francs a month, an old musician from the orchestra of the theatre, Father Vincent, who was only half as big as his double-bass, and had to climb upon a stool in order to play his instrument. He was an excellent musician, who soon enabled us to " sol-fa " at sight. Henry was gifted with a pretty counter-tenor voice, — one of those voices now in but little demand, but very useful as soprani in pieces for several voices where women are not allowed, — and I had a robust tenor. Father Vincent formed the third note in the harmony with his double-bass.

Is there anything more delightful than to take part in those beautiful musical compositions by the old masters, whose harmony penetrates and thrills you? The Colonne Concerts at Paris have their charm ; but can you compare the cold impression received by the music-lover, seated in his chair, with that of the performer, who mingles his voice with the symphonies of the choruses and the tones of the organ re-echoing from the arches of a church ?

My family, made up of rigid Huguenots, were not pleased at my visits to a Catholic church. My father was born at Sommières, a small town in Gard at the foot of the Cevennes, the scene of bloody battles during the war of the Protestant peasants against the soldiers of Louis XIV. ; and my mater-

nal grandfather, Louis Gourgas, was a bonded ware-
house-keeper of salt, and possessor of vineyards at
Lunel, not far from Nismes, where such fearful
dramas took place during the long period of the
Camisard war. My mother scolded me well for
missing the Protestant service on Sunday morning
and going to the Papists; but I won her forgive-
ness by accompanying her that same Sunday
afternoon to the Protestant Church.

Thursday of each week was devoted by us to long
excursions into the country. There was once, just
outside of Montpellier, a lonely valley planted with
great trees and watered by a pretty stream, — I
mean Valette Woods, now vanished. We would
start at six in the morning, — Henry with his naturalist's box for plants and insects, I with my net for
butterflies. What pleasant hours we passed, bathed
in sunshine and verdure, seeking for insects and
plants! I have seen many collections of insects
and butterflies since then. I have examined those
of Holland and the Museum at Paris; I have admired the specimens collected by Dr. Chenu, in the
Delessert Museum, and those of Dr. Sichel, the ocu-
list, who was also a bold hunter of butterflies. But
nothing can ever make me forget the little box of
painted wood into which I pinned my insects; for
each of those specimens recalled an incident in my
morning strolls in Valette Woods.

When obliged by fatigue to stop and rest, we
stretched ourselves in the shade of an oak or a

chestnut, each with a book. Mine was a volume of J. J. Rousseau, — the Confessions, Émile, or the New Heloise ; for in my youth I had a genuine passion for the writings of the Genevese philosopher. Henry, more matter of fact, read some anatomical treatise.

Another favorite spot for our natural-history trips was the shore of the Mediterranean. Now a railroad takes us in twenty minutes from Montpellier to Palavas, where a seashore resort has sprung up, with elegant cottages and luxurious hotels. But at that time Palavas, situated at the mouth of the Lez and at the meeting of the canals near the salt marshes, was only a fishing-village. It was known as the *Cabins*, and consisted of not more than a score of huts. We followed the banks of the Lez to reach the Cabins, because we could gather on our way the plants that grew on its shores before we gathered those of the beach, which formed an interesting flora at all seasons.

When our botanical harvest was finished, we entered the hut of some fisherman and dined on a good plate of *bouillabaisse,* cooked by the master of the house.

Bouillabaisse is not what people foolishly imagine. It has nothing in common with what is served under that name in Parisian restaurants, which is made up of a few lobster claws and scraps of mullet and bar, with a suspicion of saffron. Southern bouillabaisse is a fish-chowder. For the meat of beef-

7

stew is substituted fish of all sorts, made unfit for sale by the accidents of the take or by their quality. These are boiled in water for a long time; the flavor is enhanced by saffron and various spices, and the whole is then poured over slices of bread. The bread and broth are eaten first, — that is the *fish-chowder*. The boiled fish comes afterward; and when you have swallowed a fisherman's bouilla-baisse, you can, I assure you, go all day without having your stomach cry out for more food.

Henry and I entered the medical school as students. Henry devoted himself to anatomy, under Dubreuil; and I to chemistry, with Balard. As he was an indefatigable worker, he won the position of anatomical preparator after a successful competition. Under his direction and instructions I prepared for the examination in anatomy, the second examination in medicine, without making any break in my chemical and physical studies, for which I began to feel a liking, which was greatly to increase later on, and to lead me to teach chemistry at the Montpellier School of Pharmacy and afterward in Paris.

However, Henry had no money; and his parents urged him to choose a profession which would insure him a future. He decided on military surgery. He passed the examination for surgeon's assistant with honor, and having gained his degree, put himself at the disposal of his military chiefs. He was sent to Constantine. I escorted him to the stage-coach for Marseilles, and took leave of him with a sad and secret presentiment, which was but too well justified.

In fact, no sooner had he reached Constantine, than he was attacked by one of those violent fevers so common in Algeria in the early days of colonization, and he had great difficulty in shaking it off. Later, the Crimean War breaking out, he was ordered to the hospital at Varna. But two months after the beginning of his service he was attacked by typhus, which raged as an epidemic in the hospital, and he died.

I received this sad news at Paris, and my heart was torn.

My readers will pardon these personal memories. My purpose is to call up in their minds similar impressions, to recall to their memory those whom they have loved and who have been torn from them, and to give birth within them to the consoling thought that they shall yet meet again those who have been taken away from their tenderness.

Yes, our friends, our parents, our children, our wives, — all those we have loved and lost, — we shall meet them all in our heavenly home. They will greet us on the threshold of eternity ; they will be our guides in those new domains, with which they have had time to grow familiar ; and we will again take up with them the chain of happiness broken by our separation. Can anything be more potent to soften the apprehension of our end than the certainty of soon meeting the beings whom we have loved and who have preceded us to the tomb?

Can that be happiness which is not shared with those we love? Must not heavenly affections be the continuation and complement of those here below? As we established in "The To-morrow of Death," the memory of our previous existences, which we lack on earth, will be our privilege in heaven. Memory is, in truth, the faculty essential and indispensable to our individuality when raised from the dead. Without memory, there would be no identity, and to be born again with no recollection of our past existence would not be to be born again, but to fall into oblivion. Memory being the privilege of a man arisen from the dead, he will have perfectly present to his thought the feelings which he cherished during his earthly life, for his friends, for his relations, for those whose character and virtues he admired. Our heart will not be changed after death ; it will remain what it was, loving and remembering that it loved, even disposed to love yet more than on earth, to double its friendship, its love, its gratitude, and its admiration, — for the obstacles which the incidents and difficulties of life here below opposed to its feelings will cease to exist in spheres above.

Two friends have lived on earth, united by a close and constant affection. They have suffered together; they have battled, side by side, in the struggle for life. The existence of one was that of the other. They had their work, their desires, their ambitions, their efforts, their hopes, in common. They looked forward to the same goal; they walked in the same path. They understood their duties to their country and their fellow-beings in one and the same way. They prayed to the same God. They had but a single heart and a single thought. Death alone could separate them. And do you think that the mere accident of death, which counts for so little in the plan of Nature, could break all the ties which existed between them? Do you think that they could thereafter be strangers, unknown to each other? Lost, each for himself, in the realms of space, are they to begin, far from each other, a new and independent career? Shall they be refused the just reward of their mutual devotion, which consists in their eternal reunion and in the resumption of their former affection? It cannot be. Everything in the universe is constant, eternal. The moral world can be no exception to the physical world.

Father, who hast formed the wisdom, the honor, the soul of a beloved son, shalt thou not enjoy in celestial homes the joy of reunion with him who was, alas the day! torn from thy arms by relentless death?

Son, who hast watched with ceaseless tenderness and solicitude over a venerated father and hast lost him, shalt thou not, when thy turn comes to make thy way to heavenly homes, be reunited to him whom thy heart has never ceased to love ?

Husband and wife, you who have trodden together the thorny paths of life ; who have found in your reciprocal love, your touching abnegation, efficient help against deception, bitterness, grief, and misfortune ; who have worshipped together that God who inspires the sacred sentiment of love in the hearts of human couples, — shall you be deprived of the reward due to your virtues, which consists in enjoying together the pleasures of the new life reserved, on celestial shores, for virtuous souls ?

If it were so, then heaven were not heaven, that is the place for the just reward and beatitude of human beings risen again in power and glory.

Ah ! let us not doubt it, death interrupts nothing : it does but improve and perfect ; it does but complete and strengthen the relations of beings who felt mutual sympathy upon earth. All that was good, healthy, and generous in hearts bound together by close friendship, shall be preserved in the new life, as an integral part of their being. The sentiments of the soul will not be changed ; they will merely be purified, freed from every imperfection, every weakness, every impure alloy. And instead of being transient and ephemeral, as here, they will have all eternity before them.

Let us, therefore, cease to weep for the dead ; they are happier than we. *Beati qui requiescant!*

You have closed the eyes of an aged father or a beloved mother; you have seen them sleeping their last sleep; you have kissed for the last time, with gratitude and respect, that hand which formed and guided your youth, which taught you the ways of life, which watched over your days and cared for your existence. Later on, you buried in its sad shroud your own child, the sweet child that you cradled on your knee, that you watched through its nights of illness, that intoxicated you with its smile, that clasped you in its tiny arms to express to you its gratitude and love. You have seen the dimming of those soft eyes which reflected its young soul, full of love for you; and you have seen your dearest hopes go out with its little coffin. You have seen your young wife laid on the funeral bier, and the half of yourself harvested by pitiless death. You have seen your brothers, your sisters, your friends, the loved companions of your childhood stretched on their last bed, and you have cried aloud: "Oh, my God, how heavy is Thy arm, how bitter is Thy will! Why hast Thou condemned me to lose the objects of my best affections? Why hast Thou given me a son, if I must so soon see him torn from my arms? What had he done, my poor child, whom I formed myself, to merit so cruel a fate? Why hast Thou robbed me of so many friends, so many kind relations? Why couldst Thou not let me enjoy yet longer the joy of living beside them, with them, in the constant intimacy which was our common delight? They would have dispelled all my sorrows, they would have comforted all my griefs. I should have lived for them, as they lived for me. And they are gone! Death has cast over them his gloomy pall. Those souls, who were so deeply devoted to me, are parted from mine, leaving it torn and bleeding. I would have given my life to keep them, and they have left me. Their heart has ceased to beat, and mine still throbs on. Oh, Lord, why hast Thou thus changed our destinies? Why didst Thou not recall me to Thyself, in their place? They were good, sensitive, virtuous; they practised the precepts of morality and religion; they were worthy to remain on earth, to serve as examples to other men. Why hast Thou removed them from life, leaving me hopeless and alone?"

So speaks in his sorrow the unfortunate being who has fallen a victim to the sad conditions of earth; but let him listen to the voices of reason and philosophy, and he will be consoled, and hope will return to his heart.

Why indeed dost thou weep, desolate husband, upon the coffin-lid of her whom thou hast lost; and thou, luckless orphan, why shed tears upon the tomb of thy father? Disconsolate mother, why lament at every memory of thy child; and you, sad friends, why should you grieve at the thought of those whom you loved and whom you see no more? What was it truly which was borne to the grave? Was it the soul of those for whom you weep ? No ; it was their mere material remains, a nameless remnant, useless dust. When life forsakes the body and no longer defends it against outward influences, it is decomposed and reduced to its chemical elements ; but the soul, an immaterial substance, escapes all destruction, and is set free from this dead matter.

It is not, then, to the tomb that you should look to see him for whom you weep ; it is to heaven. The earth that covers his coffin does not cover him. He does not sleep six feet under ground ; he lives in infinite space. It is there that he awaits you. That soul which smiled upon you, for which you mourn, for which you long, has flown to higher spheres, where it shall lead an existence full of bliss. Why, then, consider the tomb ? The body buried there is not the being whom you knew. That body was only a transitory garment, which he has cast off to put on raiment more beautiful, more glorious far. His soul has ended its earthly career. His virtues, his purity, having earned for him the crown of immortality, he now enjoys unmixed happiness in infinite space.

Then dry your tears, my friend ; take fresh courage. *Sursum corda !* Lift up your heart and your eyes ! Admire Nature and bless the Creator, who demands of us a brief struggle only that He may crown our earthly career with immortality.

Be comforted, O father, O mother, who weep for a beloved child ; and you, unhappy widow, whose days are henceforth vowed to solitude and sorrow! Cease to afflict yourself, tender sister, with memories of a deeply regretted brother! Friends, deplore no more the loss of those who have left you! Bleeding wounds in lacerated hearts, close beneath the balm of hope. Your beloved dead have not ceased to live. They exist in other spheres, inaccessible to our eyes, but not to the light of reason and philosophy. Behold them where they are, — that is, in the seraphic world, which is their everlasting home.

No doubt you do not see them; but could you see them when they were parted from you by the incidents and obligations of life? They have set out on a distant journey into an unknown land in a higher world: that is all the difference. But we are still, both of us, inhabitants of the same solar system. They are in heaven, we are on earth; that is all that divides us. But they live; they think of us, as we think of them; they see us; they are interested in our actions; they look forward to the moment of our reunion in the happy realm where they abide, and which shall some day be our home.

In short, to die is not to perish; it is to change our form, to pass into another state; it is to array our personality, our individuality, in a fresh dress; it is to leave the earth to enter the universal home.

Thus considered, death can raise no fears in the

heart of man, who should no longer regard it as the destruction of his being, but as its physical and moral renewing; who should no longer consider it as the end of his life, but as the sequence and natural continuation of his earthly existence, as the chain which binds the inhabitants of our globe to the people of the skies.

CHAPTER VII.

JOYS BEYOND THE THRESHOLD CONTINUED. — STUDIES
AND TASKS INTERRUPTED ON EARTH WILL BE CON-
TINUED IN THE ABODE OF THE BLEST. — VOCATIONS
MISSED HERE WILL FIND FULL SCOPE AFTER DEATH.
— SCHEMES CUT SHORT WILL BE CARRIED OUT IN
HIGHER WORLDS.

LET us go on with our account of the joys reserved for us on the farther side of the
tomb.

A man has devoted his life to the study of a science, an art, an industry, or any work whatsoever
having genuine importance, — he has used all the
strength of his intellect to become an illustrious
scientist, an eminent artist, an eloquent orator, a
composer of melodious songs and sweet harmonies, a
poet with lofty aspirations, — and all at once death
lays him low! The dark spot which dimmed the
horizon of his life has become the black cloud en-
wrapping his last days. Do you think that an accident so insignificant as death, which is but a
transitory phase in human existence, should deprive the scientist, the orator, the painter, the poet,
of the superior qualities with which he had fur-

nished his soul by his labor and perseverance? Do you believe that talents won by so much fatigue, suffering, self-sacrifice, and sorrow can be forever lost to him and his fellow-creatures? It is impossible. God does not create the choicest intellects to destroy them almost at once; such an inference would contradict his supreme logic. Nothing is lost in the material world, say the chemists; nothing is destroyed in intellectual creation, philosophy tells us. The brilliant tribute of knowledge, intellect, and varied faculties which man has acquired at the cost of so many efforts, cannot be taken from him. He will retain them when he passes to the farther side of the tomb. Mozart died at thirty-five, after amazing and delighting his contemporaries by the productions of his precocious genius; and shall his genius and his personality vanish forever because death prematurely arrested his earthly career? We cannot think so; we believe that Mozart, risen again, now charms celestial phalanxes by his bewildering melodies. Raphael at thirty-seven dropped into the night of the tomb the brush which had created so many masterpieces, and must he therefore stop short in his sublime career? No! his soul continues, doubt it not, to scatter masterpieces among the happy beings who people the ethereal fields. Has Victor Hugo ceased to write because death has chilled his hand? No! the work of genius is not interrupted by the cessation of earthly life. What we have begun here be-

low is continued above. Our poor globe, inhabited
by commonplace or wicked beings, is unfit for the
noble efforts, the lofty productions of intellect.
The radiant realm of ethereal space is a sojourn
better suited to the emanations of the spirit. We
cannot admit that he who dies in the possession of
vast knowledge and varied talents shall be as destitute of faculties and intellectual power when he
enters into immortality, as he who lived in ignorance, indifferent to himself and others, unac-
quainted with Nature and with God. The latter
will be born again as imperfect, from a spiritual
point of view, as he was on earth ; for each of us
will begin his second existence with the intellectual
and moral patrimony which he acquired on this
globe. If that patrimony be nought, he will have
to earn it by toil and study ; if it be, on the contrary,
rich, extensive, and varied, he will perfect it yet
further.

In proportion as man advances in life, he becomes more skilful in his art or his trade, as well
as in the conduct of his affairs. He has a more
profound knowledge of men and things. Homer
describes the council of old men, at the siege of
Troy, as the asylum of prudence, experience, and
wisdom. Wisdom is indeed the lot of age ; while
youth is the period of inexperience, errors, mistakes,
and awkward blunders. We believe that the old
man's wisdom will accompany him after death, and

that it will serve in his new abode to guide his second existence aright, to preserve him from the dangers which it doubtless offers, in common with the earthly life.

Why does the old man, near his end, still cherish hopes which seem foolish and ridiculous to every one else? Why do bold schemes, pleasant projects, dispel the melancholy of his latter years? Because he has a vague and secret presentiment that after the shadows of the evening of life shall come the bright lights of a new dawn, and a hope that the plans which he secretly ponders may some day be realized. It is not in vain that he has labored and suffered here below; his experience and his wisdom shall not be taken from him. Then let him dream, during his last days of life, of enterprises to be realized when he has crossed the terrible bridge that leads to eternity.

Why does the consumptive, yielding at last to the inroads of disease apparent to all and hidden from him alone, make the most enchanting projects for the future at the very moment when death is about to clasp him? Because he unconsciously perceives the frontiers of the celestial kingdom which he is soon to enter, and where the things of which he has dreamed in his last hours shall yet be realized.

Still another consideration. Each of us comes into the world with some aptitude, vocation, or natural talent. A man is born a poet, painter, sculptor, architect, mathematician, trader, etc. Now, nothing is more unusual, in this existence, than for a man to practise the art or profession which he loves. One man feels within him the faculties of a poet, and the necessities or the chances of life make him a baker, like Reboul at Nismes, or a hair-dresser, like Jasmin at Agen. One who re- ceived from nature the gift of musical inspiration, who could write the orchestral parts for an opera off-hand, is a grocer. Another made for travelling, who has all the qualities requisite for remote expeditions, spends his life in selling calico and measuring off cloth at the back of a shop.

It is useless to multiply these common instances, which we can all recall, in an individual experience. It is certain that we, almost all of us, practise pro- fessions contrary to our tastes; and that this is one of the greatest torments of existence. But the new world which is to receive us after death is arranged quite otherwise than the earth, to give satisfaction to personal vocations. There, there shall be no more poverty, no more inequality of goods, no more social iniquities, no more hatred or envy, no more imperious necessity for providing for our daily subsistence, no more professions carried on quite contrary to our natural tastes. Each will follow his inclination and obey his calling. He who was obliged throughout his earthly life to do violence to his personal inclinations shall give them free rein, when he has put on the bright array of the celestial oattalions. The baker or the hair-dresser who was forced to stifle his poetic genius will give it free vent, and compose the verses which he pondered in his back-shop. The grocer who, born for musical composition, has dreamed of harmony and melody, of fugue and counterpoint, his whole life long, and has endured the pangs of one who has missed his vocation, will have leisure to cultivate his natural talent, and will charm the natives of space by his compositions. The lover of travels who lived in a stupid office will unfold his wings, and visit the farthest shores of the ethereal kingdom.

While he is still within his mother's womb, the child is already provided with various organs which are of no use to him. He has eyes, to see nothing; feet, with which he may not walk; ears, to hear nothing; a stomach, to digest nothing; a brain, to think of nothing. And yet wait a few weeks, and these various organs, useless to him by reason of the liquid medium wherein he floated and of the limited space wherein he was confined, will serve him to see, to hear, to move from place to place, to act, to conceive thoughts. It is thus with men living on the earth. They possess in their innermost being higher faculties, which are generally useless to them, because they are counteracted by the accidents of life, by misery, by suffering, by the evil conditions of the society into which they were born. But wait a little, — that is, until the moment comes for the separation of body and soul, — and these faculties, which were useless on earth, will be of great service in the higher realms to be attained. Then the individual will have the supreme satisfaction of living in accord with his natural tastes, and of following out the vocation which he was forced to ignore during his earthly life.

How many noble plans are prevented, on earth, by the evil conditions of human society, by hatred or envy, by opposing interests, by the resistance of obstinate routine ? Let not the authors of noble plans, nipped in the bud by these different causes, be discouraged ; let them continue to work, until their last day, at the task which they fondly dreamed of executing, and which they never succeeded in completing. The undertaking which they began here below shall be continued by them after death. Never lose courage, bold pioneers of a new idea, crushed at its birth by the ignorance or the malice of men. Cut short in its advance among humanity, it shall be developed in the society of superhuman beings, and the success which it lacked on earth shall be won in higher spheres.

Personal instances always speak more forcibly than general considerations. I may therefore be permitted to refer here to the attempt which has occupied me for many years, to create a *scientific theatre*, and to tell what has come of it.

The theatre might, in my opinion, exert a most happy influence over public morals. The dramatic writer holds the attention of the crowd nightly for several hours. Can any stronger means be asked to expand the intellect and increase knowledge? And yet in no country has either government, municipality, academy, philanthropist, or friend of progress ever dreamed of using this mighty lever for the purpose of instruction and morality. It is with a heedless eye that we in France see the theatre swerving from the paths of literature once its glory, occupied merely in appealing to the eye, striving only to seek all sorts of sensual stimulants for the spectator. Nor do they heed the fact that among all nations of Europe the masses of the people flock to music-hall concerts to dull their senses with alcohol and tobacco, to feast on platitudes and indecencies.

I have always thought that the theatre might contribute to reclaim the people by setting before them the great lessons to be learned from the life and work of illustrious scientists, by teaching them great scientific truths under cover of dramatic action.

Science has in our day transformed the world. Sharing more and more in our existence, it has largely increased individual well-being. It has facilitated friendly relations between nations, and vastly multiplied the means of transportation and communication. It has revolutionized manufactures, changed the spirit and basis of trade, and modified the art of war in its various forms. Literature and philosophy begin to feel its influence, and cannot afford to neglect either its principles or its discoveries. Making its way everywhere, science must needs find a place in the theatre ; and it may create a new style of drama, characterized by honesty, morality, and information.

In a democratic State like France, where, thanks to universal suffrage, the people are supreme rulers, the people must be educated. There should therefore be a constant endeavor to instruct them ; and when a means hitherto unsuspected offers us at the same time theatrical amusement, scientific instruction, and examples of the highest morality, the partisans of social progress, those who desire fresh horizons for a new society, should hail this innovation with gratitude.

As we have already said, governments, rulers of States, city officials, take too little interest in theatrical matters. They neglect one of the most powerful means for enlightening, instructing, and reclaiming the masses. Music-halls swarm on every hand, and will at last take the place of theatres. It is impossible, we are told, to struggle against these places, protected as they are by free trade. But side by side with the material interests of the purveyors of vulgarities, are the moral interests of the nation and care for the public good. To require the creation in the great cities of France of popular theatres for drama and comedy, to be devoted solely to the performance of moral and instructive plays, would, no doubt, be too much to ask of the present frivolity of public taste ; but we may be allowed to ask the sympathetic aid of all friends of progress for the institution, in theatres, of dramatic and scientific afternoon performances, which would afford both instruction and amusement to the youth of our schools.

As an instance of the utility of the scientific theatre from the standpoint of popular instruction, I will take one of my scientific comedies, " Franklin's Marriage," in which I strove to bring together the entire series of physical, mechanical, and psychological effects peculiar to thunder and lightning. No one who saw a performance of this comedy would ever be tempted to regard thunder as a supernatural manifestation, as a sign of celestial wrath ; as the ancients held, and as many weak, ignorant, or superstitious minds, slaves to the traditions of the past, still hold. All who saw my play must regard it as merely a grand and beautiful phenomenon of Nature, which should be admired and studied, without other thought than to pay homage to science, which revealed to us its causes, and to the genius of Franklin, who gave us in the lightning-rod the means of warding off its dangers.

Doubtless books on popular science aid in dispelling public prejudices concerning thunder ; but a book is cold and silent. A dramatic performance which shows the spectator the physical phenomena related to thunder and lightning in a material and striking form, would impress this class of ideas more strongly upon the mind of youth.

Besides the knowledge of certain facts in physical or natural science, such a theatre as we speak of would put upon the stage the life of famous scholars. Instead of taking as the chief character of a drama Cromwell, Louis XIV., Richelieu, or Mazarin, we should bring upon the stage Denis Papin, Gutenberg, Kepler, Benjamin Franklin, or Robert Fulton. I am the first to use any of these men as the hero of a play, because dramatic authors are usually unfamiliar with events in the life of naturalists and physicists. Still, illustrious scholars are quite as well fitted for interesting dramas or amusing comedies as political personages or soldiers. A scientist is a man. Like all men he has his time for youth and love, his moments of pain and depression. Should he interest us less than an imaginary character, because he has enriched his age and his country with an immortal work? There are, in the various periods of the existence of scientific men, subjects for dramas or comedies, subjects capable of rousing or touching, of stirring to laughter or to tears. Others might, compose, as I have done, from the combined data of history and science, interesting plays, which would at the same time possess the advantage of being instructive. Every one nowadays deplores the stagnation of dramatic art in Europe, and loudly demands something fresh. The heroes of science transported to the stage would clearly afford a theme which would in part answer the desire expressed by the cities of every nation, to see the theatre enter upon a new line.

The government of the French republic has done wonders to diffuse education throughout all classes of society; nor has there been so vast an impulse given to universal education since the time of Charlemagne. The State gives free education to the people of town and country. Besides official instruction, — that is, primary and secondary education, whose circle is constantly enlarging — private efforts are most zealously made to multiply the means of instruction. Public libraries are everywhere built; scientific lectures are given on every hand for both young and old. Cannot the theatre be added to all these resources of instruction? If we succeed in teaching some useful truth, in explaining some important scientific fact, by a drama or comedy, we shall realize the ancient adage, *utile dulci*, we shall contribute to the education of youth, and at the same time extend the limits of the dramatic art.

Such are the considerations which led me to attempt the creation of the *scientific theatre*.

I devoted ten years of my life to this ungrateful task. I have learned the trade of dramatic author, and I have had performed upon various stages in Paris and abroad, —

1st. *The Six Parts of the World*, an amusing piece, with fine stage setting and scenery, based on Dumont d'Urville's expedition to the South Pole. This piece, first played at the Cluny Theatre, under the management of Paul Clèves, was afterward given, in a tour through the provinces, under the direction of M. Dupoux-Hilaire.

2d. *Denis Papin*, an historical play in five acts, given in June and July, 1882, at the Gayety Theatre, Paris, where it ran for fifty performances.

3d. *Gutenberg*, an historical play in five acts, given for the first time at Strasburg, in December, 1886, then in a tour through Holland and Alsace-Lorraine.

4th. Four scientific comedies, *Franklin's Marriage*, introducing the historical fact of Franklin's marriage to Deborah Read, as well as the amusing production on the stage of the various effects of thunder; *Trianon Garden*, based on the historic fact of the creation of the various families of vegetables by Bernard de Jussieu; *Miss Telegraph*, which represents, in the form of comic scenes, a singular episode in the invention of the electric telegraph by Samuel Morse; *The Turco's Blood*, a comic piece based on the transfusion of blood.

These plays were given at afternoon performances, in 1889, at the Menus-Plaisirs Theatre.

Such is the sum of the labors and efforts which I have for ten years devoted to an attempt to found a scientific theatre, hoping to enrich French literature with a style hitherto unsuspected.[1]

I was well aware of the vast difficulties to be contended against in so novel an enterprise. Routine, everywhere so powerful, is peculiarly persistent and active in the theatre. The smallest theatrical innovation confuses every one, or threatens existing interests. We flock to the Comédie Française, to applaud Sophocles' King Œdipus, a tragedy twenty-four centuries old; while the most unpretending novelty risked upon the stage makes the entire literary and dramatic staff frown, and instantly produces an attitude of distrust. Dramatic critics continually cry out for something new; and when it is produced at the theatre, they cannot be too eager to kill it by their ridicule or their reproach.

But I hoped to triumph over these prejudices, this opposition, as I surmounted the obstacles which I encountered thirty years before, when I inaugurated the publication of works on popular science. Success has cast a veil of oblivion over the opposition against which the popularization of science originally had to contend; but it is none the less true that the struggle was long and severe.

[1] My scientific plays performed up to this date are collected in two volumes in 18mo, published in 1889, by Tresse and Stock, under the title, "Science on the Stage (Comedies and Dramas)."

When, encouraged by the great success won from scholars and the public by François Arago's " Scientific News," published in the " Annual Report of the State Observatory," I began my first publications of familiar science, I was professor of chemistry at the Paris School of Pharmacy. All my colleagues blamed my ambition to popularize science ; for a bold fellow who had attempted it, Julia de Fontenelle, failed lamentably, throwing that sort of thing into great discredit. My friends held aloof ; my relatives found fault with me ; editors of great scientific works were alarmed ; experts reproached me for lowering the dignity of science, by bringing it within the reach of all ; and the big wigs of the Institute, Chevreul and Claude Bernard at their head, uttered cries of " Profanation !" Claude Bernard, in particular, never ceased to cast discredit on what he called my " hand-books !" I was forced to quit the university, whose every door was closed against me, and to offer my resignation as professor at the School of Pharmacy, where I was lecturing on chemistry as Professor Bussy's substitute.

To-day the popularization of science is looked upon as a public benefit ; and he who originated it and forced it to triumph is amply rewarded for his efforts by the universal success of his work. Fashionable people, to whom science was formerly a dead letter, now know that they may take an interest in all that relates to it ; and they enjoy

reading books which give them a general smatter-
ing of and a taste for scientific knowledge. The
publication of works on popular science, which appear in such numbers, in every shape and at every
price, helps to educate the laborer and to amuse the
enlightened. Used in all schools, they play a large
part in the list of studies. The fine works due to
my more fortunate successors, De Parville, Guillemin, Meunier, Tissandier, Felix Hément, De Fon-
vielle, my learned rivals and constant friends, keep
up the public taste for the useful and agreeable
sides of science. Nor should we forget the eminent
writer Camille Flammarion, who had the merit to
popularize astronomy without debasing it, to inspire
the masses with a taste for that beautiful science,
and to create in its favor the great movement
which is so well known to all.

In consequence of this general taste for books of
popular science, a wholly new branch of the bookseller's trade — of vast importance, since it annu-
ally amounts to millions — has been created in
France within the past twenty years, and rapidly
spread throughout all nations of both worlds where
French books are translated, imitated, or written
expressly in the original languages.

The same success has not, unfortunately, crowned
my attempt to create a scientific theatre.

I did not, however, flatter myself that I could
succeed in such a task by my own unaided efforts.
A great work of popular instruction being involved,

the devotion and services of a mere private individual, obliged at once to write plays and to direct their
performance, could not suffice. Such an undertaking belonged to the government and municipali-
ties, supposing them to be convinced of the utility
of introducing science as a part of the education of
youth and of the people. Dramatic and scientific
matinées, such as I gave in 1889 at the Menus-
Plaisirs Theatre, should be established for the pupils
of the colleges and city schools of Paris and other
great cities of France. Unluckily, I have been unable to convert to this idea either the ministers of
the government, or the city council of Paris, or the
directors of the subsidized theatres of the Odeon
and the Comédie Française, who might very easily
have added one or other of my little plays to the
classic works which they give every Sunday afternoon. Lastly, contrary to my expectations, no
philanthropist has been found, no friend of science
and progress, who was willing to patronize this
dramatic effort and to carry it out successfully.

The idea was too novel, too far removed from the
commonplaces of current literature. No one understood it, no one supported it. Only fancy! To
desire to make a stage hero of a physicist or a
chemist; to desire to diffuse science by a new
method; to flatter yourself that you could move or
interest the spectator by incidents from the life of
a benefactor of humanity, — what a mistake! Tradition declares that a scientist should always be

greeted with ridicule, not admiration, by the crowd. And as for wishing to instruct the public by a play, what a queer idea! The theatre is meant to amuse, and not for anything else!

So spoke the wise men, and the scientific theatre vanished like a cloud. Who now knows of its existence?

Well, dear reader, that scheme, which failed in my hands upon earth, I shall again take up later, — that is, when I am dead! I am fully persuaded that it will be easy for me to carry out on high the plan which absorbed me so deeply here below.

Do we, indeed, ever do more than make plans in this world? The average duration of life in Europe is about thirty-three years; but the third of that time is devoted to sleep. We have therefore, on an average, but twenty-one years to give to work. Is so brief an interval enough to carry out anything serious? And should we not rest content with making plans, sketches, attempts, — with conceiving general ideas? We have scarce succeeded in an undertaking when death overtakes us. "When the house is built," says the Arab proverb, "death enters in."

Earth is only a place for preparation; heaven is the domain of execution. Let not the painter fear to multiply his studies of landscape or from the living model, and to train himself in drawing, by thorough study of the works of the great masters; let him cover the walls of his studio with sketches;

he will paint the picture after his death. Let literary men trace plans for novels and stories, dramatic authors write skeleton plays. Let poets practise rhyming, and accustom themselves to think in verse; the finished poems will come later. Let musical composers write series after series of harmonies without a theme, operas without words; their works shall some day be completed. Let architects draw plans with no determinate purpose; the monuments and buildings shall rise somewhere. Everything shall be perfected when we have left behind this imperfect globe, where all is difficulty, hindrance, and discomfort, to soar to higher regions, where our corrected works shall shine forth. That which was painfully begun on earth shall be easily and gloriously completed in heaven.

CHAPTER VIII.

The Idea of Justice and Truth innate in us will be realized in our Second Life.

THERE is in the heart of man a natural feeling of justice and truth, of affection and secret poetry. Now, all these desires find no satisfaction on earth. The idea of goodness and beauty, the sense of justice, the love of truth, the craving for sympathetic affection, fill our soul from our earliest youth, and in the dawn of life furnish us with delightful dreams, true heart ecstasies. But soon the ideal of which we have dreamed is shattered by rude contact with the interests, passions, and vices of humanity. Thus the thinker holds himself aloof from noisy crowds; and in woodland solitudes or on the seashore, he lets his spirit roam amid the vast horizons and the grand spectacles of Nature. He listens to the murmurous noises of living and inanimate creation, the song of the birds, the music of the tumultuous waves, or the brook that flows peacefully through the valley. He soars, in his lonely reveries, up to the sublime Author of worlds. He strives to penetrate the mysteries of human destinies; and his soul, stirred by the harmonies of

earth and heaven, asks the secret of his own existence of the solitary beach, of the wind that blows,
of the bird that flies through the air, of the star
that shines in the calm serenity of night.   But if
he would meditate in peace, he must steal away
from the importunate, the idle, the sceptic, the
bored, the sarcastic, and the wicked.   The more
lofty are his thoughts concerning Nature and divinity, the more deeply is he wounded by painful
contact with the meannesses, pettinesses, jealousies,
hatreds, and jests of strangers.

On the other hand, the idea of justice, honor,
pity for the sufferings of his fellow-men, which man
cherishes in his innermost heart, is constantly and
cruelly offended.   He sees vice triumphant, and virtue unrecognized.   He sees misfortune follow all
that is noble, generous, innocent ; friendship turn
to hate, love become a cause of torment and regret,
human justice the reverse of equity ; and his soul
at last is crushed by these continual contradictions
between his ideal and the realities that surround it.

No doubt that in the higher homes where all
purity and love dwell, the ideal dreamed of by
our heart will be realized.   There will be no
more hate, no more care, no more war, no more
injustice, no more ingratitude, perfidy, or cruel
misunderstanding.   Friendship is free from all dis-
simulation, and justice is true to its definition.

On the other hand, the physical cataclysms, the
atmospheric disturbances, which too often terrify

the inhabitants of earth, as well as the evil climatic conditions which cause them such suffering, are unknown in the serene regions of space. There, where there is no earth, there are no earthquakes; there, where there is no aqueous vapor, there is neither rain nor storm; there, where there is only an ethereal medium, of a density nearly null, there is neither wind nor tempest. All is harmony, tranquillity, and calm in the physical nature of celestial space.

In a word, the moral and physical ideal dreamed of by romantic souls will be fully realized in the blessed regions which are to be our refuge at the close of our earthly existence. We desire no other proof of this than that sense of the ideal of which we speak. If this sense be anchored in our souls, it is because God put it there. Now God, who is all goodness and all justice, cannot have deceived us; he cannot flatter us with a hope which is not to be realized. Strive, therefore, inhabitants of our globe, to perfect your soul by the practice of duties and of virtue; extend the limits of your mind by the study of science; ennoble your conscience by charity and goodness, in order to make yourselves worthy to enter the celestial Eldorado, where your entire ideal of happiness shall be accomplished.

CHAPTER IX.

AFTER the joys of meeting in our new life those who are dear to us, of following out our chosen calling and of seeing the ideal of our dreams made real, comes a satisfaction of another kind, — that of becoming acquainted with the great men who have occupied an important place in the history of humanity by their genius, by their virtues, or by the great part which they played, as legislators, leaders of an army, conquerors, scientists, or artists, in the movement of the life of the people.

Here we ask the reader's leave to enter for a space the domain of hypothesis and imagination. We will suppose, to give substance to our ideas, that one newly arisen from the dead has arrived in the ethereal regions, and desires to enter into relations with certain great historic shades. We will call this imaginary being Eusebius.

Eusebius, having laid aside his human personality to put on that of an inhabitant of ether, enters the first region of the heavenly empyrean where his second life is to be spent.

We may suppose that he will remain there five or six centuries before undergoing a second death, followed by a corresponding resurrection, which will conduct him to the second round of the celestial ladder. In the medium which is for the time being his home, he will find those persons who played an important part on earth during the five or six hundred years previous; and as our newly elect was endowed during his earthly existence with a highly cultured mind, as his knowledge embraced the history, politics, legislation, and science of his time, he looks forward with delight to a closer acquaintance with the great men, especially the scientific men, of that period.

He must give up all idea, we must note, of finding in the zone which he occupies the heroes of an earlier epoch, — that is, the great men of antiquity, — for the reason that the sojourn in any one ethereal stratum being but five or six centuries, the great men and the people of previous ages have long since flown to other levels; but the sight of the famous scholars of the last centuries will amply suffice to satisfy his curiosity.

It is natural enough that in the celestial empyrean the men who filled a certain place in the important events of history should meet together, according to their former professions and their special class of study: that politicians and legislators should gather together to talk of the things of their time; that scientists should collect in groups, to recall the peculiar circumstances of the perfecting of science, and that artists should enjoy arguing together upon questions of painting and sculpture.

There must, therefore, exist groups of these various natures.

Eusebius prefers to turn toward the group of scientific men. With one flutter of his wings he reaches that group, and he is happy enough to find himself face to face with men whose genius and works he has long admired.[1]

He first sought, he longed to see first, in this reunion of the heroes of science and the arts, Gutenberg, the inventor of printing, the creator of that marvellous art which in the fifteenth century began to revolutionize the society of Europe, and soon after that of the entire world. He who on earth was known as John Gutenberg, stood beside his valiant spouse, Annette de la Porte-de-Fer, who upheld him at every period of his stormy career, and who was the providence of his destiny. Gutenberg seemed to be thanking her for her constant devotion and the unchanging attachment to which he owed the success of his undertaking.

Eusebius addressed Gutenberg, congratulating him on the vast dimensions assumed, after his day,

[1] We ask pardon for using here, for greater clearness, the literary artifice known under the name of "Dialogues with the Dead," for which Lucian and Plato are distinguished among the ancients, and which great French writers, like Fontenelle, Voltaire, and Fénelon, have used to set forth important or new truths in an original way.

by printing, which in the nineteenth century became the most powerful and most flourishing industry in both worlds. He told him of newspapers, thanks to printing-machines, printing more than a million copies daily, in France, England, and America ; and he added that such was the immeasurable quantity of paper devoured by these printing-presses that the nineteenth century might well be styled the *paper age.*

Gutenberg smiled at this flattering proof of the importance of his invention, but he drew his interlocutor's attention to the fact that he was far from having had such lofty ideas. When he created printing, his ambition went no further than the imitation of manuscripts, — to substitute for the books which copyists wrote out laboriously by hand in Gothic characters, pages composed of movable metallic letters, which by mechanical pressure on the paper would furnish a certain number of reproductions. Laurens Coster, the Dutch image-painter, preceded him, in this trade, by inventing movable type. Gutenberg took up the art of imitating manuscript at the point where Laurens Coster left it, and succeeded in making a practical industry of this manufacture. It was Scheffer who replaced Gothic letters by Roman characters, and gave books their present form, which has changed but little since their first origin.

As Gutenberg uttered Scheffer's name, a person who had been standing near by stepped forward and joined in the conversation.

Scheffer thanked Gutenberg for his kindness in reminding Eusebius, a new-comer on those shores, of his share in the perfecting of printing. His object in adopting Roman characters was to make books more legible, and simplify the manufacture of type.

Gutenberg readily accepted Scheffer's compliments and modest self-denial; but he saw not far off John Faust, who, having at first held aloof, finally joined Scheffer.

Gutenberg could not hide a movement of annoyance, which Faust instantly perceived, and addressed him thus : —

" Is it possible that after our departure from earth and the change in our destinies, you still retain your old grudge against me ? I thought that a stay in heaven did away with all the ill-feelings of earth."

" I am wrong, no doubt," replied Gutenberg, " not to forgive you even yet for the wicked measures of which you made use toward me, and which rendered my career so painful. But how can I forget your conduct, marked by such treachery and disloyalty ? Is it not true that when I had succeeded, thanks to the help of my friends Heilmann, Dritzen, and Riff, in establishing a printing-office at the gates of Strasburg, I was treacherously driven forth by you, my deceitful sleeping partner, who merely advanced me money that you might have power to seize my invention later on, for non-payment of the amount lent? Is it not true that after I was driven out, you made capital of the new trade in my place? And lastly, is it not true that I was forced to quit Strasburg, utterly without resources, and to return, poor and discouraged, to Mayence, my native city, at the very time that you were reaping a rich return from my invention?"

"I have been bitterly punished, Master Gutenberg," replied Faust, "for my conduct to you; for on going to Paris to sell the manuscripts which you printed at Strasburg, I was attacked by the plague, and died while all my affairs were most prosperous."

"You were punished by Providence for your disloyal conduct to me," answered Gutenberg; "but that did not prevent your son-in-law, Scheffer, from continuing to make books at Mayence, and selling them at very high prices; for every one took them to be written by hand."

"You forget, master," rejoined Scheffer, "that I was careful to proclaim you as the inventor of printing, in one of the books which I published at Mayence, and that had it not been for this, the world would never have known that you were the creator of that art."

"True, my good Scheffer," said Gutenberg, somewhat mollified by the remembrance of that noble act, "I owe you a lively gratitude for such generous frankness, and that disposes me to forgive Faust for his wrongdoing."

Faust and Gutenberg were undoubtedly reconciled by this cordial explanation; for the three shades at once flew away together.

The historical character whom Eusebius next desired to know was he who revealed to the Old World the existence of a new continent, and, so to speak, doubled the extent of the habitable earth. We refer, of course, to Christopher Columbus. Eusebius went in search of him, and found him in the company of another person, whom we must admit he treated somewhat coldly.

This was Americus Vespucius. Christopher Columbus could not forgive him for giving his name to the New World, to his own detriment. In vain did Vespucius declare his good faith, and repel all idea of wishing to lessen the glory of Columbus, when he allowed the new continent to be baptized in his name. Columbus could not forgive what he called a felony.

Eusebius arrived in the midst of the lively conversation that absorbed the two shades, and he listened curiously.

"Was it proper for you," said Columbus, — "you, a mere ship's clerk, an inferior employee at trading-ports; you who had merely made a few voyages as agent, — to allow the name *America* to appear on the first maps of the New World, in place of *Columbia?*"

"In the first place, dear Christopher," said the

shade of Vespucius, " it was not I who circulated that name. It was without my knowledge that Hylacomilus the bookseller chose to speak of the New World thus in his account of my fourth voyage ; and you must know that the first map which appeared with the name *America* was not drawn until 1550, twenty years after my death. But, besides," added Vespucius, who began to grow impatient under the reproaches of Columbus, " was there any real reason why your name should be given to the new continent ?   When you set sail on the *Dark Sea*, with three-decked ships, regular cockle-shells, had you any thought of discovering a new world ?   You were simply trying to find a short cut to the Indies.   Starting from the fact that the earth is a sphere, you informed the ecclesiastical council assembled at the Robida Convent, that by sailing from east to west you must necessarily reach the Indies by water, — a route which would be much shorter than the old one.   After a miraculous passage, due to the fine weather which continued to favor you, you reached land.   But did you ever state that this land belonged to a world hitherto unknown ?   No ; you always supposed it to be a part of the Indies, and you took the sea which washed its shores for the Japan Sea.   The islands which you discovered were never during your lifetime described as other than a portion of India ; and the continent afterward discovered by Pizarro, Cortez, and other navigators was always held to belong to the Indies. For this reason the inhabitants of these new countries were called *Indians,* a name which they have always retained. Fernando Cortez was the first to recognize these regions as a new continent; and when I had proved by my voyages the truth of his assertions, and described those new countries, people were led to give them my name."

"True," replied Columbus, "I believed my whole life long that I had merely discovered a portion of the Indies, and the only purpose of my journey was to discover a maritime route to that country; but is it not also true that the New World would never have been known had it not been for me?"

"Allow me to contradict you on that point, my dear Christopher. Undoubtedly you were the first to land upon an island of the New World; but that same country was visited, three centuries before, by Norwegians; and we are now well aware that a lively intercourse existed between the inhabitants of the northern part of the New World and the Norwegians. Moreover, when the Spanish conquerors invaded it, the centre of America (allow me to call it so) was inhabited by very civilized people, who had built splendid monuments, made roads, and possessed a navy. If you had not discovered the New World, rest assured that the Americans would have discovered Europe; that is, the inhabitants of the New World would some fine day have landed on our continent. I have, however, no desire to contest your glory; and I am the first to recognize the boldness of your conjectures and your courage in setting sail on unknown seas with such frail vessels. In return, forgive me for allowing my name to be given to the regions which you discovered."

During this conversation Eusebius approached the two navigators. In excuse of his interruption, he gave Columbus an account of his centenary, celebrated by Spain with great pomp at the Convent of Robida in September, 1892. That he might also find favor with Vespucius, he insinuated that the hundredth anniversary of the death of the Florentine navigator might be celebrated likewise, in 1912, by his countrymen, eager to consecrate the memory of his glory.

Vespucius received this flattering prospect with undisguised pleasure.

Finally, taking advantage of his indirect introduction to Columbus, Eusebius ventured to ask him a question which has long been the subject of dissension among scholars, and has never been satisfactorily solved. It referred to the city where Columbus was born. We know, indeed, that six different cities dispute the honor of Homer's birth. Genoa, as well as the village of Cogoletto, in Italy, and Calvi, in Corsica, claim the glory of being the birthplace of Columbus.

"I can satisfy every one," gayly replied the shade of Columbus. "I was not born at Genoa, at

Cogoletto, nor at Calvi. My mother brought me into the world on the open seas during a voyage from Genoa to Corsica. This, I suppose, will settle all disputes."

At this jest the shade of Columbus began to laugh, and familiarly taking Vespucius as his fellow-traveller, he flew away with him toward other shores.

Having talked with the discoverer of America, Eusebius wished to know the father of modern astronomy, John Kepler. We know that this astronomer discovered in the sixteenth century the laws of the movement of the planets around the sun, — laws which gave astronomy the wonderful precision which now marks it.

Our new-comer made his way through the crowd of scientific celebrities who frequented that corner of heaven, and succeeded in finding Kepler. But the astronomer was not alone. He was accompanied by another person, who seemed trying to keep up a conversation with him, to which, however, Kepler paid little heed ; and all at once, without a word of warning, the ethereal shade of him who was John Kepler took flight, leaving his companion somewhat amazed at this abrupt departure.

Eusebius took advantage of the movement of surprise made by Kepler's companion, and approached him, saying, —

"It strikes me that Kepler took rather an odd leave of you."

"Yes," returned the person thus addressed; "but it does not surprise me, for I know my illustrious pupil's ways."

"Your pupil?" asked Eusebius in astonishment.

"Yes; I am Moestlin, — or rather I was, when on earth, — Moestlin, Kepler's master; and having followed him throughout the greater part of his existence, I am more competent than any one else to explain his character and actions. Such as he was on earth —- that is to say, mystical, contempla-tive, and dreamy — he has remained in our new abode. I presume that he is at work on a sequel to his last book, 'Kepler's Dream.' In fact, he seems continually absorbed in celestial views; and I often see him soar aloft with one stroke of his wings, as he just now did, to visit remote worlds, and doubtless to study constellations unknown to him. His existence on earth was so unhappy, so stormy, and his passionate love for planetary sci-ence met with such lamentable obstacles, that he never tires of the pleasure of giving free course here to his genius for mathematics and to the fancies of his brilliant imagination."

"You say, Moestlin," replied the shade of Euse-bius, "that Kepler led an unhappy life on earth? Still, the joy at having discovered the laws that govern the movement of the planets must have filled his soul with infinite content."

"Of course; but what price did he pay for that satisfaction? Misfortune overtook him in his cradle, and never left him till he reached the tomb. No doubt you know the chief events in his life, and you can appreciate the truth of my words."

"I know Kepler's life in a general way; but I did not know that he had endured such serious misfortunes."

"His misfortunes were such that I do not believe a man of genius was ever forced to submit to such painful trials. If you wish, dear new shade," added Moestlin, "I will tell you the particulars of our astronomer's life, in which I myself played a part; which enables me to be very truthful."

At these words, Moestlin and Eusebius sought a retired spot where they would not be disturbed by tiresome conversations; and Moestlin went on as follows : —

"I told you that Kepler's misfortunes began in his childhood. In fact, had you visited, about 1580, the little inn in the Suabian village of Ermendingen, you might have seen a lad of twelve or thirteen going to and fro among the people at the tables, pouring out wine and beer for them."

"And was this little waiter Kepler?" exclaimed Eusebius, overcome with surprise.

"Just so. He who was destined to discover the laws of the universe spent his childhood in serving drinkers in a village inn."

"And how was he rescued from that wretched position?"

"After employing him about the inn, he was sent

to work in the fields; but he could not bear the fatigues of husbandry. It was then that having heard from public report, of the boy's extraordinary mathematical powers, I obtained his parents' leave to take him to the University of Tubingen, where I taught mathematics. I gave him lessons, and the Duke of Würtemberg paid his board. It was I who introduced him to the higher mathematics and to the new system of astronomy just originated by Copernicus, the famous Canon of Thorn, which upset the old doctrine of the immobility of the earth. Young Kepler profited so well by my lessons that he was soon called to the chair of mathematics at Graetz, in Styria.

" But the people of Styria were then divided into Protestants and Catholics. The latter being the more numerous and active, trouble was inevitable. In fact, toward the end of the year 1599 persecution of the Protestants began. There were threats of driving them out of Graetz. Kepler decided to seek shelter in Hungary, where he could freely follow his own religious creed, and quietly devote himself to the study of astronomy. The banished professor was allowed but forty-five days to sell or rent his estates. His property found no purchasers save at the lowest price; so that from that moment Kepler was ruined.

" The famous Danish astronomer, Tycho Brahe, who left Norway in consequence of the persecution of his enemies, had accepted from the German emperor, Rudolph II., the post of keeper of the observatory at Prague. Tycho Brahe, knowing Kepler's merits both as a mathematician and an observer, invited him to join him at Prague, and to share the advantages which he himself enjoyed. The invitation was accepted, and in 1600 Kepler went to Prague, where Tycho Brahe received him with marks of the sincerest friendship.

"Tycho Brahe dying during the following year, Kepler inherited his position, and was made astronomer to the Emperor of Germany, Rudolph II. He established himself at the town of Linz, in Austria.

" But in 1611 he had the misfortune to lose his wife, Barbara von Müller, who became insane after the death of three of her children.

" Private cares were soon added to the misfortunes which overwhelmed him. First, it was Emperor Rudolph, who was displeased that his licensed astronomer should give himself up to pure science, and devote to calculations time which he should have used for astrological prognostics. Next, it was a long list of nobles eager for horoscopes, who wearied him with their importunities. Their constant demands for astrologic predictions being ill-received, the courtiers of Rudolph II. were never tired of protesting against the large salary paid to Kepler.

" But as a matter of fact, this salary with which Kepler was reproached was but very ill-paid. The arrears due to him in 1613 amounted to twelve thousand crowns. Even when he travelled in the emperor's train, his only means of support was his almanacs, which he sold himself or through others, and the few horoscopes which he consented to draw for the lords and gentlemen of the court."

" What!" exclaimed Eusebius, " was such the part which the caprices of fortune and the ignorance of men assigned to one of the greatest geniuses of his time?"

" Kepler," resumed Moestlin, " continued to hold his office under Emperor Matthias, successor to Rudolph II. In 1643 he was summoned to the diet of Ratisbon to settle the corrections in the Gregorian Calendar. He pleaded the cause of Gregorian reform, and you know that he succeeded in gaining a victory for it.

" It was a happy moment for him, a gleam of glory, to have attached his name to a reform which marked an epoch in the annals of civilization. But on his return from Ratisbon, his life was again vexed with trials, griefs, and misery. His salary as court astronomer was never paid; and his means of existence, reduced to the sale of his almanac, became more and more precarious. His present was constant privation, and his future a continual subject of distress. He was therefore forced to accept a professorship of mathematics offered him at the school of Linz.

" But soon an unforeseen misfortune befell him.

10

His mother, accused of witchcraft, was thrown into prison at Stuttgart. All the charges usually made against the wretched victims of this terrible accusation were brought against the old woman. She was said to have been taught the magic art by her aunt, who was burned at Weil as a witch. She was accused of having frequent intercourse with the devil; of never shedding tears; of destroying the pigs of the neighborhood, on whose backs she took midnight rides; of never looking any one in the face; and of having made the grave-digger agree to give her her husband's skull, to make a cup, which she proposed to present to her son, John Kepler.

" This fearful trial went on for five years; the wretched victim might die in prison. Kepler vainly exerted himself to the utmost on his mother's behalf. He implored the Duke of Würtemberg, in writing, to put a stop to this persecution. Unable to obtain any answer to his petitions, he left Linz in 1630, and went to Stuttgart. He did not succeed in freeing his mother; he only succeeded in hastening the result of the trial.

" Had it not been for his interposition, and the regard inspired by his merits, Catherine would have been put to death; for the charges brought against her would have been quite enough to kindle many other stakes, even in Protestant and learned Germany. Moreover, Catherine Kepler had aggravated her position by her haughty bearing toward the court. Outraged by the impertinent absurdity of the questions put to her by the judge, she became accuser, in her turn, and scornfully reproached that judge himself with his ill-gotten riches.

" Sentence was at last pronounced. It declared that Catherine was not to suffer physical, but only moral torture.

" According to the decision of the judges, the executioner terrified the old woman by showing her, one by one, the various instruments of torture, — the rack, red-hot irons, thumb-screw, etc., at the same time explaining their use and the progressive increase of agony. Trials for witchcraft sometimes ended in this comminatory way. The prisoner, although acquitted, was made to feel the terror of torture.

" Kepler, on his return to Linz, was unable to resume his professorship. The charge of sorcery brought against his mother, and the long trial that followed, had left the most unfavorable impressions against him. His enemies overwhelmed him publicly with the injurious epithet of ' the witch's son.' Such was the power of prejudice and the ignorance of that age that he could not leave his house without being exposed to the gravest insult. He was therefore obliged to leave Linz.

" Without any means of subsistence, what was to become of the luckless Kepler, who had several children by his second marriage ? A few friends obtained for him the necessary means to leave the

city. Twenty years before, his life was troubled, in
Styria, by religious wars; and he was obliged to
give up his chair at Graetz. Now, hatred of so-
called sorcery drove him from Austria. On leaving Linz he wrote bitterly to one of his friends:
' Where shall I take refuge now? Am I to seek
out a province already laid waste, or one of those
which will erelong be devastated?'

"He next entered, as official astronomer, the court
of the Duke of Wallenstein, who had become a
prince of the empire, after having long been a powerful and dreaded adventurer. But parted from his
wife and children, whom he had left in Austria, he
could not accustom himself to the noisy, lawless
life of a camp. Moreover, although of gentle and
easy-going temper, he had too strong a sense of his
own superiority to bend readily to the caprices of
an imperious and haughty master, who desired to
make his will prevail even in heaven.

"Duke Wallenstein soon saw that Kepler had but
little faith in the language of the planets, and that
in his predictions he was far too indifferent to
flatter his master's desires. Like Philip of Mace-
don of old, he would fain himself have dictated the
oracles of fate. Not finding Kepler as submissive
as he required, he dismissed him and replaced him
by an Italian astronomer, Zeno, who could make
the planets speak in terms more suited to the ideas
of princes.

"To procure payment of his back salary, Kepler

made frequent journeys on horseback between Linz and Ratisbon, and passed the rest of his life in useless exertions. At last, worn out by fatigue and sorrow, he died of want, perhaps of hunger, in an inn at Ratisbon, at the age of fifty-eight.

"Few men, you see, ever led a life at once more laborious and more full of sorrow and trouble. How many disappointments, changes of dwelling, journeys, and heartrending solicitudes! And all to end in naught but misery! Grief and exhaustion shortened his existence; and he died, leaving to his wife and children nothing but the glory of his name."

Moestlin's tale had been a long one. Our two friends hoped that Kepler might return, after their conversation, from his excursion to distant worlds; but he did not appear, and Eusebius was forced to leave his kind informant without seeing him who made himself so illustrious by giving to astronomy laws which govern the movements of the planets in our solar system.

Newton had the glory of continuing Kepler's work. We know that the great English astronomer generalized Kepler's laws, by demonstrating the fact of universal gravitation, and proving that the force which causes the fall of bodies to the surface of the earth is the same which makes the planets revolve around the sun, the satellites around the planets, and consequently, the moon around the

earth. Thus completing Kepler's labors, Newton
explained the mechanism of the world by general,
absolute laws, which allow of no exception. Grasping the astronomic and mathematic data won for
science by the labors of his predecessors, and thanks
to a new process of calculation which he himself
invented, infinitesimal calculus, he demonstrated
the existence of a universal principle, attraction,
which governs all matter, from the invisible atom
to the vast globes which gravitate in the skies, and
he established the law in harmony with which that
attraction is exerted. Where confusion reigned, he
introduced harmony. He restored the universe to
unity ; he revealed the grandeur and beauty of its
mechanism, and far from diminishing the Supreme
Author of Nature, he placed Him so high, he showed
such power in Him, that he compelled humanity to
admire and respect Him.

Having seen Kepler, Eusebius next eagerly
desired to be brought in contact with Newton.

He had no difficulty in recognizing him ; for he
was described as usually holding aloof from others,
busied with the studies and calculations which he
began on earth.

The shade of the English mathematician had,
indeed, retired to a lonely corner of heaven, and
was absorbed in his usual meditations. Eusebius,
not without some hesitation, decided to address him.

He began by excusing himself for disturbing the
scholar for a moment in his lofty meditations.

He knew all the details of his magnificent labors, and merely wished to inquire as to the authenticity of an anecdote which had been current for two centuries, founded on statements which seem genuine, for it is quoted by a French writer on science, a man of much authority, J. B. Biot. The reader will guess that we refer to the tradition that the idea of universal gravitation was suggested to Isaac Newton by seeing an apple fall from the tree. It is said that being seated in the garden of the farm at Woolsthorpe, which he cultivated in his youth at his mother's request, an apple dropped from a tree, and that this trifling incident led his mind to the cause of the movement of the planets around the sun and the satellites around the planets. "Why," he is supposed to have thought, "should not the power which attracts bodies toward the earth be the same as that which forces the moon to revolve about our globe?" Such, according to popular tradition, was the origin of the calculations by which Newton proved the identity of weight and of universal gravity.

Newton smiled at the question asked by Eusebius.

"The anecdote to which you allude, amiable and courteous shade," he answered, "is a charming one, and its only fault is that it is not true. It was current in my time; for it was told for the first time by Pemberton, the publisher of my works, and I contradicted it, in so far as the thing deserved. You can understand that when I lived in the country, at Woolsthorpe, in my early youth, I was not yet possessed of the process which I afterward invented, — I mean infinitesimal calculus, which was indispensable to the handling of a question as difficult as the identification of universal gravitation and weight."

Eusebius did not seem clearly to comprehend this last consideration. This induced the great mathematician to enter upon details of a nature to enlighten the mind of his interlocutor.

"The idea of identifying weight with universal gravitation does not belong to me personally," said he. "Copernicus foresaw it. Kepler compared the sun to a magnet acting on the planets to hold them in their orbits, and he found that their rate of revolution varies very nearly in inverse ratio to the square of their distance from the sun.

"Bouillaud, in a work published in 1645, formulated this law more distinctly yet, saying: 'The force of the sun acting on the planets is in inverse ratio to the square of their distance.'

"Borelly, in his work on the 'Satellites of Jupiter,' plainly showed how the planets may be held and suspended in space around the sun, as well as satellites around their planets, by the action of a central power. Thus, before the date of my labors, the honor of the first idea of the assimilation of weight to the planetary movements was attributed to Borelly. Still the principle was not mathematically demonstrated. Now, it is not enough, in science, for an idea to be suggested ; its reality must be demonstrated by figures. In the absence of this proof, the opinion can only be accepted as a conjecture.

"The general problem of universal gravitation had therefore been pointed out and studied before my time by astronomers and physicists ; but it had not been proved. I then took up the idea, subjected it to calculation, and solved the question with mathematical precision."

"May I venture to ask you, dear and great master," said Eusebius, "by just what means you reached that solution ?"

"I was struck," replied Newton, "by the fact that weight is just as potent in the lowest spots on earth as on the loftiest mountains, and I was led to inquire if it did not extend to the moon, — that is to say, whether it might not be the same power that caused heavy bodies to fall to the earth and that held the moon in its orbit. Following my indications, I thought that, this first view being correct, the planets which move about the sun must also be maintained in their orbits by the action of the same planet. 'If a general principle, which I will call weight, exists,' said I to myself, ' the planets must have different rates of speed at different points of their orbits, for the reason that all points of the ellipse are situated at different distances from the sun.' Now, Kepler had established a relation between the rates of the revolutions of the planets

and their distances from the sun. We might therefore conclude from this the law of the growth and
decrease of speed, and, consequently, that of solar
weight. Starting from Kepler's law, I found, in
fact, that the energy of the solar weight decreases
in proportion to the square of the distance. The
calculus gave me the key to the system of the
world! Having determined this law, I desired to
apply it to the moon, and did so as follows:
knowing how far a body falls toward the earth's
surface in the first second of its fall, I could calculate how far the moon would fall in the same time,
by diminishing the weight according to the law of
the square of the distance. That element obtained,
I could deduce from it the speed of the circular motion of the moon, or the length of its revolution;
and if this rate of speed agreed with that given by
observation, we must conclude that the earth exerted an attractive influence over our satellite. To
make these calculations, I had to know the exact
measure of the earth's radius, and the distance from
the earth to the moon, expressed in fractions of that
measure. Unfortunately, at that time we had no
exact measure of the earth's dimensions. The degree of the meridian was estimated at sixty English
miles (297,251 French feet). From this I inferred
that the earth's radius was 17,031,230 feet, and I
based my calculations on that figure. In this way
I found a value one sixth greater than observation
gives, for the power that holds the moon in its or-

bit. This result of my calculations, varying so much from observation, puzzled me and led me to doubt the value of my hypothesis. 'I am mistaken,' said I ; ' weight does not attract the moon in inverse ratio to the square of the distance. There is some other cause which escapes me, and which modifies, for the earth and moon, the law which I have discovered.' I therefore abandoned the matter, and devoted myself to mathematical and optical research. It was not till thirteen years later that chance gave me the explanation of my error, and clearly proved that my first calculations were correct."

" Chance ? " asked Eusebius, in surprise.

" You shall hear. One day in the month of June, 1682, being in the hall of the Royal Society of London, while waiting for the opening of the meeting, I heard those about me talking of the new measurement of the meridian just made in France by the astronomer Picard, and of the peculiar care which he had taken in the work. Picard's operations made a serious alteration in the length of the meridian, and consequently an important rectification in the measure of the earth hitherto adopted. I was greatly startled. Was the error in my calculations relating to universal gravitation wholly due to popular ignorance of the true dimensions of the earth ? I at once noted Picard's figures, and hurriedly returned home, to resume my calculations of 1666, with the new estimate of the meridian. As I went on with my task, the agreement that I sought became more and more clearly manifest. Soon it was so evident that, overcome by the deepest emotion, I was unable to go on with my calculations, and had to beg one of my colleagues in the Royal Society to finish them for me.

"There was now no possibility of a doubt; the analogy of weight as manifested on the earth's surface, and of the attractive power which balances the centrifugal force of the moon in order to retain it in its orbit, was now as plain as possible. I instantly saw unrolled before me, as in a rapid vision, all the consequences of this discovery. I saw the entire universe subject to the laws of gravitation, and understood at a glance the true system of the world. This discovery opened so superb a field to astronomy and physics that I was stunned, and it was some time before I regained my senses. My hands trembled, and I was dizzy."

"You were," answered Eusebius, "like Archimedes, who, when he had unveiled the trick of the maker of King Hiero's gold crown, by taking the weight of that crown submerged in water, ran half naked and like a madman through the streets of Syracuse, crying, 'Eureka!'"

Having thus fully satisfied his questioner's curiosity, Newton signified, by a polite gesture, that he desired to resume his meditations. Eusebius accordingly left him, greatly edified in regard to the legend of the apple and Woolsthorpe garden, and happy to have had a serious conversation with one of the men of genius who have done most to honor earthly humanity.

The steam-engine is the great instrument of the renovation of trade in the nineteenth century. Before that period men had no powerful motor which could be handled easily. Wind-power, water-falls, springs, human power, and horse-power were the only means of mechanical energy of which any practical use was made. The steam-engine replaced these insufficient agents, with incalculable advantages over all of them. During the early years of this century manufactories and mills made use of the steam-engine, and, thanks to its aid, multiplied their products in proportions hitherto unknown. This powerful motor distributed power to the different work-rooms, adapting it to a great variety of tools, now setting in motion enormous masses, and now performing the most delicate tasks, here lifting huge hammers, there winding threads of linen, cotton, or silk. By its economical application in all sorts of manufactures the steam-engine revolutionized trade, and brought within the reach of all products until then reserved for the favorites of fortune alone. It improved dress, lodging, and food, and created industries never before thought of.

From manufactories and mills, the steam-engine passed to rivers and seas. It was introduced into boats and ships, which parted the waters of streams or the waves of the sea without the aid of oars or sails, and triumphed, as if in play, over contrary currents and winds.

The same machine was soon applied to transportation by land; and steam was substituted for draught-horses. Locomotives were seen, pouring forth clouds of smoke, cinders, and steam as they passed, drawing long trains heavily loaded, moving on iron rails.

The steam-engine, therefore, was the soul of trade in the nineteenth century.

Eusebius, who, while on earth, was possessed of wide scientific knowledge, desired to make the acquaintance of the famous English machinist who made the steam-engine a universal motor. This machinist was James Watt, who, by perfecting Newcomen's imperfect machine, — that is, by substituting steam condensed in a separate vessel for the injection of cold water into the interior of the steam cylinder, — made the machine now in use; and thanks to the many improvements which he introduced later, made a motor at once powerful and economical, which was rapidly introduced into all the mechanical industries of Europe.

Eusebius accordingly inquired for James Watt; and he was pointed out to him, with the remark that he was with his *inseparable companion*.

This somewhat puzzled Eusebius; but he soon had an explanation. The shade of James Watt was in company with another inhabitant of the celestial Eldorado, and they seemed to be united by a most cordial affection. Thus, when Eusebius introduced himself to him who was once James Watt, the latter answered him in these words, —

" I accept your praises, dear new shade, but I beg of you to transfer the greater part to my friend."

And as Eusebius gazed curiously at the person mentioned by Watt, the latter added, —

" You have before you one who was Denis Papin, the man of genius to whom we owe the discovery of the principle of the steam-engine. As Denis Papin was one of the most unfortunate men of his age, a true martyr to science, I desire that justice, which was refused him on the imperfect sphere which was for a time his dwelling, should be fully done him in the blest abode where all truths are made known, where all wrongs are repaired, where rewards are bestowed. Therefore I never leave Denis Papin without comforting him for his misfortunes, congratulating him on his constancy and courage during the sad years of his earthly life, and proclaiming him before all the true inventor of the steam-engine, which his successors marvellously improved, but whose first idea was wholly due to him."

The shade of Denis Papin smiled at this ardent declaration from one who so gloried in doing him homage, and addressing Eusebius, said, —

" You see, by these generous words, how true it is that genius is always allied to goodness. James

Watt exaggerates my merits to diminish his own ; he makes of his own glory a mantle for mine ; he makes me an aureole from his own halo, for I cannot deny that my machine was but a rough sketch, while his was a masterpiece."

" I exaggerate nothing, dear shade," replied James Watt. " You say your machine was only a rough sketch ? I suppose you refer to the plain cylinder and piston, containing a layer of water at the base, which was reduced to steam by means of a furnace, and was chilled by interior radiation. Simple as this arrangement was, it raised considerable weights, by means of a cord fastened to the handle of the piston ; but no one ever thought of offering it as a machine for every-day practical use. It was only a means of demonstration, invented by you, to show the fact of the mechanical power existing in the elastic force of aqueous vapor. I do not, therefore, refer to that demonstratory apparatus, but to the really practical machine which you constructed, and in which steam, directed into a cylinder full of water, itself connected with the water of a river or pond, exerted a pressure on the water contained in the cylinder, and expelled the liquid, which fell back upon the buckets of a hydraulic wheel and set it in motion. It was actually a water-mill worked by steam, and the paddle-shaft of the hydraulic wheel, as it turned, formed a motor which could be used to work various tools."

" No doubt," said Eusebius, addressing Papin,

" it was the same apparatus that you adapted to the boat which you transported from Germany to England, when the boatmen of the Weser stopped you at the mouth of that river, and upon your insisting on continuing your journey up the Weser, stove your boat to pieces."

" Yes," replied Papin, " that was the machinery which was to turn the wheels of my boat ; and the stupid fury of the sailors destroyed, with my boat, all my hopes."

" The blow which you received on that fatal day, dear friend and master," said James Watt, " was the beginning of all the misfortunes which you endured throughout the rest of your existence ; the cause of your misery, your sorrows, and your lonely death. But your grief should now be assuaged by the thought that you left your country, forsaking fortune, position, future, and friends, in order to remain true to your religious convictions, and that you need not conform to the commands of the Edict of Nantes. You were a martyr to the religion of your fathers ; and the trials which you underwent to escape the persecution of the Catholics gained for you immediate admission to the blest abode where you now dwell. The affection that I feel for you is due as much to the memory of your sufferings, nobly borne for the sake of the Protestant religion, as to your scientific genius."

With these words the two shades vanished, exchanging tokens of mutual affection, and leaving

Eusebius fully convinced that equity, gratitude, and
disinterested friendship are the native virtues of the
happy inhabitants of the astronomic paradise.

He was still more convinced of this truth on listening to the conversation just then going on
between two other celestials, whom he readily recognized by their words as the English engineer, George
Stephenson, and the French engineer, Marc Seguin.

Every one knows that the locomotive that drags
our trains over iron rails owes its creation to two
distinct inventions, equally beautiful and original:
the tubular boiler, which furnishes vast quantities
of steam in an instant; and the steam blast, — that
is, the jet of steam forced from the boiler into the
flue of the chimney, which produces a tremendous
draught, an enormous demand upon the gases of
the fire-box, and thus increases, in extraordinary
proportions, the quantity of steam produced by the
generator.

These two inventions contributed equally to create the locomotive, for they complete each other
marvellously well. One of these arrangements
alone would not be enough to attain the desired
end; but their union furnished the solution of the
problem of the speed of locomotives.

But which invention did more toward solving the
problem, — the steam blast or the tubular boiler?
This is a question which has always divided scientists, or rather nations, — the French maintaining
that Marc Seguin's tubular boiler played the larger

part in the creation of the locomotive ; the English
asserting that the supremacy belongs to George
Stephenson's steam blast.

Now, do you know what the shades of Stephenson
and Marc Seguin were saying when Eusebius over-
heard their talk ? Stephenson maintained that the
French engineer's invention was far more important than his own ; while Marc Seguin insisted that
all the glory belonged to Stephenson, for his invention of the steam blast, which would have alone
sufficed to provide the strong draught necessary for
the production of large quantities of steam in the
boiler.

The elect of heaven therefore held views the
reverse of those prevalent on earth. They carried
justice so far as to efface themselves in honor of a
rival.

From this delightful self-sacrifice, Eusebius
learned what supreme virtues are the privilege of
the inhabitants of ether.

Continuing his review of the scholars who have
left the most enduring impress on the history of
humanity, Eusebius wished to know, after the inventors of the locomotive, the inventors of steam
navigation.

Three shades were chatting together, not far
away. Eusebius approached them, and listening to
their words, discovered that he had before him
the three discoverers of navigation by steam ;

namely, the Frenchman, Claude de Jouffroy, the American, John Fitch, and the American, Robert Fulton.

To understand why we mention the names of three men as the creators of navigation by steam, we must know the somewhat complex history of steam navigation. It will therefore be necessary to give a rapid summary of the origin and progress of that discovery, before coming to the conversation which Eusebius was so fortunate as to have with the three great shades.

James Watt having, about 1770, made considerable improvements in Newcomen's steam-engine, that machine was used, as a motive power, in many workshops and manufactories throughout Europe. Its application on board boats, in place of oars, was clearly indicated. Therefore, in both worlds machinists and constructors were making every effort to apply James Watt's steam-engine in navigation.

However, there were great difficulties in the way, if we may judge by the long interval which passed between the invention of Watt's steam-engine, and its final application to navigation on rivers and streams, which was not until 1807, on Fulton's boat, the " Clermont," which ran from New York to Albany.

The history of science has recorded with scrupulous care the names of the various machinists who worked together to create steam navigation, from its origin to its final success.

A Frenchman, Marquis Claude de Jouffroy d'Abbans, an officer in the King's troops, was the first to make a boat move by steam power.

The propeller used at the outset by the Marquis de Jouffroy to transmit the motive power of steam to the water was a sort of jointed oar, opening to strike the liquid, and closing again, to permit the boat to advance. It was what Claude de Jouffroy called *palmated oars*, because they resembled the feet of aquatic birds. But he soon gave up this elaborate system.

July 15, 1783, he launched on the Saône, at Lyons, a huge boat, moved by paddle-wheels, themselves impelled by a steam-engine of Watt's pattern, which was made at Lyons, in 1780, in the shops of Jean Brothers.

The steam-engine which worked the paddle-wheels was of considerable size, the boiler being a foot and nine inches in diameter and the piston having a stroke of five feet. The boat containing this engine was also very large. It was no less than 140 feet long by 16 feet wide. The wheels were a foot and six inches in diameter, the paddles six feet long; and they plunged two feet deep into the river. The boat's draught of water was three feet.

The Marquis de Jouffroy made the trial-trips of this boat on the Saône at Lyons; and it plied, against the current, for several months, as far as Ile Barbe.

July 15, 1783, the boat was set in motion, in the presence of ten thousand curious spectators and before the members of the Lyons Academy of Science and Letters. It moved with the greatest ease, going up the Saône against the stream. The members of the Lyons Academy drew up a report, giving the particulars of this splendid experiment.

We can scarcely understand why, after such a result, De Jouffroy failed to obtain at once the license which he requested, for thirty years, to establish a service of steamboats on the Saône.

We must attribute to Minister Calonne the unqualified refusal returned to De Jouffroy's request. This minister carelessly refused to regard the Lyons experiment as sufficient proof of the originality of De Jouffroy's discovery. He considered it his duty to submit the petition to the Academy of Science at Paris. This latter body, exaggerating the importance of the task, demanded, through Périer and Borda, that the inventor should repeat his experiment upon the Seine, at Paris. But to have a new boat built, in order to submit it to the academic Areopagus enthroned on the banks of the Seine, was beyond the means of the inventor, who had spent his last cent in the construction of his huge boat and his steam-engine. De Jouffroy therefore could only send a small model of the Lyons boat to the commissioners of the Academy; which was not considered sufficient by those terrible judges.

Jouffroy's big boat continued to navigate the

Saône for some sixteen months, and was then abandoned.

Just about this time almost all the nobility of France emigrated. The Marquis de Jouffroy went abroad in 1790. He afterward took service in the armies of the Empire, and gave no further heed to steam navigation. He took it up again, however, in 1815, after the return of the Bourbons. But the invention had then made vast progress in other hands than his; still, it can never be denied that he was the first person in the world who built and navigated a steamboat upon a river.

Here let us note certain attempts, of no great import, made in Scotland in 1788 by two native engineers, Taylor and Simington, to navigate a pleasure-boat on the Port Clyde Canal by means of an imperfect steam-engine.

In 1787 John Fitch, a Philadelphia builder, launched a little boat upon the Delaware, in which wheels attached to a horizontal bar running length-wise of the planks were moved by steam. The engine was built, with great trouble, by native blacksmiths.

In 1789 Fitch navigated a larger boat on the same stream, propelled by a good Watt's engine; and this boat made a very long trip. Franklin and the learned Rittenhouse were present at the experiment, and they planned a line of steam transports to run between Philadelphia and Trenton.

The difficulty of constructing good steam-engines

cut short Fitch's scheme. Not finding the hoped-for encouragement in Philadelphia, and deserted by those who had thus far supported him, he decided to go to Europe. In 1792 he set sail for France, and landed at Lorient.

He had known, in Philadelphia, Brissot, who was living in America with the Quakers. He sought out Brissot in Paris, where he had now become a member of the National Convention, and asked his help, which was not refused.

Escorted by Brissot, he appeared at a session of the National Convention, somewhat ostentatiously holding in his hand the flag of the American Republic, with which the Governor of the State of Pennsylvania decorated his boat after its trial-trip by steam on the waters of the Delaware, in 1789.

The Convention received the American ship-builder with due honor, and saluted the United States flag with cheers.

But Brissot, the Girondist, died on the scaffold Oct. 31, 1793; and with him, Fitch lost his sole support.

Unable to prolong his stay in France, Fitch resolved to return home; but his destitution was such that he had not the means to pay his passage, and he was glad to get the cost of his journey from the United States Consul at Lorient.

However, he was forgotten in Philadelphia. He made vain efforts to re-establish his undertaking; no one would listen to him, and in despair he committed suicide.

In his will he left his manuscripts, plans, and the sketches for his machines to the Philosophical Society of Pennsylvania, that some one might carry on his work, — " if he have the courage," he added bitterly in this his last testament.

At Paris, in 1803, a journeyman gold-beater, Charles Dallery, tried to build a steamboat, to be moved, not by wheels, but by a screw, a propulsive motor then in its infancy ; but he could not manage to build the steam-engine, and in a fit of despair he broke his boat to pieces with his own hands.

Meantime Robert Fulton, an American engineer, built on those same banks of the Seine a steamboat combining all the requirements necessary for navigation ; and it moved triumphantly over the very waters where the fragments of the boat shattered by the unhappy Dallery still floated.

The son of poor Irish emigrants, at first apprenticed to a Philadelphia jeweller, young Fulton, endowed with some talent for drawing and painting, soon supported himself by his pencil. At the age of twenty, he was a miniature-painter in Philadelphia. In 1786 he went to Europe, landing in England, where, his taste for mechanics becoming more and more pronounced, he gave up the profession of painter for that of engineer.

During his fifteen years' stay in Europe (in England and France) he won distinction by a large number of mechanical inventions of varied order. To him we owe the invention of torpedoes, intended to blow up ships by a submarine explosion, — a terrible weapon which, being again taken up in our day by the navies of all nations, produced a complete revolution in the construction and armament of military fleets, both for offensive and defensive purposes.

The problem of navigation by steam, which Fulton began to study in 1796, was another object of his efforts.

Owing to the deep study of the causes which had prevented the success of the previous attempts made by his many rivals, Fulton contrived to succeed where so many others failed. In the month of August, 1803, a steamboat built by him journeyed up the Seine, as we have already stated, in the very midst of Paris.

He submitted this boat to the examination of the directors of the Conservatory of Arts and Manufactures, as well as to the Academy of Sciences at Paris.

The Academy was very far, as has often been stated, from despising or ignoring the importance of the invention of steamboats. It named a commission, made up of scientific men of high rank (Bougainville, Abbé Bossut, Carnot, and Périer), whose duty it was to visit Fulton's steamboat, which was stationed on the Seine. Several members of the Institute, among whom were Abbé Bossut, Carnot, De Brouy, and Volney, went on board of her on the 20th of Thermidor, 1803.

If the invention of steamboats was not recognized in France, was scorned and rejected, it was — history is compelled to admit — owing to the Emperor Napoleon I.

Having refused to examine into torpedoes, — invented, as we said, by Robert Fulton, and tested by him at Brest, — Napoleon refused to receive Fulton, whom he treated as a " charlatan, whose only desire was to make money."

Napoleon was at this time preparing for a descent on England. Fulton offered to build steamboats for him, to transport an army to Dover, instead of scattering them in the small flatboats, each carrying one cannon, then in process of construction at Boulogne. We know that the foolish idea of gunboats failed miserably, after several years' delay and enormous expenditure.

Repulsed in France, Fulton went to England, where his ideas were no better received by the Admiralty, who looked with horror on an invention so full of menace for English war-ships and commercial vessels. Fulton, wearied out, returned to America.

Thanks to the financial support of a former French consul, Livingstone, he managed to build at New York a splendid boat, the " Clermont," which, on April 10, 1807, made a most successful trial-trip up the Hudson, from New York to Albany.

From that moment the steam-engine took possession of boats navigating American rivers and lakes. It was soon to be introduced into ships and to plough all seas.

Thus we see how long a series of labors was required to realize the application of steam power to navigation.

Eusebius was fully acquainted with the history of navigation by steam, and with the relative parts played by Claude de Jouffroy, John Fitch, and Robert Fulton. He was therefore not surprised to find these three great shades together.

After excusing himself for addressing them, Eusebius said that he supposed, no doubt, like Papin and James Watt, they had met to exchange recollections, to congratulate one another on their respective triumphs, and to forget their past rivalries.

But at the word " rivalries," he was interrupted by the shade of Jouffroy, who reminded him that Fitch, Fulton, and himself were never rivals ; that they worked independently, without any knowledge of each other, at a common task, at different times ; and that it was by the Supreme will that they had successively devoted their lives to the same study.

Eusebius considered this latter assertion, seemingly unable to understand it. Then John Fitch said, —

" New-comer to our Empyrean, you cannot yet be initiated into all the joys which fall to the lot of the dwellers in this abode. One of the most precious is that we know the reason of the various events of civilization, politics, war, science, and the arts, which occur on earth, and which seem inexplicable, or contrary to the unfailing justice of Providence. You have a proof of this in the fate allotted to us on earth. We were all cruelly treated by destiny; and in spite of our constant devotion to searching out what would be for the general welfare, we were scorned or persecuted. Our misfortunes seem to have been contrary to the justice and eternal wisdom which rule over all worlds. And yet it was the Divine will that successively combined the periods of our three existences, to attain a great humanitarian end."

And as Eusebius seemed anxious for further explanation, the shade of Jouffroy went on : —

" I do not know whether or not you lived before the introduction of steam-engines on board boats and ships ; but if you had seen what seafaring then was, you would have been struck by the dangers and vast inconveniences which it presented. In ancient times, when men were reduced to oars and sails, they could navigate only along shore, never going out of sight of land ; and when it was known that a Roman fleet, composed of hundreds of triremes and thousands of rowers, had crossed the sea from Syracuse to the coast of Africa, there was a universal cry of surprise and admiration. It was not until the thirteenth century that the compass gave its first impulse to the art of navigation. The magnetic needle, combined with observation of the Pole Star, pointed out the way to the navigator, who thenceforth ventured to trust himself on the open sea, and to undertake quite long voyages on the ocean or inland seas. It was by this means — that is, thanks to the compass — that Christopher Columbus was enabled to navigate without swerving from his route, westward, until he found a new land. But how imperfect, how full of dangers and cares, navigation still was, limited to the compass and observation of the North Star! Contrary winds held vessels in port indefinitely. In the open sea, when there was a calm, ships were forced to lie still for lack of wind to swell the sails. Their stay in the same latitude seemed eternal, exposing the crew to lack of provisions, to die of hunger and thirst. To tack or beat to windward was the forced expedient of every sea-voyage. It was so hard to decide beforehand on the length of a passage that traders could make no calculation as to the date for the return of a vessel. The voyage from America to Europe and back, was a daring experiment, seldom enough ventured. How many human existences have been devoured by the Minotaur ocean! How many ships perished with all on board during the long period that followed the discovery of the magnetic needle, down to our age! Thus all eagerly longed for the time when sailors should possess some means of propelling their ships which should not be at the mercy of the caprice of the winds.

"Well," continued the shade of Jouffroy, "here God's hand is revealed. Steam applied to the propulsion of vessels, in place of sails and oars, was to afford navigators the dreamed-of desideratum. By using steam to move ships, there would be no time lost in waiting for a favorable wind, in tacking or in beating to windward. Navigation would be continuous, incessant; it would mock at wind and storm. Sea-voyages would become both safe and swift, and trade would receive a tremendous impulse. But to produce steam navigation was a task replete with difficulties and dangers. The idea of putting furnaces and a boiler into wooden ships aroused universal fear. All dreaded the explosion of the engine, and fire on board. Contrary interests, consequent on prosperous sea-traffic, created obstacles of another sort, over which it was not easy to triumph. The successive action of the three generous men was, therefore, none too much to insure victory. And those men were certainly doomed to the trials, the sufferings, the martyrdom to which every inventor, every creator of a new work, is condemned on earth. I was the first victim," added Jouffroy's shade; "for my long watches, my incessant toil, my courage, were unavailing to insure success, and I had the sorrow of growing old, unknown, while my invention grew and was perfected without me and remote from me."

" I was the second victim," added John Fitch ; " for after a life wholly devoted to working for the welfare and safety of sailors, I received in return only the indifference or the hatred of mankind. Rejected by all, ruined, discouraged, I was forced to destroy a life whose sufferings and regrets I could no longer endure."

" My fate was scarcely happier," said Fulton, " although I finally succeeded in my undertaking. But what fatigues and agonies did I not endure during my long stay in Europe ! Overwhelmed with mortifications, repulsed by all, I was glad to return and offer to my own country the new industry rejected by old Europe."

" Thus, you see," said Jouffroy, " that three eager and devoted men were none too many to accomplish this humanitarian task ; and that it was indeed with a providential purpose that we handed down this mission, one to the other, ourselves unconscious of it, but blindly obeying a premeditated plan, which was to insure a precious benefit to mankind."

" Sea-voyages, once so dangerous," added Fulton, " are now perfectly safe. Transatlantic steamers make the journey from one world to another in a week, while in my time it took two months, and there is now nothing to be feared from wind or storm. Learn from this instance, new-comer to our happy shores, that the secret designs of Providence in regard to earthly events are here revealed."

Eusebius, who had, indeed, much to learn concerning the conditions of the new existence upon which he had entered, thanked the three learned and kindly shades, and took leave of them to continue his visits to famous men made happy in the astronomic paradise.

If the nineteenth century witnessed the triumph of the steam-engine, which produced an entire social and industrial change in both worlds, electricity is now beginning to supersede steam ; and it is probable that the twentieth century will see the electric current take the place of the elastic power of steam, and used as a motor in factories and shops; to transport travellers and merchandise over steel rails, instead of horses in carriages on ordinary roads ; to propel boats and ships ; to light houses, public buildings, and streets, in place of the reagents which are the base of the present chemical trade ; to extract metals from their minerals ; to dye and print stuffs ; to dress leather ; in fact, by a marvellous phenomenon unsuspected until now, to transport natural forces, and utilize from a distance the mechanical power resident in water-falls and the wind.

The electric current, which will be the great industrial power of the twentieth century, was discovered in the beginning of this century, — that is, about 1800. Insignificant at first, so that it was limited to static effects, produced by rubbing-machines, electricity took a sudden start when it assumed the form of a current. The discovery of the electric current is due to Galvani and Volta. Eusebius was therefore very impatient to know the paradisal shades of those two great men.

He had no trouble in finding them, and in finding them together, for they seldom parted. By listening to their conversation, he gathered the curious topic of their talk, which referred to the circumstances that led to the discovery of the electric current.

"No one," said Volta, "admires more than I do the genius and particularly the perseverance displayed by you during the long series of years which you devoted to the study of *animal electricity*, which I called *metallic electricity*. To you is surely due the great discovery of electricity in motion, which you placed in the body of animals and which I placed in the mineral world. But, call it by what name you please, you were the first to point out the existence of the electric current, — a form very unlike purely static electricity, furnished by frictional machines; and you described certain of its characteristics. But allow me to suggest that it was not your wisdom alone which led to your success, but it was particularly the result of a series of fortunate chances."

"It was not mere chance that led to my discovery," quickly replied Galvani; "for you must confess that I had done much to help that chance by my twenty years' studies."

" Agreed," replied the shade of Volta ; " but you will not deny that the fundamental fact upon which all your research was based, was revealed to you by a wholly accidental circumstance. Is not it true that your wife, Lucia Galvani, was the first to observe the phenomenon of the contraction of a frog's body under the influence of electricity, and that this phenomenon occurred in your presence under singular circumstances ? One of your pupils was drawing sparks by friction from an electric machine, while another was engaged close by that same electric machine in preparing a frog for the anatomical studies which you had for some time been making with regard to the nervous irritability of those animals. It was the instantaneous reunion of those two acts that caused the contraction of the frog's body."

" That is true," answered Galvani's shade. " In order to study the nervous irritability of frogs, I had prepared one of those animals, as I frequently did, by dividing with the scissors the lower limbs from the upper part of the body, retaining only the two nerves of the thigh, which, being left intact, united by this frail link the upper and lower limbs. At that instant another observer, a friend of mine, was making some experiments of his own in regard to the spark of the electric machine. The frog being prepared, I laid it, without any special purpose, on the wooden board used as a support for the electric machine ; then I left the laboratory, and went to another part of the house. Now, it happened that one of my pupils, whom I had directed to finish the dissection and separation of the crural nerves of the frog, touched those nerves with the point of his scalpel. Instantly he saw with surprise that the animal's lower limbs were contracted as if seized with an attack of lockjaw. All those present were astounded. Among them was my wife, Lucia Galvani. While the others eagerly strove to reproduce the singular phenomenon which had so amazed them, my wife thought she saw that the contractions occurred only at the precise moment when a spark was drawn from the electric machine close by. In fact, when a spark was drawn from the machine, and at the same time the tip of a scalpel was applied to the nerve of the frog, lying at some distance from the apparatus though it was, the animal's body was convulsed; and these convulsions ceased to appear when the glass plate of the electric machine was no longer rotated. Surprised at this fact, my wife hastened to tell me of it; for I was just then engaged elsewhere. I ran to verify the phenomenon of which she informed me, and could not but acknowledge its reality. When I put the frog on the support of the machine, and approached the tip of a scalpel to one of its crural nerves, while another person drew the spark from the machine, the animal's lower limbs were seized with violent contractions."

"The phenomenon which surprised you so much,"

said Volta, " was very simple. It was produced by
the *back stroke*, — that is to say, the electric shock
which may be felt by animals at a long distance
from the spot where the lightning strikes. When
a cloud is charged with positive electricity, for
instance, it acts by influence on all bodies situated
on the surface of the earth; it decomposes their
natural electricity, and attracts their negative
electricity. But if the lightning finally strikes,
and thus releases the free electricity in the cloud,
it ceases to influence bodies placed in its sphere of
action. These latter then suddenly return to a
state of neutral electricity. This abrupt return to
a neutral state, this sudden recomposition of two
electricities, when it acts through the bodies of men
or animals, produces in them a shock, a violent and
sometimes fatal commotion ; this is the *back stroke*.
It was a phenomenon of this kind which occurred
in your experiment. Placed in the vicinity of an
electric machine in an active state, and being thus
within its sphere of attraction, the body of the frog
was electrified by influence, and continued in that
electric state so long as the conductor of the
machine was charged with positive electricity. But
when they came, by drawing the spark, to strip the
conductor of the machine suddenly of all its free
electricity, the recomposition of the two electricities
took place at the same time through the animal's
body. This rapid movement of the electricity
determined a commotion in the limbs of the frog,

because the body of a frog recently killed always undergoes these motions of muscular contractability, under the influence of electricity in motion. A fresh-killed frog is, in fact, a capital electroscope; it reveals the presence of the faintest traces of electricity in a free state."

"I saw perfectly," replied Galvani, "that the phenomenon of the frog's contraction might be explained by the *back stroke*, but I did not feel satisfied to stop at that explanation."

"Very luckily," hastily replied Volta; "for had you been content with that interpretation, you would not have carried your investigations any further. You would have admired the electric sensibility of the frog's body, and the service which it might render as an *electroscope*, but you would have stopped there. It was because you did not choose to accept that theory, which was nevertheless the true one, that you imagined you were on an absolutely new road, which would lead to a total revolution in physics and physiology. But let us pass over this point, and come to your greatest discovery, that of the electric current. You will not deny the powerful intervention of chance on this occasion."

"Yes," said Galvani, "on Sept. 20, 1786, in order to study the influence of atmospheric electricity on the motions of the frog, under a sky exempt from electricity, I prepared one of those animals as usual, and having passed a copper hook through its spinal marrow, I hung it on the iron railing which ran along the terrace of my house. I had already tried the same experiment several times, with no unusual result. Toward the end of the day, wearied by the length and futility of my observations, I seized the copper hook imbedded in the frog's spinal marrow, and applied it to the iron railing, which I rubbed rapidly, by means of the hook, in order to produce a closer contact between the two metals. At once the animal's lower limbs underwent violent shocks and contractions, which were repeated at every fresh contact of the copper hook with the iron railing. And yet there was nothing to indicate the presence of free electricity in the atmosphere. This observation was of great importance, inasmuch as it showed that atmospheric electricity had nothing to do with the phenomenon of the frog's contractions, which were independent of all exterior cause, and undoubtedly proceeded from some force innate in the frog. To set at rest all doubt on this head, I repeated the same experiment in my laboratory, merely substituting a sheet of polished iron for the iron railing. I hung a freshly prepared frog on an iron rod, and passed a small copper hook through the mass of the lumbar muscles and the fasciæ of the spinal marrow. As soon as the copper hook touched the iron, the contractions took place, just as I had witnessed them on the terrace. This latter observation was fundamental. By this experiment I entered into possession of an absolutely new order of facts. Hitherto I had sought the cause of the frog's muscular contractions in some external electric influence. Here atmospheric electricity played no part, and the fact was reduced to these two simple terms, — a metal arch in contact with the frog's nerves at one of its extremities, and with its muscular system at the other extremity. It was by dwelling on these facts that I believed I had proved beyond a doubt the existence of a form of electricity peculiar to the living organism, and established that the body of animals is an organic Leyden jar, that positive electricity circulates from muscles to nerves and from nerves to muscles, and that when we unite muscles and nerves by a metal arch, we produce muscular contraction, by establishing a communication between the two electricities. I thus put beyond a doubt the existence of an electric current in the body of animals."

"I have never accepted," returned Volta, "your *animal electricity ;* but be its nature what it may, it was an electric current, and you thus discovered that particular form assumed by electricity. It is none the less true, however, that you owed this latter discovery quite as much as the first one to chance."

Somewhat piqued by these remarks, Galvani replied as follows : —

"I am, illustrious and revered shade, one of the greatest admirers of your genius, and declare that the instrument which you invented, and to which your name was given in just homage, is one of the most precious which ever came from the hands of a physicist; but if I grant you that chance played a certain part in my discovery of the electric current, you must admit, on your side, that it was owing to a series of errors that you were led to invent that wonderful apparatus."

" What errors," asked Volta, not without a shade of bitterness, " can you point out, as having led to my discovery ? "

" Your contemporaries," replied Galvani, " took care to make them manifest. You gave to the learned world a description of the instrument which you call a *pile*, in a letter which you addressed, March 20, 1800, to the President of the Royal Society of London. Now, in this letter you only speak of this new instrument as suited to excite shocks in the organs of animals. You call it an *organic Leyden jar*, possessing the property of recharging itself after each emission of electricity. Misled by your principle of contact, whose fallacy was lately so well proved, you failed to note any of the many facts which overthrow your theory. You did not observe the rapid decrease that takes place in the intensity of the effects produced by your machine after the first moments of vigorous action, a decrease which is due to the diminution of the chemical effects going on between the metals and acid liquids composing the pile. How could you fail to be struck by the decrease in intensity of the

pile which takes place after a certain period of
activity, and how was it that you were not led to
seek the cause of this decrease ? You said nothing,
in your memoir, of the profound alteration undergone by one of the metals in the couple. You did
not notice the saline efflorescence which forms
around the metal disks, and which consists of
sulphate of zinc, produced by the dissolution of the
metal by the acidulated water. Indeed, in a pile
which has been used for any length of time, all the
zinc plates are worn away, and lose considerable of
their weight, in consequence of the dissolving of the
metal in the acidulated liquid. The copper plates,
on the contrary, remain intact. How was it that
you were not struck by this fact, which was so self-
evident to the observer ? Neither did you remark
the singular fact, which it was almost impossible to
overlook, of chemical decompositions, with the
production of gas, which took place during the
action of the pile. You repeated many times
the experiment of the interrupted circuit with machines of one hundred and twenty couples, communication being established by means of a smooth
copper plate submerged in a solution of sea salt,
and you noticed neither the formation of bubbles
of gas on the plate in contact with the negative pole,
nor the oxidation of the plate at the positive pole.
More yet, you made a battery consisting of a series
of cups arranged in a circle of two hundred and
forty-one couples ; you left the elements in place

for a very long time, now opening and now closing the circuit, and you did not observe the escape of hydrogen which occurs during the movement of the pile. This strange theory of contact — a sort of physical abstraction, now utterly forgotten — was long held in high repute; but you were shown in your own lifetime that it was wholly inexact. In fact, to demonstrate the principle — that is, the development of electricity by the mere contact of two metals — you took a metal rod composed of two bits of copper and zinc soldered together, and holding it in your fingers by the zinc end, you applied the copper end to the upper plate of an electroscope-condenser of gold leaf. At the same time you raised the upper plate of the electroscope by its insulating handle, and the gold leaf of the instrument at once deviated from the line, owing to the effect of the electricity existing on the lower plate. This experiment served, according to you, to prove the presence of free electricity in every metal plate composed of two different metals. But to destroy all the value of this experiment, it is only necessary to show that the escape of electricity revealed by the electroscope under these circumstances is produced solely by the chemical action going on between the operator's finger, always soaked in some acid liquid, or acid perspiration, and zinc, a most oxidable metal. In fact, this experiment succeeds only when the plate of the electroscope is touched with a finger previously moistened.

If instead of touching the metal plate with the finger, you touch it with a bit of dry wood; if instead of grasping the voltaic couple by the zinc end, you take it by the copper end, that metal being less oxidable than zinc; lastly, if instead of working in the air, you try this experiment in a vacuum, or in a gas other than oxygen, such as carbonic acid gas or nitrogen, — in these various cases the electroscope ceases to show the presence of electricity. The experiment upon which you based so many hopes was, therefore, but ill observed. Carried out under strict precautions, it proves exactly the opposite, — that is to say, the absence of all electricity in a plate made of two different metals. The objections to your theory of contact were, however, stated as soon as you made known your hypothesis. The chemist Fabroni, in your own country, and Gautherot, in France, destroyed it, by showing that all the effects of the pile are produced by the chemical action of the sulphuric acid upon the zinc; which proved that your explanation rested on facts but ill-noted."

" In short, you claim," replied Volta, " that the invention of the electric pile was merely the result of a series of errors on my part. I will not undertake to argue the question fully, but I would like to remind you of the vast consequences of the discovery of the apparatus which sets the electric current in action. Do you know, either in inanimate or living nature, any agent to be compared with the electric current, either for the power or the originality of its effects? If the two ends of the pile are joined, these effects, as varied as they are remarkable, are obtained. Between these terminal wires, brought very close together, a flame appears which, when produced under special conditions, is to be likened only to the full blaze of the sun. If the two poles of the pile are connected by a fine wire conductor, so that the wire interposed merely serves for the flow of the electricity, we have a powerful centre of heat. The most stubborn metals may be fused by this means: iron, platinum; non-metallic bodies, such as silica or aluminum, commonly supposed to be absolutely infusible; even diamonds; in a word, without exception, almost every substance belonging to the mineral kingdom. The electric current travels to any distance with incalculable speed. It acts a thousand miles from its starting-point, and no obstacle is strong enough to keep it from travelling any distance. Its action may be suspended and renewed, in the twinkling of an eye, at will and with a wave of the hand. The electric current decomposes composite substances, such as water, and all other composites are subject to the same decomposition through which water passes under the influence of the voltaic current. Metal oxides are reduced to their elements; the oxygen escapes at the zinc pole, the metal is deposited at the other pole. Saline composites are also destroyed by the effect of the same force. The electric current has enabled chemists to reveal the nature of countless composites. Potash being subjected to its action, that alkali is decomposed. All basic oxides are, in turn, divided into two parts, — into oxygen and a peculiar metal. The true nature of alkaline and earthy bases was thus revealed ; and all other chemical substances being successively subjected to this powerful means of analysis, unknown metals were discovered. The electric current, which produces such wonderful physical and chemical results, also produces important physiological results. By circulating through our organs, it reproduces that peculiar commotion which it is the peculiarity of innervation to excite, and rouses our dormant faculties. The electric current revives in the corpse of an animal the organic actions destroyed by death. By sending it through the pectoral muscles of a fresh-killed animal, the mechanical act of respiration is reproduced in the dead body. Criminals who have been executed have been subjected to the same order of experiment, and performed all the phenomena of organic life ; the hands moved and lifted weights, the body rose and sat erect, and the facial muscles went through such fearful contortions that the witnesses of the singular scene fled in terror. The electric current is, therefore, at once a source of light and heat, an agent of motive power, a powerful means of chemical action, and an instrument for various physiological phenomena. To produce heat and light, create motive powers, restore bodies to their original elements, and combine them together, — such are the effects of the electric current, whose unique characteristic is that it is universal in its applications. By its aid we confine and condense in one and the same point a continual source of electricity, that is to say, of a physical agent equal to caloric in the number and importance of its attributes; and we can employ, by turns, its various effects, — that is to say, heat, light, mechanical action, or physiological effects. We can, at will, make use of any one of these effects, to the exclusion of the others; and all, separately or simultaneously, meekly obey our orders. It is a submissive servant, who sets forth, hastens to obey, and pauses at a sign."

" I do not deny," answered Galvani, " the immense importance of the apparatus which sprang from your industrious hands; and the effects which you enumerate, some of which were known in my day, excited a just admiration. I merely wished to remind you, and I hope that you will excuse the slight lack of courtesy which my long dissertation on physics may show, that you were led to invent the electric pile through a chain of facts but half observed."

During the conversation which we have repeated, another celestial had approached our two friends, and had caught their last words. This was the English physicist, Michael Faraday.

" You just now acknowledged with much frank-ness," he said to Galvani, " how much accident had to do with your discovery of the electric current. I would add that it is to the same cause that we owe the discoveries which have so marvellously increased the effects and applications of the electric current. The great discovery of the action of the electric current upon magnets was certainly the re-sult of chance. Men had almost exhausted the study of the effects of an *open* electric current, — that is to say, when the two poles of the electric pile are removed, one from the other, for a certain space, so as to produce an electric discharge between those two poles, with the production of a luminous arch or a spark ; but no one had paid any heed to the *closed* electric current, — that is, where the electricity flows continuously without any outward manifestation. It was thought to be deprived of all action under these conditions. Chance led to the discovery of electro-magnetism, at the hands of a Danish physicist, Oersted, a professor at the Uni-versity of Copenhagen. In 1820, during one of his lectures on physics, Oersted was showing his audience the calorific power of the electric pile, by heating a fine platinum wire joining the two poles, red-hot by the effect of the current. A magnetic needle accidentally lay some distance away from the pile. Now, as soon as the pile began to act, — that is, as soon as the current was *closed*, — the magnetic needle began to fluctuate in a singular fashion, which greatly surprised the spectators. They believed, indeed, that just because the two poles of the pile were joined, therefore the current was destroyed, and it could no longer produce any result. The fact, however, could not be denied, since every one saw that the magnetic needle was moved, at a distance, by a *closed* current. When the students had gone, Oersted made haste to repeat the experiment, which had thus, as it were, performed itself, before the eyes of the public. He again set the pile in action, and held a movable magnetic needle near it. This needle moved most vigorously whenever it approached the wire uniting the two poles of the pile.

" This discovery," continued Faraday, " was soon vastly extended. Oersted had created *electro-magnetism*, Ampère established its mathematical and physical laws, and Arago discovered the fundamental fact of the power of *closed* currents to magnetize iron and steel. Here again it was chance that revealed this important phenomenon. On repeating Oersted's experiment, Arago observed that the uniting wire of the pile attracted iron filings just as iron might a magnet, but that it did not attract the filings of other metals. The current, therefore, gave rise to the magnetic force in iron; and Arago proved that this force disappeared when the current was interrupted. By winding the wire uniting the two poles of a screw-shaped pile around an iron or steel rod, the rod became a magnet, — that

is, it attracted iron, and this magnetization ceased
as soon as the current ceased to circulate through
the wire.   On this temporary magnetization of iron
by the Voltaic current, depends the electro-me-
chanic principle of the electric telegraph, and of a
whole series of inventions of similar order.

"Lastly," continued Faraday, "it was by continuing the study of similar phenomena that I discovered the *induced currents*, and constructed the
first *magneto-electric* machine, known as the *machine de Pixii*, which was destined later on, thanks
to wonderful improvements, to increase the power
of the electric current a hundred fold, and to lead,
a few years later, to the appearance of superb instruments, known as electric dynamos, such as are
now used for electric lighting, as well as for the
transportation to a distance of natural or artificial
forces.   And all this, I repeat, arose by chance,
which led Oersted to discover the action of the
closed current upon the magnetic needle, which
fully confirms the statement which you just now
maintained ; namely, the large part which chance
has played in the discovery of the electric current
and its effects."

Eusebius, who had followed the close of this
learned conversation with great attention, as he
had the first part of it, now ventured to join in the
discourse of these Elysian shades ; and after excusing himself for taking part in their scholarly de-
bate, he asked what conclusion was to be drawn

from the fact that chance had so often presided over discoveries relating to the electric current and its uses.

" What conclusion, dear novice ? " answered the shade of Faraday. " Why, the conclusion that what we call chance on earth, because of the moral blindness peculiar to humanity, does not exist ; but is a means peculiar to Providence, which is inaccessible to the feeble understanding of men. As for us, — that is, the inhabitants of the celestial regions, who are in possession of a part of the secrets of the physical world, — we do not admit that there is such a thing as chance. We regard it as the premeditated will of God. You have had a striking proof of this in the so-called chances or errors accompanying the discovery of the electric current, which were really only events foreordained by the Divine will for the purpose of putting earthly humanity in possession of a new power, and of one resource the more for the welfare and activity of man."

With these words the discussion closed, and each of the ethereal shades withdrew.

In continuation of his visits to the celebrated men of the nineteenth century, Eusebius desired to make the acquaintance of the two Montgolfiers, the inventors of aerostation, — an art which in his opinion would one day put humanity in possession of a fresh benefit of immense compass, that is, aerial navigation. The shades of the two inventors of aerostation, the two Montgolfiers, were pointed out to him as they chatted together; and he addressed them, begging them to tell him under what circumstances they conceived the idea of making balloons.

"Nothing simpler," replied the shade of Stephen Montgolfier; "the idea occurred to me during a moment of revery and repose. I was on the terrace of my paper-mill at Annonay, and I amused myself by watching the clouds move across the sky. I admired their strange shapes, their rapid changes, their brilliant colors; and it suddenly occurred to me to make some artificial clouds, which, in imitation of natural clouds, would rise into the upper regions of the air. Close beside me I saw the smoke from the chimneys of our factory rise and float in the air exactly like clouds. Putting these two facts together, it seemed to me not impossible to make artificial clouds similar to those found in Nature. I made small globes of paper, and filled them with smoke by burning damp straw. Smoke, like aqueous vapor of which clouds are made, is lighter than air. It would therefore rise above the earth, bearing with it my light paper balloons. I tried the experiment, and it succeeded. From that time forth I often amused myself by making little balloons of white, pink, and silver paper, which I launched into the air. I delighted in doing, with my weak hands, what Nature with her grandeur and majesty achieved. The people of the region round about, seeing my sports, called my little balloons *montgolfières*. But my brother Joseph, the clever one of the family, who had studied scientific things at Paris, corrected my explanation. He substituted a scientific theory for the poetry of my clouds. He showed me that if my little spheres rose, it was because I filled them with hot air, lighter than the outside air. To prove this to me, he heated my little paper balloons over a charcoal stove which produced no smoke; and the balloons thus heated flew as high as those which I filled with smoke. I was mistaken in my explanation of the phenomenon; but I had invented a new art, that of aerostation."

Eusebius was curious to know the opinion of the two Montgolfiers in regard to the steering of balloons. He turned to Joseph Montgolfier, and asked him whether he thought that it would ever be possible to make air-ships move in a given direction.

"Reflect, dear new shade," replied Joseph Montgolfier, "that if balloons rise and float in the atmosphere, it is because the gas which they contain is much lighter than air; which signifies, from a mechanical point of view, that the dynamic power of the air is considerably greater than that of the gas contained in the air-ship. If these two forces were equal, we might strive to oppose one to the other; but the difference between the mechanical force of hydrogen gas and that of air is too pronounced, pure hydrogen being fourteen times lighter than air. Therefore the faintest current of air prevents the advance of an air-ship filled with hydrogen gas in a direction opposite to that current."

"But," replied Eusebius, "an air-ship might be provided with a motor which would make up for the lack of power in the hydrogen gas, to fight against the force of the wind. Kept in equilibrium in the air by the specific lightness of the hydrogen gas, the air-ship might be urged forward by the motor."

"Yes," answered Joseph Montgolfier; "that would require a motor at the same time very strong, in order to resist the impetus of the wind, and very light, in order not to diminish the ascensional power of the air-ship. But where are we to find such a motor, both strong and very light, — for power and light weight scarcely go together? This providential motor has for a hundred years been vainly sought for. I have kept myself informed of all the efforts made in this direction during the past century in different parts of the globe, — for we have, you know, the ability to see and know all that occurs on the planet which we once inhabited. Well, every motor tried has proved incapable of overcoming the resistance of the air."

"Still," objected Eusebius, "the electric motor gave excellent results."

"You do not refer, I suppose, to the accumulators; for their enormous weight could not be sustained by a balloon."

"No; I mean the motor worked by a bichromate of potash Voltaic pile."

"That has, indeed, been tried by many aeronauts during the last twenty years. Unfortunately, the action of the pile is quickly exhausted. At the end of a few hours it ceases. The source of the electricity is dried up, and the motor has no more power. The aeronaut must either descend or abandon himself to the mercy of the wind. This is the reason that all the experiments which made so much talk were limited to an aerial stroll of two or three hours, after which the balloons were obliged to return to earth. And yet the electric motor was the agent on which most hope was based."

"That is, unfortunately, true; but what do you say to the system of *heavier than air?* Is it not possible, with a wheel or screw endued with sufficient speed, to act upon the air in such a way as to keep the air-ship in equilibrium, or to move it in a given direction?"

Stephen Montgolfier smiled at these words, but at once became serious again.

"I would not, dear novice," said he, "discourage any one; but when I think of the strange expectation of raising a heavy body into the air, I cannot help smiling. What a tremendous rate of speed would be required for such a reaction on a gas like air, which escapes under pressure, and reacts little if at all! Moreover, hundreds of machines answering to this system have been tried, for a half-century back, and none has succeeded. This is the best argument against the paradoxal system of 'heavier than the air.'"

"The body of a bird," replied Eusebius, "is very heavy, with its bones, flesh, and cartilage; and yet it floats in the air, merely by the action of its pectoral muscles. Here, you must admit, we have a fine instance of heavier than air. May not art attain what Nature produces daily?"

"When the bird is dead," rejoined Montgolfier, "can you, by any means whatsoever, make it fly? There must therefore be in the bird's pectoral muscles some peculiar element which our machines cannot reproduce. That element is vital force. Find a motor as powerful as that which active life bestows on the body of a bird, and you will realize in your air-ships the system of 'heavier than the air.' But Nature has not revealed to you her secret."

"Yet many efforts have been made," replied Eusebius, "to imitate the flight of birds; during these latter years physicists, not destitute of merit, have made *artificial birds*, in which an electric motor moves vast surfaces imitating a bird's wing. We are told that these machines float in the air."

"Yes," said Montgolfier, "such is the claim put forth by certain inventors; but hitherto all has been reduced to empty promises. Besides, what duration could such a machine have, with an electric motor whose action is so soon exhausted?

To fall from a height with more security than was afforded by the old parachute, — which I have often seen in use, and which brought an aeronaut to the ground apart from his balloon, — to this must be reduced the use of the *artificial bird,* so long announced but never appearing."

Eusebius was somewhat crestfallen at finding that the inventors of aerostation had so little confidence in the future advance of their own discovery; and he left them to visit other inventors.

The art that interested him most, on account of his recent progress, and concerning which he desired some special information, was photography, so humble at its birth, so marvellous in its results. He was told of the presence, not far distant, of the three inventors of photography, Joseph Niepce, Daguerre, and Fox Talbot, who were in the habit of meeting to talk over the progress of their art. He had no difficulty in finding the group ; and without sharing in it, he listened to their conversation.

It bore upon the extraordinary advance made during fifty years in the invention which owed its birth to them. Every one knows that Joseph Niepce, of Chalons on the Saône, was the first inventor of photography on metal ; that the Parisian painter, Daguerre, was his partner and assistant ; and that Fox Talbot, the Englishman, made the first photograph on paper.

The three friends had just taken a look at the earth, to see the photographic work done in the open air by countless amateurs of different lands, and they could not recover from their surprise.

"What do you think, dear Daguerre," asked the shade of Niepce of his former partner, "of the advance in the art which originated with us? Do you remember how, after numberless attempts, we succeeded — in what? In getting a reproduction of some natural object upon a silvered plate. But each operation furnished only one copy; a fresh operation and a fresh metallic plate was required for every picture. Now a single plate supplies thousands of pictures."

"I obtained the same result," eagerly exclaimed the shade of Fox Talbot; "for by inventing photography on paper, I furnished the means of obtaining from a negative picture as many positive pictures as were required."

"We know it," answered Daguerre, "and we have no idea of attributing to any one but you the merits of that great conquest of art, although one of our countrymen, the over-modest Bayard, is said to have made photographs on paper at the same time that you did. But a discovery to which you will not lay claim, as it occurred half a century later than you, is *instantaneous photography*, with gelatino-bromide of silver, which crowns a long series of successive improvements. The miraculous results of instantaneous photography are now the pride of artists and the delight of amateurs."

"Yes," said Talbot, "in the rapid glance which

we took of earth, I saw extraordinary things. An amateur paused for an instant on a sidewalk; he caught sight of a young woman whose portrait he wanted. To get it, he drew out his watch. But this watch was not a watch; it was a minute photographic apparatus. Knowing the distance between himself and the young woman, he held the machine towards the model for a second. Then he withdrew, no one having any suspicion of what he had done, and went home to develop at his leisure the picture taken in so strange a way."

"Like you," said Daguerre, "I saw amateurs working in the open air, pointing at a building or a passer-by a camera concealed under a waistcoat, or even stuck in a cravat, like a pin. The amateur, without stopping for an instant, uncovered the lens of a liliputian machine, then went his way with the desired picture. I saw others who seemed to be looking at some one or something through an opera-glass which they held to their eyes. But this opera-glass was not an opera-glass; it was a camera, which they used to take a picture."

"If you want another queer case of instantaneous photography," said Niepce, "hear this. I was watching a balloon ascension in the Champ de Mars, at Paris, when I saw a parachute cut loose from the balloon, and drop rapidly to the earth. Now what do you think the parachute contained in its descent? A camera. The parachute having reached the ground, a photographer, who was waiting, hastily picked it up. Then he went to his studio, to develop the picture of the landscape taken by the machine during the descent."

"I saw more than that," he added. "A velocipede passed by, devouring distance, as it is the property of these amazing vehicles to do; and all at once, without suspending his speed, the rider aimed a camera at a little fair-haired girl standing in the street. Then continuing his journey, he went home to develop and fix the picture taken on the gallop."

"It only remains," merrily added Daguerre, "to photograph a cannon-ball flying through the air from the mouth of a gun."

"That will come," said Talbot. "Is there not an electro-mechanical machine which registers, to the *thousandth part of a second*, the instant of a projectile's passage? The course of a cannon-ball may some day be photographed by this same instrument, combined with photographic lenses."

"That will be progress with a vengeance," said the shade of Niepce, laughing.

"Would you like to hear, my friends," said Fox Talbot, coming nearer, "the wonders of *automatic photography?* Hear this. A few months ago I was hovering over the Tuileries gardens, in Paris, to watch the always amusing spectacle of the people who frequent those beautiful avenues of an afternoon. The broad walk which borders the Rue de Rivoli, and which is planted with fine young chestnut-trees, was filled with a crowd of mothers, nurses, and babies, rolling hoops and spinning tops between the legs of every new-comer. Little goat-carriages and childish teams, with long red reins, covered with noisy bells, moving through the throng, added to the general confusion. I was about to fly away from the din, when I saw, hidden by the trees, a sort of kiosk, with two dial-plates on the front wall, each crossed by hands like those of a clock. In the middle, forming a projection, was a short telescope, which plainly contained a camera. A red and white striped parasol covered the tiny machine, and opposite to it was an arm-chair, leaning against a concave metal surface, painted white. The whole made up the machinery of an *automatic photographer*, executing all the operations of photography without the necessity for any intervention on the part of an operator. You slip a ten-cent piece into a slot near the dial-plate, you take your seat, and in a very short time you receive your photograph all framed. Is not this the last wonder of art?"

"Of course you saw a picture taken?" said Niepce.

"To be sure," replied Fox Talbot. "The owner of the machine was a sort of Cheap Jack, in a straw hat, but decently dressed and tolerably well-mannered. He explained the merits and advantages of his machine, and a circle of curious people gathered around him. A young nurse-girl, somewhat confused at being the centre of attraction for so many eyes, stepped forward, and taking a ten-cent piece from a shabby purse, offered it to the Cheap Jack, who instantly dropped it into the slot. At once the hands on one of the dials began to move, and the girl seated herself in the photographer's chair. While the hand moved and the girl smoothed her hair, pulled down her cuffs, arranged her skirts, and put on the proper expression, the mysterious operation was accomplished within the machine, hidden from the gaze of the profane. The plate was covered automatically with gelatino-bromide of silver, and took its place behind the lens, hidden by a movable diaphragm. When the hand completed its course, a bell rang within. ' Don't move!' cried the man. The girl never stirred; she was as rigid as a soldier under arms. Hardly ten seconds had elapsed when the bell stopped ringing. ' All done!' said the man. The nurse rose and mingled with the curious spectators. They waited five minutes amid universal silence; and those who stood on the right side of the box saw a very thin sheet-iron plate some two and a half inches long by seven and a half wide, which contained the portrait, come out of a slot. Meantime the Cheap Jack had prepared a little frame of stamped brass for the picture, and had put into it a sheet of transparent gelatine to preserve it from rough handling. When the photograph issued from the magic box, he seized it delicately, blew on it for a few moments to dry it, for it was still wet from the bath, and putting it into the frame, he handed it to his customer, to the great admiration of the spectators, who crowded round her to gaze at the masterpiece."

" And was it a good likeness ?" asked Daguerre.

" I could only get a hasty glance at it," replied Fox Talbot ; " but you will think it was successful when you hear the rest of my story. Putting the tiny picture in her pocket, the nurse for the second time opened her purse, took out another ten-cent piece, herself dropped it into the slot ; then she again seated herself in the photographer's chair and asked for a second picture. You will admit, friends, that the first picture must have been satisfactory, since the girl desired another."

" And for whom did she intend this second portrait ?" said Niepce, with a smile.

" You ask me too much," answered Talbot. " I am too discreet to question a young servant-maid's heart."

" Let that go," replied Daguerre. " But," he added, " in what you have just told us there is one point which strikes me particularly. It follows from your story that to get a picture by the automatic process, a new operation must be gone through with each time ; for this process gives but a single copy, and, moreover, the picture is made on a metal plate. This is exactly what Niepce and I did when we invented photography on metal."

" You are a thousand times right," cried Niepce, with warmth. " So photography, having reached its height of perfection, — that is to say, instantaneity, — borrows our processes, our primitive method. Having grown to manhood, it returns to its childhood days. Let us congratulate ourselves, my dear Daguerre, on this singular return to that which constituted our glory, to the starting-point of photography."

All will understand, without further insistence upon it, the heartfelt joy of the two shades who thus saw the discovery which had cost them so much time and labor again restored to favor.

The conversation was at an end ; each withdrew, and Eusebius, fluttering his wings, set out for new regions of air, in search of other inventors or creators in the scientific order.

We will not follow him in his future wanderings, satisfied with having in these imaginary dialogues given an idea of the happiness peculiar to inhabitants of the astronomic paradise, which consists of coming into relation with great persons who have left important traces in the history of humanity.

In the foregoing pages we have considered the happiness reserved, in our opinion, for celestial spirits, of holding communion with the souls of illustrious scientists, because science has been the special object of our study ; but is it necessary to add that the same kind of satisfaction is allotted to artists, who will enter into relations with the souls of great celebrities in the world of painting, drawing, sculpture, engraving, and architecture? Is it not unequalled happiness to see face to face the souls of Delacroix, Ingres, David, Vernet, Meissonier; to hear the lessons, enjoy the conversations and recollections of Houdon, Canova, Barye, and Pradier; to receive the counsels of the great architects who built the famous monuments of both worlds? The same may be said of the great legislators, renowned politicians, celebrated historians. And will it be a matter of indifference to men of war to converse with the soul of Napoleon I., or with the galaxy of illustrious generals of the First Empire, and to live side by side with the great captain who so long filled the world with the fame of his genius and his victories?

14

CHAPTER X.

WE have now reviewed the joys reserved, according to our way of thinking, for the
human race raised from the dead, — joys which
atone for the misfortunes experienced during our
earthly existence, and which are also the reward
for the virtues of the individual and the perfection
to which his soul may have attained on earth by the
efforts of his will. We shall now try to prove that
our system of the resurrection and transmigration
of souls is the only one — if we except, from a certain point of view, Christianity — which furnishes
man with any genuine solace against the fear of
death ; the only one suited to dispel the apprehen-
sions which that critical instant inspires in all men,
and which replaces that fear by the prospect of
eternal bliss.

Various statisticians have attempted to enumerate and classify the many religions now practised
on the earth. We quote, to give some determinate

idea, the distribution of religions recently printed by Hübner, a German geographer.

Supposing that the number of the earth's inhabitants is 1,400,000,000, Hübner gives the following table of the sum total of religions professed by man : —

Buddhists	500,000,000
Catholics	200,000,000
Brahmins	150,000,000
Protestants	110,000,000
Greek Church	80,000,000
Mahometans	80,000,000
Israelites	6,500,000
Christian Sects	10,000,000
Various known religions	244,000,000
Unknown religions	19,500,000
Total	1,400,000,000

The same statement may be given in the following form, to make it more synthetic : —

Buddhists			500,000,000
Christians {	Catholics	200,000,000	
	Protestants	110,000,000	400,000,000
	Greek Church	80,000,000	
	Christian Sects	10,000,000	
Brahmins			150,000,000
Mahometans			80,000,000
Israelites			6,500,000
Various known religions			244,000,000
" unknown religions			19,500,000
Total			1,400,000,000

In comparing our cosmogonic system with those religions actually existing, with regard to the consolations offered against the fear of death, we will take up each religion in its order of numeric importance. Buddhism being the most prevalent upon our globe, since it is followed by more than a third of the human race (500,000,000), we shall begin our comparisons by a statement of the system of Buddha.

Buddhism.

Like Christianity and Islamism, Buddhism was founded by a man of genius, who preached to the people the desertion of idolatry, and substituted for it a new conception of the divinity. Buddha, Jesus, and Mahomet are the three founders of the religious systems that bear their names. If we would understand their doctrines, we must know the events of their lives. We therefore begin by a sketch of the life of Buddha.

It was in the seventh century before our era (from 622 to 542 before Jesus Christ) that the devout personage lived who endowed India and Oriental Asia with a new religion, substituted by him for the ancient dogmas of Brahminism. His family name was Siddhârtha. He was born at Kapilavastu, at the foot of the Himalaya Mountains, in a small independent kingdom bordering on India. He was no less than the son of the king of this country. A supernatural origin was attributed to his birth. He was said to have entered the body of his mother, Mayadevi, under the form of a young white elephant; and he was said to have been born, ten months later, causing the death of her who gave him birth.

As the three magi, according to the legend, worshipped the infant Jesus in the manger, so too Brahma and Indra, Indian divinities, assisted at the birth of Siddhârtha, which was followed by various miracles. No sooner was he born, than the child took seven steps in the four directions of north, south, east, and west, proclaiming himself as the destroyer of disease, old age, and death.

The new-born child bore on his body the thirty-two chief signs and the eighty secondary signs which, according to Indian tradition, characterize the great man, and prophesy for him absolute wisdom. Accordingly he gave proof of unparalleled precocity from his earliest childhood. When he was sent to school, the writing-master wishing to teach him to form the letters of the alphabet, the precocious lad repeated to him a list of sixty-four different kinds of writing, of which the professor had never heard. Imagine the master's surprise at the sight of this polyglot in miniature!

However, in spite of the satisfaction which the brilliant qualities of his mind must have afforded him, Siddhârtha, on attaining to early manhood, fell a prey to unconquerable melancholy. To distract him, his relatives married him. But marriage could not dispel his sorrow, or rather, it doubled it; for the young pair having parted on account of incompatibility of temper, after six years' separation, Gotha — that was the wife's name — had a son !

His conjugal misfortunes deeply affected the young prince ; but what filled up the measure of his grief — what determined him to quit the court, and shut himself up in a retreat — was what Buddhist tradition calls the *Four Encounters.*

Wearied of being detained within his palace by friends too assiduous in amusing him, Siddhârtha went out one morning for a walk. · But he met by the way an old man, feeble in body, with tottering gait and stupid air. Alarmed by these painful attributes of age, Siddhârtha returned to his palace, to mourn over the unhappy destiny of man, condemned to grow old.

Next day, starting out at the same hour for a second walk, he met a sick man, carried on a litter. The pallor of his features, the emaciation of his limbs, the hideous wounds with which his body was covered, deeply affected the mind of the young prince, who hastened home to deplore the fate of humanity, dedicated to suffering and sickness.

During a third walk he met a funeral train ; the parents in tears, the friends in mourning-dress, the women uttering loud lamentations, and the face of the corpse exposed to view. This spectacle terrified the sensitive youth, who from that moment resolved in his own mind to seek some remedy against old age, disease, and death.

A fourth walk offered him what he sought. He saw coming toward him a Brahmin monk, whose calm, serious face struck him with admiration. The remedy for disease and death was found: it was the monastic life!

Siddhârtha implored the king, his father, to give him leave to quit the court, and lead a hermit's life in some remote solitude. But the king utterly refusing to grant this unusual request, the young prince dispensed with his permission. Shielded by night, he secretly left the city, accompanied by one servant only, and mounted on a car drawn by a single horse. The wheels of the car were muffled with cloth to deaden all sound.

When they had reached a forest, some hours distant from the city, Siddhârtha dismissed his servant and the car; then he exchanged his rich robes for a coarse, dark dress, and cut off his hair.

Thus disguised, he began to follow the teachings of certain learned men of that region; but their instructions did not meet his expectations. Weary of the false doctrines of these masters in regard to the world and Nature, he decided to seek for himself, by maceration and mortification of the flesh, the revelation of absolute wisdom.

Withdrawing to Mount Gatya, he condemned himself to eat nothing but a little rice, and to hold his breath that he might fall ill. In this he succeeded perfectly; for after a few years of this regimen he was fearfully thin; his body, which had become quite black, being reduced to the state of a skeleton. The friends and disciples whom he had made in the neighborhood said one to the other: "Sramana Gotama is quite black; Sramana Gotama is perfectly blue; Sramana Gotama is just the color of a fish!" Sramana Gotama — that is, Gotama the ascetic — was the name by which our anchorite was known in the country round about.

The laughter of his friends showed Siddhârtha that his mortification of the flesh had not revealed to him the principles of eternal wisdom. He therefore renounced his dangerous mode of life and his solitude. He went down to Uruvilva, on the banks of the Nairandjanâ, and taking leave of his retreat as well as the austerities which he had practised for six years, he returned to every-day life, observing a happy mean, equally removed from a depressing asceticism and from wearisome pleasures.

He then resolved to seek in religious ecstasy the revelation of the secret of eternal wisdom. He took up his position at the foot of a fig-tree (*Ficus India*), and seated himself on a carpet of grass, his legs crossed, determined not to quit that position until he had found "Buddhi;" that is, had gained possession of supreme truth, which causes a man to become a "Buddha," a term signifying the possession of all moral perfection.

While he was absorbed in this ecstasy, he was a prey to the attacks of Mâra, the demon of evil, who let loose upon him rain, storm, and tempest, and who then overwhelmed him with every sort of projectile and engine of destruction. But nothing could rouse the immovable thinker from his fixed and meditative attitude. Seeing that violence was of no avail, the demon sent an army of young girls, who strove to lure him away; but, like a worthy predecessor of Saint Anthony, he opposed an utter passivity to all the seductions of their charms.

After having passed through this final proof, Siddhârtha at length attained the object of his desires. He became "Buddha,"—that is to say, possessed of supreme wisdom, which includes (1) the knowledge of his exterior existences; (2) the destruction of all evil desire in his soul; (3) the knowledge and concatenation of the twelve causes; (4) absolute knowledge, divided into three sections.

It was now essential that he should win disciples, preach the doctrine, and found a school. While he gave himself up to mortification of the flesh on Mount Gatya, he had, as disciples and friends, five inhabitants of the country, who took part in his devout practices. He sought them out to make them apostles of the new religion. These five auxiliaries then went from town to town, in groups of two or three, to beg food for their master and his disciples.

Such was the nucleus of the first confraternity of which Siddhârtha was the founder; for you must know that besides the institution of a religion which took the place of that of Brahma, Siddhârtha was the creator of the monastic mendicant orders which now swarm throughout India and Eastern Asia.

The Buddha passed his days as follows. He rose early in the morning, put on his cloak, and with his alms-basin in his hand, begged from door to door. All his disciples did the same. Returning to his monastery at noon, he took his only meal, and devoted the rest of the day to preaching. He commonly collected about him from twelve to fifteen hundred hearers at each gathering.

Thus, for a period of forty-five years, Siddhârtha preached his doctrines in the north of the Indian peninsula, constantly adding more and more disciples to his confraternity, and making powerful friends, eager to retail his ideas throughout all India and Eastern Asia. Brahminism, planned for the use of the upper classes, was hated by the Indian people. Buddhism, which proclaimed the equality of men, fraternity, charity, morality, and justice for all, was everywhere received with delight, and spread abroad, not only by people of low condition, but by princes and rajahs.

It is impossible to form any idea of the enthusiasm excited by the ardent and untiring converter. The new religion, opposed to antique Brahminism, spread like a train of powder. When Siddhârtha visited the province and city of Rajagriha, King Bimbisara went out to meet him. He received him most cordially, and gave him as a residence for himself and his monks a magnificent park. Throughout his entire reign he granted him most efficient protection.

The arrival of Buddha at Sravassi excited exceptional curiosity, as it did everywhere. King Prasenadjeti could not believe that so much wisdom could be combined with so much youth in the new apostle. Buddha dispelled all his doubts by one of his most famous sermons, the *Sutra* (pattern) *for young people.*

From Sravassi he went to Kapilavastu, the capital of the kingdom of his father, whom he had not seen for ten years. He was received with the highest honors, and he and his monks were lodged in a vast park; for devoted as he was to the cause of the people, he would never have consented to cross the threshold of the royal palace where his father lived. His preaching roused universal enthusiasm at Kapilavastu. Everybody wanted to leave the world and enter the Buddhist brotherhood. The king, his father, himself set the example of abnegation by resigning his crown. Deserted by their husbands, fathers, and sons, the women made the city ring with their laments. As this dangerous current had to be stopped, those who could enter the brotherhood were limited to one member of each family.

The establishment of sisterhoods for women dates from this journey of Buddha to Kapilavastu. Thenceforth there were as many " Bhikchounis " (nuns) as there were " Bhickous " (mendicant friars).

After his journeys to Sravassi and Kapilavastu. the new apostle returned to Rajagriha, where he spent the second, third, and fourth years of his career as a preacher. During the fifth he went to Vazed, where the Garden of Mangoes was given him for a residence.

We will not follow him in his many journeys, which kept him busy for thirty years more, during which time he everywhere received the same homage. Princes and rajahs, as well as the crowd, were converted in a body. Thus he succeeded in founding the new religion which, after his death, spread from India to China and Japan, and then to most of the countries of Eastern Asia.

Recent estimates give the following table of adherents to Buddhism, including both monastic fraternities and mere individuals. We will divide them into Northern and Southern Buddhists; for it is important to know that the teaching of Buddha has met with many schisms, and that various schools now exist, which may be divided into those of the North and those of the South.

South.

Ceylon	1,520,575
Burmah	5,447,831
Siam	10,000,000
Annam	12,000,000
India Proper	485,000
	29,453,406

North.

Dutch Indies	50,000
British India	500,000
Russian Asia (Kalmucks, etc.)	600,000
Loo-Choo Islands	1,000,000
Corea	8,000,000
Bhotan and Sikkim	1,000,000
Cashmere	200,000
Thibet	6,000,000
Mongolia	2,000,000
Mantchuria	3,000,000
Japan	32,794,897
Nepaul	500,000
China	414,686,994
Total	470,331,891
With those of the South, that is .	29,453,406
General total	499,785,297

This gives us a figure not far from the five hundred million, which we gave in the beginning of this chapter.

After a very long life, twenty-nine years of which were spent at the court of the king, his father, six in the practice of asceticism, and forty-five in preaching, Siddhârtha died, at the age of eighty, in the country of the Mallas, near the city of Kusina-gara. His faithful disciple, Ananda, was the only person present at his death-bed, and received his last breath.

His death caused universal mourning among the inhabitants of India. His body was burned ; and the ashes were divided into eight parts, which were placed in as many funeral monuments.

Siddhârtha wrought the wonder of converting millions to his doctrine, by the unaided power of his words, and by the virtues of which he set an example. He never pretended to be sent by God, and performed no miracles. These two things clearly distinguish Buddha from Jesus and Mahomet.

At his death his disciples and the apostles of his ideas collected together the facts of his life and his sermons with a view to writing them out. They then called a meeting of five hundred monks, which was held at Râjagriha, and was the first Buddhist council.

The chief dogmas of the Buddhist religion were formulated at this meeting; but the secondary points not being touched upon, divergent doctrines soon arose. In order to give the new religion the unity which it threatened to lose, the most ardent propagandist of Buddhistic views in India, the King of Pataliputra (Asoka was his name), called a second council, composed of seven hundred monks. This assembly, which met one hundred and ten years after the death of Buddha, settled the chief dogmas, and made out a list of canonical books.

However, eighteen new sects having been formed between the decisions of the second council, a third council had to be held four hundred years after the death of the founder of the faith, which reconciled all these dogmas.   These councils were all previous to the Christian era.

We have not yet spoken of Buddha's doctrines. It is now time to take up this point.

We will divide our brief sketch into three parts : *Buddha's System of Morals and Philosophy; Buddha's Theodicy; Man's Destiny.*

System of Morals and Philosophy. — Buddha's system of morals was perfectly correct, and one of the most beautiful ever taught to man.   Obedience to parents, love of children, devotion to friends, indulgence to inferiors, kindness to animals, respect for Brahmins and learned people, — in short, tolerance, charity, and universal brotherhood, — such are the chief teachings of the Buddhistic system of morals.   They are to be put in practice by the suppression of passions and desires, which are the first cause of all our ills.

We hasten to add that an impenetrable obscurity surrounds Buddhism so soon as we leave the region of pure morality.   For centuries, writers of all lands have vainly striven to dispel these clouds. We will not enter upon the abstruse study of Buddha's philosophy, which would take us away from our object; for what we chiefly wish to consider is the Buddhist theodicy, — that is to say, the idea which that religion gives us of God and the Creation.

Theodicy. — It is easy to prove that atheism and nihilism are the end and aim of the so-called religious dogmas of Buddhism. We shall see, indeed, that the gods accepted by Buddha are intimately associated in all their acts with the inhabitants of the earth. They may be deprived of their celestial existence, and again assume bodily form on our globe. There is thus a perpetual interchange between divinity and man, between earth and heaven. Such promiscuity is simply atheism.

The wise men of Indian councils have established a sort of hierarchy among the gods (*devas*), in which these devas are divided into successive grades, as the officers are in a battalion.

Heaven is the abode of the gods, or genii (devas), — that is, those beings who by their merits have won a privileged position, a position which they may lose if they cease to deserve it. If the vicissitudes of their celestial existence lead them to commit faults, they again descend to earth, and by a transmigration backward, once more begin their earthly career. Devas, therefore, are not, properly speaking, gods, but beings enjoying the fruit of their virtues.

The Buddhist books of China contain a sketch showing, by a series of lines running from top to bottom of the page, the places occupied by the gods in the various departments of heaven.

Three regions, one above the other, are the abode of the three categories of gods. The lower region is called the *region of desire*, the middle one the *region of form*, and the upper one the *region without form*. The higher they ascend, the more fully are the dwellers in these three regions purified from the stains of existence. There are even, in each region, certain stages, answering to the various states of purification; for these stages, to the number of twenty-eight, contain gods of different degrees of merit.

In the region of desire, where the purity of the gods is least, we find six stages. The genii, or gods, who dwell here are, reckoning from below upward: (1) the *four great kings* and their *subjects*, settled on the sides of Mount Meru, which bears up the sky; (2) the god Indra and the thirty-three gods; (3) the *yamas* (the vigilants); (4) the *tushitas* (the satisfied), — it was from this region of the sky that Siddhârtha, the founder of Buddhism, descended, to fulfil his final earthly existence; (5) the *Nirmanaratis* (those who delight in transformations); (6) the *Paranirmânavas* (those who delight in transforming their centres). The region of form, which is next above that of desire, is divided into several stages, whose singular names we omit.

The region without form receives those beings in whom life is reduced to its minimum. The first stage of this region is called *void;* the second, *absolute knowledge;* the third, *the stage where nothing is;* the fourth, that *where each is conscious of self.* Here the gods reach the term of their de-

15

liverance: they sink into nothingness. We shall
see presently that nothingness (Nirvâna) is, indeed,
the supreme good, reserved, according to Buddhist
doctrines, for those who have deserved, by their
trials and their virtues, the end of existence, and
eternal rest.

This strange distribution of gods, or genii, which
divides the ruling and regulating power of the
world among so many individualities, is not at all
illogical. But to admit a divinity capable of a fall,
of loss of merit, is contrary to the idea of divine
perfection. In brief, the system laid down by
Buddhist sages is nothing but atheism and moral
nihilism. Thus the Indian, the Chinese, the Japanese, the Singalese, the Annamite, the native of
Tonquin, etc., care very little about the divinity and
his influence over human actions. Religious worship, with them, is reduced to the greatest simplicity.
The Buddhist temple (*stupa*) is only intended to
contain a part of the relics of Buddha or to exhibit
his image. No sacrifice is ever made there, and no
prayers of any sort are uttered. Everything is
reduced to commemorative offerings, which are
placed before the master's image. Worship is
purely honorific, and excludes all superstitious cer-
emony ; for Buddha declared that religious worship
was contrary to morality.

Destiny of Man. — We know that the learned
Orientalist, Eugene Bournouf, made a profound
study of Buddhism. According to his works,

the principles of that doctrine, concerning human destiny, may be summed up in the following
propositions : —

I. There is no creation ; consequently there is no
creator. The world, made up of matter and forces,
is eternal. There is no immortal soul ; individuals
are temporary incarnations of forms, which are
themselves in a perpetual state of change.

II. The visible world is incessantly changing its
form ; death incessantly succeeds to life, and life
to death.

III. Men and animals pass through an unending
series of transmigrations. Man passes successively
through all forms of life, from the lower animals
up to himself ; and the place which he occupies in
the series of beings depends upon the merit of the
deeds that he has done. Thus the virtuous man is
born again, after this life, in the body of a god ;
the guilty man in the body of one damned.

IV. Man's good actions are rewarded by his
sojourn in heaven, the abode of genii and gods.
But nothing is eternal ; time exhausts the merit
of virtuous deeds, just as it effaces the wrong of
evil deeds. The law of change, therefore, inevitably brings gods and condemned back to earth,
both being placed in a state to begin once more
the test of purity, and to pass through a new
period of transmigrations, from animal species to
animal species and to human beings.

V. The reward and supreme end of trials victoriously met is to enter oblivion, where all suffering ends, where being attains the goal of its long transmigrations, griefs, and joys. Buddhists call this final annihilation of individuality *Nirvâna.*

VI. Man's speedy entrance to Nirvâna — that is, nothingness — is made known by the possession of unlimited knowledge, which gives him an exact perception of the world as it is, and the possession of transcendent perfections, which are: charity, purity, knowledge, energy, patience, and benevolence.

From this statement we see that Buddhism is based on two fundamental ideas: *the transmigration of beings*, a period of trials and expiations, of indefinite extent, the only meaning of our existence; and *Nirvâna*, or the annihilation of the individual, which is our final reward, the end of our trials or expiations, which terminates forever the circle of our existences.

The principles of Buddhism are contained in the collection of sermons by Siddhârtha, the founder of the system. The collection of Buddhist books consists of two great works, — the Kandjur (108 volumes folio), and the Dandjur (240 volumes folio). These are the equivalent of the Christian Bible and the Mahometan Koran.

Is it necessary to dwell upon the point to make our readers understand all the horrors of Buddhist philosophy? It is pure atheism; it is pessimism, which is usually thought to be a modern invention, but which was professed in the Orient, twenty-five centuries before the advent of Auguste Comte, Büchner and Darwin, the leaders of modern materialism and positivism in Europe. Nonentity, elevated into a dogma, and given as the reward of virtue, offered to men as the supreme object of all their aspirations; nonentity, *nothing*, after an existence of unmerited misery; nonentity, set up at the close of reincarnations, as the recompense of unrecognized honesty and devotion, of much abused resignation, of innocence oppressed, — can we conceive of a people who would profess such a religion? What society, outside of Asia, could bear with impunity the shock of such monstrous ideas?

Compare the doctrine of the rewards and pleasures reserved for the virtuous, in our system of celestial transmigrations, with the gloomy theory of Buddha, and look at their comparative consequences. Take two men, one a convert to the idea of the second birth of humanity in the ethereal medium, in the enjoyment of the many felicities attached to this new period of his existence; the other believing the doctrine of the Buddhist Nirvâna.

The former, regarding the difficulties of his earthly life as transitory accidents, looking forward to the blissful existences which he is to lead in planetary ether, accepts, with composure, his share of the misfortunes which may befall him during his sojourn here below. He will labor courageously to enlarge the sphere of his knowledge; and having acquired a number of new aptitudes, he will await with philosophic calm the close of his earthly career.

The other, the Buddhist, — the partisan of the *dismal comforter*, to whom moral perfection, knowledge, and virtue offer no other prospect or reward than the annihilation of his being, — will endure the burden of life with indifference and impassivity. He will lose all interest in his surroundings. He will reflect that the good or the evil which he may do in this life are much alike, since all that awaits him, after death, all for which he can hope, is the final suppression of his being. " What is the use of being virtuous," he will say, " since nonentity is the equal lot of all; since labor, knowledge and honor, goodness and beauty, lead straight to annihilation? Let us pass our life in idleness and amusement; let us use all the resources of our mind to satisfy our passions, our desires, our caprices. Let us pay no heed to the rest of humanity; what will humanity be to us, when we sink into oblivion?" The unfortunate Indian pariah, scorned, condemned to the vilest tasks, shunned by society, has no hope of finding, after his death, compensation for the evils which he has endured. Frightful despair must take possession of his soul; since all that he can expect, as the reward of his pains and his submission, is the destruction of his person.

And this is the doctrine which holds beneath its

yoke five hundred million men, — that is to say,
one third of the human race !

Do you wonder, now, at the indifference, moral
inertia, and contempt for life, which we find among
Indians, Cingalese, Chinese, Japanese, Burmese,
Thibetans, etc., if those people put genuine confidence in the principles of the religion of their
fathers ?   It is difficult for us to believe that this
gloomy dogma, which has ruled over the greater part
of Eastern Asia for two thousand years, can retain
in our day the same supremacy which it possessed
at its origin ; for such beliefs, judged from our standpoint as men of the Occident, are repugnant to human nature, and must cause us to shrink in horror
and disgust.

Brahminism.

Brahminism is closely allied to Buddhism, and
it would not be possible to separate them without
injuring the clearness of the statement.   In fact,
Brahminism is the religion of India, as Buddhism
is that of the rest of Asia and its dependencies.

Brahminism, one of the oldest religions in the
world, reigned exclusively in Asia, when in the
seventh century before Christ there appeared the
great reformer who in his persuasive addresses
promised salvation to the multitude without distinction of castes, and exalted universal charity and
brotherly love.   As we have said, the greater part of
Asia was won over to the new religion.   The Indian

peninsula alone resisted the religious revolution; but even this was for a time led away by the general movement. The startling conversion of rajahs and Indian princes deprived the Brahmins of many of their adherents. And yet the ancestral religion fought hard. Foreign invasion of India (by Greeks and Scythians) made it easier to resist; for the Brahmins, with their caste spirit, detested the barbarian, the stranger, who, mixing with the inhabitants, shocked national instincts and offended against fundamental customs of Hindoo society. Brahminism therefore finally resumed its sway, and that religion is now almost the only one professed in Hindostan.

And yet it was not without some changes that Brahminism remained the dominant religion. Old customs prescribed for private worship in public fell into disuse, and sacrifices were wholly changed or simplified.

Added to this, in our day, an important schism has arisen in the Hindoo religion. A rival of Buddha, the reformer Keshub Chunder Sen, who was born in 1838 and died in 1884, preceded and taught by another man of genius, Ram-Mohun-Roy, founded the " Brahmo-Somaj," which has a great number of followers, who publish magazines and books, and hold conferences intended to give a definite form to the new ideas. The work entitled " Navâ Bidhân " (New Doctrine), which appeared in 1880, gives the synthesis of the Brahmo religion. But we shall not enter here upon any examination of this attempt at reform.   We shall rest content with stating the general dogmas of the time-honored religion professed by Hindoos.

The word *Brahma* means the supreme being, the only God; for monotheism, in opposition to Buddhist polytheism, is the characteristic of the Indian religion.

This supreme and only being is, however, divided into three equal potentialities; just as, in the Christian religion, the supreme being is divided into God the Father, God the Son, and God the Holy Ghost.

Brahma, Vishnu, and Siva are the three divine personalities who by their union make up the supreme being of the Hindoos.

The sun is the emblem of Brahma, who is the creator of the universe, and represents the work accomplished in the past.

Water is the emblem of Vishnu, who represents the present, preservation, space.

Fire is the emblem of Siva, the destructive principle, who also represents time, or the future, as well as avenging justice.

These three gods exercise their power through the intermediation of an endless number of secondary divinities.

It is to recall this trinity of attributes that the Hindoos, in their images of the supreme God, represent him with four heads, ornamented with lotus leaves.   He holds in his four hands a chain, which supports the world, the book of the law, the bodkin used in writing, and the sacrificial fire.

According to Indian tradition, the castes into which the country is divided are of divine origin; and this it is that makes this social institution immovable.

It is supposed that Brahma had four sons, whose descendants form the existing castes. These four sons, in fact, gave birth: (1) to *Brahmins*, the highest, most aristocratic caste, which supplies priests, scholars, and public officials; (2) to *Kshatriyas*, or warriors, whence come rajahs and princes; (3) to *Vaishyas*, who produce merchants and farmers; (4) to *Sudras*, that is, workmen and artisans.

The Brahmins sprang from the mouth of Brahma; the Kshatriyas, Vaishyas, and Sudras issued from his arms, thighs, and feet.

Thus were created and brought into the world the ancestors of the four castes which make up the Hindoo population. It is forbidden to leave these castes, or to mix them by marriage.

Pariahs is the name applied to those persons who belong to none of these four social classes, because their ancestors, or they themselves, have been cast out of them in consequence of their demerits. Rejected by society, these unfortunates are considered unclean beings, all contact and intercourse with whom must be avoided. They are banished to solitary places, and are forced to carry on the vilest trades.

The Vedas, the books of Vishnu, and the " Code of the Laws of Manu " are the sacred books of the Hindoos, as the Bible and the Koran are to Christians and Mahometans written guides containing revelations from God.

Public worship is addressed not to Brahma, who is regarded as inaccessible to the prayers of men, but to Siva, Vishnu, and secondary divinities. Pagodas or temples are consecrated to them ; but public worship is not carried on in these pagodas, which merely serve to receive offerings to Brahma or secondary divinities.

Worship is wholly private, and is performed either at home or in the open air, upon altars reared for the purpose, and moved from place to place, as necessity requires.

The rites of the Brahmin worship are very complicated. They are performed by Brahmin priests, and vary singularly. One rite requires the milk of a black cow who has given birth to a white calf. The kind of wood to be used for the sacrificial fire is rigorously prescribed. The accent and pronunciation of the verses from the Vedas which accompany sacrifices are minutely stipulated.

Sacrifices are sometimes daily, sometimes fortnightly, and sometimes only occasional. Some last but a few moments, others are prolonged for years. Ceremonies are intertangled ; introduction follows upon introduction, conclusion upon conclusion, according to the principles of a complex formalism, into which Brahmins alone are initiated. Thus the rite sometimes requires the presence of more than fifteen or twenty priests at a single sacrifice.

Religious hymns are also a peculiarity of the Brahmins.

Religious worship requires ablutions in sacred rivers, especially in the Ganges; and the holy city of Benares is the obligatory goal of pilgrimages, as Mecca is for Mussulmans.

We now come to an essential part of the religion of Brahma, — metempsychosis, which plays an important part, not only in the religion, but in the social customs of India. This doctrine interests us particularly, because it was thence that modern philosophy derived the idea of the transmigration of souls, — a doctrine which we have adopted in the "Tomorrow of Death" and in the present work.

Indian metempsychosis originated in man's original sin, just as Christianity is based upon the feigned unworthiness of man. According to the Hindoo dogma, man was created free and perfect. When the world was formed, we read in the Vedas, *spiritual prototypes* were born, who produce all life, and dwell in ether. They are pure spirits, analogous to the angels of Judaism and Christianity. These superior beings long enjoyed a state of blessedness; but some of them having through pride ceased to merit such happiness, the supreme being deprived them of their beatitude, and banished them, in order to subject them to a state of trial and renovation.

The downfall of these spirits, according to the Vedas, was fatal in its consequences for the earth. Its axis was displaced, and acquired the vicious inclination which causes inequalities of season and climate, to the great injury of human health and happiness. The stars also were turned from their course; which brought about the Flood.

The human soul is an image of divinity in memory of its original nature of pure spirit, directly created by God; but it is condemned by the will of Brahma to undergo successive migrations through the bodies of different animals and of man, even in plants, according to the merits and demerits of each soul.

These migrations will end when Brahma shall destroy our material world, to replace it by a new one. This destruction will occur in four hundred and thirty-two thousand years. Then God will appear, and replace the material world by another wholly spiritual, where every creature shall enjoy the felicity to which his merits entitle him.

The Hindoos believe so firmly in metempsychosis that there is at Bombay a magnificent refuge for old or infirm animals, and at Jeypore there is a huge pond where more than three hundred crocodiles are maintained. The rajah of the country, in spite of remonstrances from the English Government, insists on keeping them, declaring that the souls of his ancestors are contained in those animals.

The idea of metempsychosis has become a social law with the Hindoos, and the result is as follows: The Hindoo waits patiently for the renewal of the world and its transformation into a spiritual domain; but as he can hasten his entrance to the new world by his virtues, far from avoiding suffering, he seeks it as a means of making himself sooner worthy of the destiny for which he hopes. The earth being regarded as a place of expiation, the idea of sanctity is naturally attached to the privations which he imposes on himself, and the pangs which he voluntarily endures. The Hindoo condemns himself to terrible punishments in order that he may not have to atone in another life for the sin which he has committed. He even exposes himself to cruel mortifications of the flesh, when he is guilty of no sin, simply with a view to blotting out and expiating his future faults. The present life is therefore merely voluntary or preventive expiation and sanctification to him.

The character with which a Hindoo invests his life casts a gloom over his thoughts. He longs for death, as destined to hasten by successive rebirths his entrance to the spiritual world, where he will be spared all suffering, and will be reunited to his creator, Brahma.

Rebirth after death has not therefore to a Hindoo the character of reward which we give it in our system of the transmigration of souls. While we consider the present life as a preparation for the life to come, Hindoos regard it as the result of a series of previous existences ill spent. A man is placed in a social caste or in a star, according to the merits or demerits of a former life. In our system the earth is a place of trial ; in the Indian doctrine it is a place of expiation, very similar to the Catholic purgatory. According to the Brahmin religion, the soul expiates, by assuming a certain body, a certain form, faults committed in a past life.

And yet we must note that in the Brahmanic doctrine the soul has no recollection of its previous existences, or of the sins committed in them ; nor in its lives to come will it have any better memory of its present life.

Thus, in the eyes of the religion of Hindostan, man is nothing ; he has no freedom, he obeys a higher power which is not accountable to him. He is a part of general humanity, which moves by a higher decree towards a goal assigned in advance by God. A uniform law, one and the same force, bears onward all human souls, and guides them all unconsciously towards one and the same final goal.

In the Hindoo system, the rebirth of souls, the celestial metempsychosis is undoubtedly immortality ; but it is an immortality without memory, consciousness, or freedom. But is it not plain that to live again without memory of the past is not living again ? There is no real immortality where there is no continuation of individuality by memory. Expiation unaccompanied by memory is not expiation. We must have knowledge of our faults before we can regret and atone for them. The contrary is sheer nonsense.

We are careful to say in our system, that, from the moment of his resurrection, man, who had no recollection of his existences in the animal state, by reason of the weak development of the soul in animals, will possess complete memory of his past existence, when he attains to the state of super-human being. Thus immortality will be accompanied to him by continuation of individual being.

A Hindoo, persuaded that his present life is merely an expiation and forced progress towards another state, it being out of his power in any way to modify the fate reserved for him, passively endures the burden of the present life. He never for an instant dreams of leaving the caste into which he was born. He cannot complain because he is a Sudra, since he is condemned to live again in that state, in consequence of sins committed in a previous existence. He can only submit, fulfil the duties of a Sudra, and serve higher castes, in order the sooner to prepare for his soul a better position in another life.

Caste spirit takes the place of family feeling in India. Hindoos love their wives and children, but that affection is subordinated to certain principles.

Expulsion from one's family is the result of various causes, chiefly of the violation of rules laid down by religion, or of the illicit intercourse of women of high caste with men of an inferior caste.

If a man belonging to one of the three upper castes allies himself to a Sudra, — that is, to the servile caste, or worse yet, to a Pariah, and lives with her, — he cannot legally marry her, he is instantly degraded, in virtue of direct orders of the law of Vishnu; and he debases his family as well as his offspring to the condition of Sudras. If he be a Brahmin, his son as well as himself ceases to be so. No expiation is possible to him from the moment that his lips are once contaminated by a Sudra.

Brahmins and Sudras, as well as Pariahs themselves, are divided into a number of sub-castes, a member of which can neither eat, drink, nor marry with any member of any other sub-caste. If a Hindoo is degraded, *if he loses caste*, he is cast off by his relations; his wife is regarded as a widow, his children as orphans; and he need look for no help, no pity, from those who have hitherto surrounded him with most devoted care.

Europeans rank with Pariahs, because they make daily use at their meals of the flesh of oxen. Brahmins do indeed consent to shake hands with Europeans; but on returning home they are careful to change their dress and perform ablutions, in order to purify themselves of the stain which so impure a touch has left.

Every Indian village (at least in the Deccan) is invariably composed of two parts, divided by a distance of some yards. There are two wholly distinct quarters, — one reserved for people of caste, the other surrounded by hedges and intended for Pariahs. These wretched creatures are not allowed to enter the village streets without the consent of the inhabitants ; and they are forbidden to draw water elsewhere than from the wells set apart for their use. In places where the Pariahs have no wells, they set down their jars by the wells of people of caste, and wait humbly and patiently for some one to bestow the alms of a few glasses of water. It is always women who are charged with this household care.

Higher castes often give presents to Pariahs, invariably laying them on the ground for fear of contracting by mere contact that moral leprosy with which Pariahs are, in their eyes, infected. No man of caste ever accepts a gift from the hand of a Pariah.

If in physical and intellectual respects those of high caste are far superior to Pariahs, the latter are more laborious, more docile, more accessible to European influences. In the Presidency of Madras they form the best disciplined and most solid part of the native recruits to the English army.

Brahminism, as we see, is less a religion than a

social institution. characterized by the existence of castes and founded on the doctrine of metempsychosis. The life of each individual is ordered in the minutest manner, so that it may be blended with the religious duties.

From the idea of metempsychosis, which forms an essential part of the religious and social beliefs of the Hindoos, results the respect which they as a people show to animals. In fact, they are considered as possibly containing sympathetic souls, and religious laws forbid the eating of their flesh.

Faithful observers of religious ordinances, Hindoos are essentially vegetarians. They abstain from all animal food on pain of being dismissed from their caste and exiled from the bosom of their family. The Pariahs alone eat meat; they devour all sorts of animals and drink *arrack* (rice brandy).

The ordinary food of a Hindoo consists of rice boiled in water, and a mixture of vegetables with butter, saffron, and spices, known as " curry ; " occasionally eggs or milk ; rarely fish, and sometimes cakes made of banana flour and breadfruit. Morning and evening the meal is the same for rich and poor.

As a vegetable diet is very weakening to the stomach, the Hindoo is forced to make use of an astringent stimulant, to restore the powers of that organ. Areca nuts and betel pepper are therefore the necessary seasoning of every meal. It is betel that gives the lips of natives the yellow tinge so universally seen.

Like the Mahometan, the Hindoo drinks nothing but water, — tepid water for the rich, cold water for the poor. All fermented drinks are strictly forbidden by the Code of the Laws of Manu.

We must, however, state that in the Kshatriya (warrior) caste, it has been found necessary, on account of the rigors of their profession, to do away with the strict letter of these laws. A Kshatriya abstains from such meats as are considered impure, as beef, veal, and pork, but he is willing to eat fish, poultry, and even mutton; various vegetables, both green and dried, however, continue to form the staple of his daily diet.

This respect for animals, derived from the idea of metempsychosis, is carried so far that the followers of a peculiar religious sect, the Jains, to avoid killing even the microbes of the air by absorbing them in breathing, wear by day and by night a very fine linen cloth over their nose and mouth. As also no filter can wholly free water from all animal substances, they drink no water that has not been boiled. Do they understand our modern principles of hygiene?

When a Jain goes out, he is always to carry a special broom, to sweep away any insect which may cross his path. He walks with downcast eyes, lest he should crush one by mistake.[1]

[1] Anthropological Review, May 15, 1888.

We find an infinite number of persons, of high caste and of every rank, who will never kill either a fly or an ant. Such people often catch a flea which is running over their clothes and carefully carry it out of the house.

Respect for animals is thus carried to its extremest limits among the Hindoos. But by a spirit of contradiction familiar to the human mind, the Hindoo, who scruples to kill an insect, is utterly barbarous, not only to the Pariah, but to himself. He hates and persecutes the Pariah, whom he regards as an unclean being, who must be avoided if he would escape contagion and disease. He treats him harshly, in order to keep him in the miserable caste to which he belongs; and he becomes his own executioner, from a conviction that the physical sufferings which he inflicts on himself are agreeable to Brahma.

Brahminism is full of superstitions, some ridiculous, others revolting. We know that during a yearly festival — that of Juggernaut — Brahma's car crushes beneath its heavy wheels countless victims, who fling themselves into the jaws of death in order to insure themselves eternal felicity.

Fanatics assemble in temples to undergo together voluntary torture, which is to hasten their entrance into immaterial life. A widow will ascend the pyre which burns her husband's body; and although since 1830 the English have striven to put an end to this odious custom, instances are still quoted where it has been impossible to prevent it.

The terrible Sepoy insurrection, which set all India on fire, is one of the most fearful instances of Hindoo superstition. The Sepoys are the native regiments formed by the English for military service in the Indian Empire. In 1856 rifles were distributed to these Sepoys. Unfortunately, the cartridges were greased with lard. Now the pig is considered unclean by Hindoos as well as Mahometans. Any soldier who bit these cartridges in two would necessarily touch to his lips particles of the flesh forbidden by his religion.

This was quite enough to incite a general revolt of the native troops. Ninety Sepoys being sentenced to ten years in irons for refusing to touch these cartridges, the three regiments forming the garrison of Meerut rushed to the prison, freed their comrades, and massacred all the Europeans on whom they could lay hands. They then entered Delhi, a city of one hundred and fifty thousand inhabitants, roused the native population, and killed every European with horrible torture.

Other regiments followed the example of those of Meerut; and in this way a fearful insurrection of the entire native population was brought about. The war lasted two years, and was marked on both sides by unheard-of refinements of cruelty. The Sepoys flayed their prisoners alive, and disembowelled women; the English hung or shot the natives. They bound fifty or sixty men to the mouth of the cannon and fired them off every day, on the slightest pretext, — for a word, for a letter handed to an insurgent. Whole regiments of Sepoys were thus put to death, and the war was brought to an end only by the total destruction of the insurgent troops. And all this for a few pounds of lard! We may well be proud of humanity!

Christianity.

We now come to the dogmas of Christianity, viewed from the special point of view of this book, — that is to say, in regard to the consolations offered by this religion to man, to comfort him at the moment of death.

When we leave the gloomy aspects of Buddhism and Brahminism, to enter on the wholesome prospects of Christianity, we feel like the traveller who, coming from the heart of the arid desert, sees the smiling landscapes of a blossoming oasis. A moment since, mournful solitude and an endless stretch of sand, absence of all organic life on a parched ground; now the cool breath of running water, verdure, shrubs, trees, and flowers. There the distressing tenets of Oriental fatalism and nihilism; here the principles, loudly proclaimed, of the immortality of the soul, a sovereign Creator, the resurrection of men, and even the existence of beings superior to humanity, — *angels*, who watch over our destiny. We must therefore bow down before Christianity, which contains principles in accord with those advocated in the present work.

Let us hasten to say, however, that important reserves are to be made after this declaration of approval.

The dogma regarding the penalties and rewards awaiting man beyond the tomb is expressed as follows by the Church : —

" When we cease to live our body remains on earth, where it decays. The soul, set free from all material alloy, appears before God, who, seated on His throne, judges its merits or demerits. The soul of the just ascends into heaven; that of the wicked descends into hell. There they both await the hour of the last judgment, which will mark the end of the world. Then the trumpet shall sound to summon the inmates of paradise and of hell, for the second time, before the bar of God. Each man's body shall reassume the form that it wore on earth ; the soul shall return to its former dwelling, even sex shall be restored ; and God shall pronounce His final sentence as to the fate of each individual, who shall be sent back to hell or admitted to heaven, according to his deserts and the result of his first atonement."

We say nothing of *purgatory*, a middle term between heaven and hell, since it is merely a matter of money. Christian councils invented purgatory only with a view to having the souls of those detained there bought off at a high price ; so that the rich easily evade this temporary prison, but the poor can never escape it. It is useless to dwell on it !

The Church adds that when the trumpet shall sound for the last judgment, the light of sun and moon shall be extinguished and the stars snatched from the firmament.

We have already expressed our views, in the " To-morrow of Death," in regard to the Christian legend of punishments and rewards, borrowed from Pagan antiquity. The judgment of Minos, Hades, and Elysium furnished the idea of the last judgment, ending in paradise or in hell. We will not repeat the criticism of this antique conception which we published in the " To-morrow of Death." Moreover, as words always have great influence over men, theologians have hit upon a word, to avoid an impossible controversy. This is the word *faith*, which means that we must believe in the mysteries of the Christian Church, trample reason under foot, and say, *Credo quia absurdum*. We have faith when we believe in the dogma set forth above.

And yet we must have a mutual understanding. It is admitted that two and two make four, that the whole is greater than a part, that a straight line is the shortest distance between two points; that the radii of a circle are all of equal length, etc. Reason leads man to accept these self-evident truths. But if the same man admits that three are equal to one (Father, Son, and Holy Ghost are but one person, according to the Church); that the particles composing a human body may find their way together again after thousands of years, and reconstitute the original body, etc., — all things contrary to reason, — we can no longer make use of that same reason to recognize any fact as real ; and hence it is not true that two and two make four, that the whole is greater than a part, that the radii of a circle are all of equal length, etc.   Still, human society and nature itself, which is wholly mathematical, rest upon these truths, and if you destroy them there will be nothing left.

The Church adds that at the sound of the last trump the stars shall fall from the sky.   But the stars are suns which light worlds similar to ours. If they drop from heaven, where are they to go, since heaven is merely space ?   Finally, if the stars disappear, nothing will be left of the universe but our earth with its planets and its sun.   And as the orbit described around the sun by the earth is influenced by the other stars in the firmament, that orbit will necessarily be greatly disturbed in the absence of the stars.   The earth and the other planets will follow another course, and everything in our solar system will be absolutely destroyed. Thus the whole universe will crumble, because, forsooth, the merits and demerits of the inhabitants of a mere planet must be judged, — a star so small that it occupies no more space in the infinite whole of creation than a grain of sand on the seashore !

Science likewise refutes the idea of the soul's reinstallation in the old body at the moment of the last judgment.   In fact, when a body corrupts in earth or in air, it is reduced (1) into water, which remains in the ground to become a part of the atmosphere later on, as vapor, or to be absorbed by the roots of plants ; (2) into phosphate and carbonate of lime, which remain permanently in the ground ; (3) into carbonic acid gas, nitrogen, sulphuretted hydrogen, and ammonia, which escape into the air. . All these products are finally reabsorbed by the roots or leaves of plants, which use them for purposes of respiration and nutrition. They then compose the substance of plants.

Thus the same material elements successively pass through a great number of different bodies. Hannibal may have had in his body the substance of Carthaginian soldiers ; the slave Spartacus that of Roman soldiers, and Cicero may have helped to form Caligula. My bony skeleton perhaps contains phosphate of lime from the body of peasants of the Cevennes, killed during Protestant wars by the king's men ; and your graceful body, my fair young lady, may contain the material substance of peasants of La Brie.

It is therefore physically impossible that at the last judgment we can each appear arrayed in our former body ; its material substance having served to compose thousands of other bodies of men or animals in turn.

The Catholic Church should certainly correct this tenet, for the honor of good common-sense. It would be enough to make human souls appear before the tribunal of God stripped of their material body. He who tries to prove too much, proves nothing.

We will not carry these too easy arguments further. We admit that with faith anything may be accepted. You have faith, the *faith of your fathers*. Let us drop the subject!

Still, even admitting, thanks to the aforesaid and fortunate faith, the dogma of the last judgment, we can prove that the consolations offered by the Church to the dying-man are infinitely inferior to those assured to him by our system. In fact, according to the Christian idea, the elect and the damned occupy wholly different places, the latter being relegated to hell, the former lodged in paradise. But if my relative, my friend, my son, my brother, enjoy the glories of paradise while I am lodged in hell, I am parted for an indefinite period from those whom I loved in my lifetime. I must wait in order to renew the broken chain of my earthly affections for the hour of the last judgment, whose coming is most vague ; inasmuch as no one can say when and how the earth will end. Even then we must admit that after our judgment we shall all, good and bad alike, receive the same billet. Is not our system of cosmogony and theology more comforting, reuniting as it does directly after death those beings who have deserved to ascend into planetary space, where they will again find their friends, their families, the objects of their affections ?

Then, again, what do you say to that eternity of

punishment to which the Church condemns the
sinner ?   Is eternity, that frightful gulf, that insoluble problem, from which the human mind shrinks
in horror, an element of which it is allowable to
talk lightly ?   Buddha himself dared not accept
eternity : he said that nothing is eternal, — neither
sin nor merit.

Is not the eternal punishment to which the
Church condemns us for a single ill-spent existence the height of absurdity and odium ?   Is it not
simpler to admit that punishment for the guilty will
consist, as we allow in the " To-morrow of Death,"
of again beginning his existence here below, until
his perfected soul deserves to wing its way to the
celestial realms, where it will join its friends, its
relatives, the beings who are the object of its
affections and sympathies ?

As for the idea of the awful torments to which
the damned are subjected, can anything be more
monstrous ?   To be eternally tormented for a sin,
sometimes involuntary, — can you conceive of anything at once more horrible and more unjust ?
Thomas Aquinas carries things to a yet fiercer
degree of cruelty, when he says that the inmates
of Paradise gaze with delight at the sufferings of
the damned.

"The blessed," says this doctor of the Church,
" without leaving the place that they occupy, shall
yet leave it in a certain sort, by reason of their
gift of intelligence and clear sight, *in order to con-*

sider the torments of the damned, and seeing them, they not only shall not feel any pain, but they shall be full of joy, and shall give thanks unto God for their own happiness, on beholding the unspeakable calamity of the impious."

Thus the inmates of Paradise will be filled with joy when they see the agony of their friends, their relatives, their brothers, those whom they have loved, and whose absence they regret! They will rejoice at their martyrdom, they will applaud their eternal torment!

To understand how so savage a doctrine could be conceived by theologians, we must know that it was promulgated in the Middle Ages, and bears the stamp of the customs of those barbarous times. Men must be struck with terror if they were to be kept beneath the yoke of the creeds of the Church. The doctrine of eternal punishment was consecrated by the fourth Lateran Council, and by the Council of Florence, in the fifteenth century, at which the doctors and representatives of the Greek and Latin churches met together. The fifth Lateran Council and the Council of Trent adopted it later. At the time when these assemblies were held, the customs and habits of Europe were marked by universal cruelty, and the fury of prelates against heresy knew no bounds.

How far such penal atrocities were from the thoughts of the mild and tender Jesus! Could he have issued such fierce decrees, — he who was all

love, all charity, all devotion to his fellow-men;
he who dreamed of universal happiness for all
nations, and who offered the wretched and the
disinherited of the earth prospects of eternal joy
after this life? Every one knows that the Naza-
rene was not the founder of the religion which
bears his name; that he wrote nothing, originated
nothing; that he confined himself to preaching the
love of God, universal charity, sacrifice, devotion;
that he died quietly and without pretension, clearly
understanding in advance that by preaching a religion of gentleness and love he made himself a
mark for the cruel wretches who had already slain
a goodly number of reformers and prophets, his
predecessors in Judæa. The Christian religion
was created, not by Jesus, but by Saint Paul, who,
having been one of Christ's bitterest foes, became
his most fervent apostle, and founded Christianity
as a religion. Saint Paul was not, as tradition
tells us, suddenly enlightened on the road to Damascus; he was simply won over to the teachings
and the person of Jesus by the irresistible power
of the eloquence and placid virtues of that matchless charmer of souls. An unwearied preacher of
the new doctrines, Saint Paul was made a martyr
at Rome, by order of Nero; but he had time to
establish and strengthen the new-born religion.

After him, and down to the Middle Ages,
councils met to settle the dogmas, just as religious
assemblies in the Orient had settled the principles

of Brahminism and Buddhism. The chief dogmas were established at the Christian Councils of the Middle Ages, especially that which relates to eternal punishment, against which public sentiment has always protested, and which has ceased to alarm any one but children.

With the reservations which we have made, we cannot but accept the principles of Christianity, which assert that our immortal soul will rise to celestial regions, there to receive the reward of its merits, with the direct assurance that a sovereign God will watch over its destinies after its earthly end.

If therefore the dying man extend one hand to the priest, who lavishes upon him the consolations of the Church, let him offer the other to the philosopher, who opens to him prospects of a speedy rebirth in an abode where all is happiness and joy, power and peace. Let the Christian apostle and the freethinker unite their prayers in behalf of the dying.

In the table that we gave of the four hundred millions of Christians scattered over the earth, we included Catholics, Protestants, members of the Russo-Greek Church, and various Christian sects; for, in point of fact, in spite of the variety of forms of worship, the tenets are essentially the same in all these different branches of Christianity. Catholics, Protestants, members of the Greek Church, confess to the same principles concerning punishment and reward after death.

In France there is no difference between Catholics and Protestants, except in regard to the Mass, confession, the adoration of the saints, and the celibacy of the clergy. Aside from these questions, their belief is identical.

And it is for such slight religious differences that so much blood has been shed, that such hatred has been heaped up! Under Louis XIV., during the Protestant insurrection, the mountaineers of the Cevennes and the peasants of the plains refused the king but one thing, — they would not go to Mass. They refused to hear the priest talk Latin; they chose to pray in the temples where their fathers had prayed; and it was for this alone that they fought so many bloody fights!

Since Catholics and Protestants agree on the question of future punishment and rewards, since both accept the last judgment, eternal punishment, heaven and hell, there is no distinction to be made between them, from the standpoint of our argument, and of the comparison which we have established between our system and Christianity. What has been said of Christianity in the foregoing argument applies equally to Catholics, Protestants, and the Greek Church.

We must, however, hasten to make an important observation in regard to Protestantism. All Protestants do not involuntarily revert toward Catholicism, as might be inferred from the preceding lines. French, English, and American Protestants may be divided into two sects, — *Orthodox*, or *Meth-odists*, who are but latent adherents of Catholicism ; and *liberal Protestants*, who break distinctly with the doctrines of the majority of the members of the reformed religion.

Liberal Protestantism is a form of Christianity which rejects the yoke of all revelation, of all or-thodoxy, which denies the supernatural, miracles, the divinity of Jesus Christ, and which, by its pub-lications and preaching, has opened the way for the modern school of religious criticism, which produced Strauss in Germany and the illustrious Renan in France.

The liberal Christian is, in the religious order, the direct disciple of Jesus Christ, as in the philo-sophic order the Cartesian is the disciple of Descartes, and the Kantist the disciple of Kant. Liberal Christianity may be summed up, philosophi-cally speaking, in deism or pantheism, under the shield of the morality and worship of Christ.

M. Fontanès, formerly a Protestant preacher at Montpellier and Paris, now preaching at Havre, published, in 1867, "A Study of Lessing," in which he shows that this German writer was one of the fathers of liberal Christianity. To oppose freedom of discussion to the principles of traditional ortho-doxy ; to combat the reasoning of the State, or rather of the Church, in the name of the personal character of every conviction, — such was the task undertaken by Lessing. "Lessing was very justly

called," says Fontanès, " the Luther of the nineteenth century. He deserves this name for his
valor and his love of truth. He it is who freed
reform from the yoke of the letter, and brought it
back into the path of freedom."

Fontanès hails with admiration this return to
the true principles of Protestantism, this emanci-
pation of the Protestant conscience : " No more
authoritative churches," he exclaims, " no more
codes or barriers which enslave thought, no more
imposed faith ; autonomy of the conscience, a sense
of life, free movement of the spirit ! It is the peculiar feature of Protestantism that it combines with
the Christian religion all the independence of science. The Protestant is always at the breach ; he
is always examining and revising his opinions, his
beliefs. Like the saint, he never feels that he has
attained his object. We do not register ourselves
as Protestants to bind ourselves later to the letter
of a doctrine, and again become Catholics for the
rest of our life."

These words of Fontanès sum up the ideas
which the eminent Parisian preacher, Athanase
Coquerel, and his son Athanase unfolded in the
pulpit of the Oratory ; those which they both upheld in the review called " The Disciple of Jesus
Christ : a Liberal Protestant Review ;" those which
Martin Paschoud maintained after them ; those
which I shared with rapture, so soon as I gained
the precious friendship of the two Coquerels, after

attending their lectures and sermons, — ideas which I had, moreover, dimly entertained in my youth, from hearing the venerable preacher Michel, who was my religious instructor; and my constant friend, Rev. Charles Grawitz, who was an honor to the Protestant Evangelical pulpit of Montpellier, and the noblest representative of Christian charity.

Liberal Protestantism, it is needless to say, rejects the doctrine of the last judgment.. I have heard Athanase Coquerel, the son, mock in the pulpit, with witty good-nature, at the literal resurrection of human bodies ; and Charles Grawitz took the same question as the subject of one of his best sermons, which may be found in the collection of his works, published at Montpellier, by Boehm.

Mahometanism.

The vast region known as Arabia, and situated on the continent of Asia, is divided into Arabia Petræa, Arabia Deserta, and Arabia Felix, or Yemen.   Mecca and Medina are in Arabia Petræa, or Hedjaz.

It was here, early in the seventh century of our era, that that astounding revolution was first kindled, which soon fired half Asia and the North of Africa, as well as a great part of Southern Europe.

A man who in his childhood led camels, and who in order to live found it necessary to enter a commercial house as overseer or head servant, was the instigator of this memorable revolution.   But he possessed those intellectual and moral qualities which constitute great superiority over other men, and he had true genius.   This man was Mahomet.

Arabia is mentioned in the oldest histories. The primitive races inhabiting those countries were full of courage and intelligence, always animated by the sacred fire of a liberty compatible with human dignity and the maintenance of social laws. In their inaccessible mountains they never yielded to a foreign yoke.   A close connection is recognized between the Arab tongue and that of the ancient Chaldeans, Syrians, Egyptians, Hebrews, and Abyssinians.   This was one of the causes which contributed most to the spread of Islamism throughout Africa and Asia.

To understand the revolution which Mahomet brought about in Africa, Asia, and Europe, — a revolution which was at once religious, political, and literary, — we must know the chief events in the life of this extraordinary man.

His real name was Mohammed.   Born at Mecca, Aug. 29, 570 A. D., he was of very humble origin; although Arab authors, who desired to endow him with a lofty genealogy, make him descend from Abraham through Ishmael, that son of Hagar whom the jealousy of Sarah, according to the Bible, drove into exile with his mother out of the land of Canaan, whence they withdrew to Mecca. It is certain, in spite of this legend, that Mohammed was merely the youngest son of a poor family of Arabs from Mecca. Early left an orphan, he was brought up by the care of his grandfather, afterward by his uncle Abu-Talib, and in his childhood he was employed in leading or keeping camels.

The inhabitants of Mecca were, for the most part, merchants; and Abu-Taleb conducted caravans from Mecca to Syria to carry on the trade between those two countries. Mohammed was thirteen when he was taken by his uncle, with one of his caravans, to the city of Borsa, in Syria.

On reaching Borsa, the caravan was received and generously lodged by a monk, named Baherah, of Arab origin. This monk, recognizing all the young Mohammed's fine qualities, did not hesitate to foretell a brilliant future for him. It is certain that the young Arab was even then remarkable for his gravity and honesty, his regular life, and the elegance and propriety of his speech.

At the age of twenty he was hired as head servant or overseer, by a rich widow of Mecca, Kadijah, who carried on a large business with Syria. He made two journeys by caravan to Syria in Kadijah's interests. She was so pleased with the services of her assistant that she married him. He was then twenty-five, the widow forty; but his beauty was so striking, and the widow's affection was so strong, that differences of age and social position went for nothing. The marriage contract ran as follows: "Forasmuch as Kadijah loves Mohammed and Mohammed loves Kadijah . . ."

He continued to manage her affairs, and carried on the business of merchant and trader at Mecca for many years. Nothing then proclaimed in him the future reformer.

It was only at the age of forty that he began to be aware of his mission ; for several years he brooded over and tested his scheme in every detail. He learned his part ; he feigned to be inspired, and went to the cave of Hirâ, in the outskirts of Mecca, to dream of his approaching apostleship.

At this time Arabia had no other religion than idolatry ; but there were many Jews, and Christians had carried the conquests of the gospel into that country. The constant quarrels of idolaters, combined with those of arch heretics, Jews, and Christians, troubled the mind of the Arabs, who wavered, undecided, between the three forms of worship. Moreover, they were divided into incoherent tribes, with no connecting link of any sort, and with no common government. The Koreish formed a political and judicial body, which gave the people laws and regulations ; but they did not succeed in imposing them upon the many tribes scattered throughout Arabia. Mohammed conceived the vast scheme of endowing his country with a single religion, and forming by its aid a political government applicable to the whole Arab people.

He derived the principles of the religion which he planned to introduce from Christianity and Judaism.

He did not hesitate to present himself as a prophet sent by God to reform Judaism, turned aside, he declared, since the time of Moses, from its natural course, and led astray by the false claim of Jesus to divinity. As for him, he was, undoubtedly, a mere man; but being sent by God, he could reveal, in His name, a religion based on new and unassailable truths.

He found his first proselytes in his own family. The long incubations of his thought, the look of inspiration assumed by his face, under the influence of this mental struggle, struck his relatives; and he began to exert the magic charm of his genius over them. He often visited the grotto of Hirâ, to converse, as he said, with angels, and he returned in a most exalted condition. One night he had a vision; the angel Gabriel appeared to him, and said, offering him a scroll, "Read!"

"I do not know how to read," answered Mohammed.

"Read," repeated the angel Gabriel, "in the name of the Most High, who created man out of a little clotted blood. Mohammed," added the angel, "you are the apostle of God!"

By this communication from above, Mohammed felt himself confirmed in his mission.

Three years, however, elapsed, before he began his apostleship. For some time he was content to school his relatives and friends. His wife Kadijah, his slaves, his nephew Ali, and his father-in-law

Abu-Bekr, who was afterward the first caliph of the Mussulmans, were the first converts to his faith.

He then began to preach publicly in Mecca, with all the fire of his natural eloquence ; but his first discourses were ill received. The Koreish, who had the care of the temple at Mecca, looked with alarm upon a man who might some day dispossess them of their charge. They undertook an open war against the · reformer, which forced him and his followers to leave Mecca.

This was in 615, five years after the beginning of his apostleship.

The death of Abu-Talib, and shortly after, that of his wife, Kadijah, were a great grief to the prophet ; in them he lost a strong moral support. His whole family were already banished from the city. He withdrew to Taïf ; but even there he was pursued by insults and mockery, and attacked with showers of stones.

Still, he ventured to return to Mecca. Having converted some of the Koreish to his cause, he went back to the city, where he was tolerably well received. He then used more moderation and tact in his addresses. His sermons became less frequent, but more direct. He respected idols, and spoke rather of God than of his own mission.

He thus gained many proselytes. Tired of the disputes of Christian Arabs and of Christian controversies, many Arab tribes came out in his favor.

During the same year he married six wives. He

afterward raised the number to fifteen, although his religion forbade Arabs to marry more than four ; but we all know that the prophet had an unbounded love of women.

If the allies of the new religion became more and more numerous, its enemies increased in the same proportion. The situation of Mohammed and his followers finally became perilous. A part of them sought refuge at Medina. Mohammed refused to follow them ; but he came near falling a victim to his courage. The Koreish decided on his death, and men were ordered to kill him the next night at his own house. Warned in time, he escaped the sword of the hired assassins, and withdrew to a cave in Mount Tour, three miles from Mecca. The assassins pursued him and reached the cavern ; but seeing a nest of doves on the wall of the cave and spider-webs hung across the entrance, they concluded that no one had entered, and went away.

Mohammed had crawled into the cave on his hands and knees.

Three days later, his followers brought him a camel and a guide, and he gained the territory of Medina, where his numerous allies in that city gave him an enthusiastic reception.

This day, which answers to the 26th of June, 622 A. D., became the first of the Mussulman era. The date of Mahomet's flight (Hegira) was, ten years afterward, established, by Caliph Omar, as the first day of the Mussulman year.

When Mohammed entered Medina, every one desired to lodge him. "Let my camel advance," said Mohammed ; " God will guide him." The camel stopped of his own accord ; he knelt, and Mohammed stepped down. On the spot where he stopped, the first Mohammedan mosque was afterward built, and still exists.

The city, which was then called Jathrippa, took the name of Medina, — that is to say, the City above all cities. Medina and Mecca are sacred cities to all Mussulmans.

Soon the new religion had its especial rites. A month of fasting was ordained ; a *tax for the benefit of the poor* was levied ; hours for prayer and for absolution were fixed.

Then began the era of conversions by the force of arms ; and the prophet's mission assumed the warlike character which it had not hitherto worn, but which was, from this time forth, the great means of spreading Islamism.

At Medina, Mahomet formed a small army, which grew continually, and at last constituted a considerable military force.

During the second year of the Hegira, Mahomet, with his little troop, attacked a caravan of Koreish, nine hundred strong, who threatened Medina, and utterly defeated them.

Having become a military leader at the same time that he became a prophet, and emboldened by his first successes, he travelled through the countries of the various Arab tribes, sometimes using persuasion and sometimes the sword.

Desiring to win the respect of his countrymen by the fame of his name abroad, he sent messengers to the King of Persia, the King of Abyssinia, and the Emperor of the Romans, Heraclius, to inform them of his accession and mission. He went so far as to propose that they should embrace the new religion.

The King of Persia tore the letter to tatters in a rage; but the others replied with congratulations and gifts.

These relations with great empires showed the reformer's power; and Arabia recognized him, quite generally, as her leader. He resolved to strike a decisive blow at Mecca. In vain did the Koreish oppose his advance. He scattered them, and entered Mecca, almost without dealing a wound (630 A. D.). His first act was to shatter all idols.

Some days after, anxious to give the sacred city new sanctity in his laws, he made a solemn entry, in the midst of a most imposing train. His soldiers covered the country for miles, and he marched in triumph at their head. He and his escort walked seven times around the temple of the Caaba, taking the first three rounds at a quick pace, and the others at an easy gait. Since then Mussulmans perform their devotions in similar fashion at the temple of the Caaba at Medina. He ordered the *muezzin* to call the faithful to prayer, from the top of the tower of the mosque, as is still done, according to the Mussulman rite.

The surrender of the Koreish, reputed the most learned of the Arabs, and the governors of Arabia in legal and religious matters, induced the adhesion of almost the entire country. Mahomet then sent soldier-apostles to the different tribes, to regulate the new form of worship and secure the prerogatives of his political power.

In 630 he left Mecca, with ten thousand soldiers, to meet two mighty tribes who were marching against the city. He defeated them, and then besieged them in Taïf, where the vanquished had fled. He was, however, obliged to withdraw after a useless siege of twenty days.

The following year, the Christians of Nerdjran and all their clergy were compelled to pay a tax or embrace Islamism.

In order to consecrate Mecca as the capital and centre of the Mussulman world, and as it were to complete his mission in the eyes of men, Mahomet proclaimed a great pilgrimage, which took place in 632. He slew with his own hand sixty-three camels, and set free sixty-three slaves. This was the *pilgrimage of farewell* (Hajj). The prophet felt that his end was at hand.

It is claimed that poison shortened his life.

He succeeded in winning recognition from the tribes which had thus far kept their independence.

The most powerful of all was composed of Jews settled at Kaïbar, the name of a fortress built on a high mountain, some six days' journey from Medina. The number of Jews who occupied it was swelled by those of their brothers driven by Mahomet from the neighborhood of Medina. They were headed by a chief named Machab, and dignified with the title of king. At the news of the danger which threatened them, they hastily made all their preparations, and leaving the open country, shut themselves up in the fortress. But Mahomet appeared sooner than they expected, at the head of fourteen hundred foot-soldiers and two hundred cavalry. He began by attacking and destroying a certain number of castles surrounding the fortress, and strengthening its defence. The inhabitants of these castles became his prisoners, and he began a siege of the place by means of battering-rams and such instruments of war as were then in use.

Machab appeared, yataghan in hand, at the head of his troops. He was a sort of Hercules, reputed to be invincible. Ali, Mahomet's nephew, answered his challenge. Very skilful in the management of arms, he contrived to lay the colossus low with his sword. The fortress was quickly captured and occupied; the booty was divided among the soldiers.

Mahomet could only have congratulated himself on this expedition, had it not proved the speedy cause of his death. In one of the castles which he had besieged, and which surrounded the fortress, was a woman, named Zainab, sister of the warlike Machab, who was killed by Ali during the siege of the fortress, as has been related. Zainab burned with desire to avenge her brother's death. Becoming the slave of Mahomet, who had observed her beauty, she conceived the idea of putting poison in a shoulder of mutton which she served up to him. At the first mouthful that he swallowed Mahomet quickly spat it out, exclaiming, "This mutton warns me that it is poisoned!" A guest who shared his meal died almost immediately.

Mahomet refused to take any revenge for this cowardly attempt at murder. A new Holofernes, he was generous enough to pardon this second Judith; but the poison had entered his entrails, and the effects of it shortened his days.

On June 8, 632 A. D., he once more appeared at the mosque; but this expedition robbed him of his last remnant of strength. He went home, and never spoke again, except a few broken words. His head rested on the knees of one of his wives, his dear Ayesha. She suddenly felt his head grow heavier; she looked more closely at him, — he was dead. His health had failed since the attempt to poison him, and his death was attributed to the consequences of that occurrence.

The news of his death filled Medina with grief and distress. The people could not believe that the prophet was dead; and on the other hand, his

mission had lasted too short a time to allow the
new religion to be universally substituted for the
old one. Some loudly inveighed against impos-
ture; others raised doubts of the talents of his
successors; and Mahomet, with his many wives,
left no son. Urged to come to some decision,
the leaders of the army declared in favor of Abu-
Bekr, in spite of his advanced age.

Abu-Bekr collected the scattered pages of Mahomet's writings, and made the collection known
under the name of Koran, which is the gospel, we
may say, the God, of the Mussulman. When the
different parts of the Koran were put together,
they were read in the presence of all the leaders of
the army, and its authenticity was thus established.

Then, and not till then, did they proceed with
Mahomet's funeral. His body was washed, perfumed, covered with spices, wrapped in three
shrouds, and after many prayers buried on the very
spot where the prophet had expired.

We know that Mussulman law forbids the
reproduction of human features. No portrait of
Mahomet therefore exists. And yet by putting
together various descriptions, left by many authors,
of the features and person of the founder of Islamism, Barthélemy Saint-Hilaire, in his "Life of
Mahomet," published in 1865, succeeded in drawing
the following portrait: —

"Rather below the middle height, he was strongly
built. His chest and shoulders were broad; his hands

and feet remarkably strong, as was his whole frame; all his joints were very small; his limbs were fleshy without being unwieldy; his neck was long, white, very graceful; his head was very large; his forehead well developed and always serene; his nose was large and slightly aquiline, somewhat turned up at the tip; his mouth was wide, with very sound white teeth set far apart; his eyebrows were slender and separated by a vein which swelled in moments of emotion; his brilliant black eyes were shaded by long lashes; his hair, thick and jet black, fell in curls behind his ears and over his shoulders; his beard and mustache were abundant. As is often the case with very robust men, he carried himself badly and stooped; his walk, though light and quick, seemed rather heavy, and he always moved as if descending a mountain. For the rest, his whole countenance, full of power, breathed gentleness and amiability, although he seldom looked people in the face while he talked with them. His general physiognomy was very restful and calm; his complexion neither pale nor ruddy; his skin very smooth, although tanned. In a word, his whole person, without being precisely beautiful, had much charm, and every one felt drawn towards him."

After Mahomet's death, his successors, who took the name of Caliphs, continued to move from conquest to conquest. Holding the Koran in one hand and the sword in the other, they invaded, in turn, Persia, Syria, Egypt, and finally Spain. In 713 they were in full possession of the last-named country. They even entered Gaul, and advanced as far as the plains of old Poitou.

18

It would be a mistake to regard the Arabs of Mahomet's time as a wholly barbarous people. It would also be a mistake to think that their conduct towards the people upon whom they desired to impose the Koran was that of pitiless conquerors. Abu-Bekr, chosen in 632 by a majority of votes to succeed Mahomet, spoke as follows to the tribes assembled under the sacred banner : —

" Go forth, valiant warriors, go forth, and know that in fighting for religion you obey God. Take care to do nothing but what is just and equitable ; those who do otherwise shall not prosper. When you meet your enemies, bear yourself like brave men. If you are victorious, kill no women, children, or old men ; destroy no palm-trees, burn no grain, cut down no trees, do no harm to cattle, save to such animals as you are forced to kill for your food. In short, be exact in keeping faithfully the promise you have given."

The Romans laid waste the countries which they invaded. They crushed conquered nations beneath the burden of exorbitant tribute money. They destroyed the monuments of science and art almost everywhere. The Arabs behaved very differently. They were not swayed, as were the latter, by burning greed. If they strove to subjugate nations, it was not so much to enrich themselves with the spoil as to compel them to accept the Koran. In moments of exaltation they may have burned a few theological works ; but nothing, in their conduct or their customs, betrays a systematic plan of destruction. It is certain, on the contrary, that the Romans in Italy, at Carthage, and elsewhere burned a quantity of volumes of science, literature, and history, and that later, Christians, in their turn, imitating the example of the Romans, set fire to several great and rich libraries in the East during the Crusades. It is a well-established fact that the famous library at Alexandria was not, as has so often been declared, burned by Arab conquerors, after the taking of Alexandria by Omar. In fact, Albufaragus the historian, who makes the first mention of this event, lived six centuries after the taking of Alexandria. This writer is, moreover, refuted by others of less doubtful authority.

It may be added that innumerable quantities of books serving to form great Arab libraries and to instruct Europe were taken from the library at Alexandria; which goes to prove that it was not destroyed.

At the time when Arab revolution, originating in the mountains of Arabia Petræa, began to spread to Asia, Africa, and the islands of the Mediterranean, Christian civilization was rapidly declining. In Greece and Italy, scientific studies were abandoned. Arts requiring imagination and feeling gradually lapsed into barbarism. True taste had disappeared. It was almost the same in Egypt. To be sure, the famous school of Alexandria, which had long shone with vivid lustre, still produced learned men, arithmeticians, grammarians, and commentators ; but the remnant of intellectual power was wasted, to no purpose, in dissertations and controversies on subtle or foolish distinctions, on metaphysical questions, which nobody understood. The creative genius that invents, develops, and perfects, was utterly dead at Alexandria, as elsewhere.

In the physical order, at certain seasons of the year, storms — that is to say, great developments of atmospheric electricity — have the effect of reviving languid Nature, by re-establishing on the earth's surface the conditions of equilibrium essential to the functions of life. So too, in the social order, revolutions, whose immediate consequences are sometimes so sad, have the effect of reviving a half-dead civilization, or arousing a new one when the old one is worn out.

The Arabs, becoming powerful, carefully collected all monuments of science and art, precious fragments of which still existed in Egypt and Greece. They formed libraries, museums, and cabinets of natural history. They established schools, academies, and observatories. They devoted themselves to the study of astronomy, natural history, mathematics, and particularly medicine, which they found written out by Hippocrates and Galen. The best Greek scientific works were translated, commented on, and sifted, among the Arabs, by minds of the first order.

The caliphs encouraged trade, understanding its

advantages. They had ships and a navy. Soon the Arabs were in relations, by land and sea, with all civilized nations. They made their way into India, China, and Japan, and gathered precious knowledge, of which the Greeks were completely ignorant.

In Persia and Syria the Arabs found the works of Aristotle, Theophrastus, Galen, Dioscorides, etc., and translated them into their own language.

It was thus that from India to Spain, from the shores of the Tigris to those of the Guadalquivir, scientific books spread rapidly among people who already had a literature, a religious philosophy, and who were not destitute of imagination.

The intellectual level was accordingly raised wherever the Arabs succeeded in establishing themselves.

This great civilizing movement began in the eighth century. Just about the time when Charlemagne founded in France the schools called *Carlovingian*, Al-Mansur founded a great university at Bagdad.

Bagdad, a city of ancient Chaldea, built on the eastern shore of the Tigris in one of the finest situations in the world, in a few years became a flourishing city. It owed to the caliphs its splendor, its love of study, and the elegance of its customs. Oriental poets of the period speak of it under the name of "the city of peace."

We must read in the history of the caliphs descriptions of the public buildings of Bagdad, in order to get any idea of its riches, and of the masterpieces of every sort which that wonderful city contained.

Thanks to the caliphs Al-Mansor, Haroun-Al-Raschid, Al-Mamoun, and several others, who loved letters or learning, and themselves cultivated them with renown, the Arab school of Bagdad grew rapidly, and won great fame. It attained its highest degree of splendor in the ninth century after Christ.

Al-Mamoun directed the construction of an astronomical observatory at Bagdad. By his order the length of an arc of the meridian was measured on the plains of Sennaar, in order to determine the true dimensions of the earth.

Early in the eleventh century the Bagdad school gradually lost its importance, and at last died out entirely.

Political revolutions incessantly harassed Asia. As early as 997, Mahmoud, the Ghiznevide, seceded from the Sultan, and founded a new empire. This secession became the signal for the division of the Arab empire into little independent sultanies, like those of Kerman, Aleppo, and Damascus, which, unfit for self-defence, soon became tributaries of Persia.

In the midst of these political dissensions, the torch of learning did not go out. It merely changed place; it deserted Asia. Henceforth it burned in Africa, and later in Spain.

Then the Cairo school was formed. Ben-Al-Mahdi, who lived at Cairo, tells us that the library of that city contained six thousand manuscript works on astronomy and mathematics. Elon-Iounis, who died in 1007, was the founder of this school. The most illustrious of his successors was Hassem-Ben-Hackem, an astronomer who wrote more than eighty books, made a vast quantity of astronomical observations, and wrote notes on Ptolemy's "Almagest."

We have no exact information on the subject of the works of the Arab scientists of the Egyptian and West African schools.

Spain, conquered by the Arabs, also speedily became the centre of a brilliant civilization. It was soon filled with splendid public buildings. Granada, Cordova, and Toledo were enriched by sumptuous palaces, glittering with gold and marble. In all these structures it was elegance and taste, rather than a display of wealth, that called forth universal admiration.

The perpetual contrast between extreme opulence and abject want, which saddens us in modern European cities, was not to be found in Arab cities. Neither the kindly customs of the Orient or the teachings of the Koran, at a time when the law of the prophet was scrupulously obeyed, would have sanctioned this. Temperance and toil readily placed ease and comfort within the reach of all among the lower classes.

In every great city occupied or ruled by Arabs, there were schools to which pupils flocked. The Cordova school in Spain had a reputation which soon spread, not only throughout Europe, but also through a great part of Asia. People sent there, from all sides, for the most skilful professors, scientists, artists, and doctors. People went there from Egypt, Persia, even from Bagdad, although Bagdad had gained great fame for her cultivation of the arts and sciences. And one proof that Arab civilization would have spread readily throughout Western Europe had not the Arabs been driven out of Spain by Christians far less civilized than they, is the fact that illustrious Catholics, some- times even princes, went to Cordova to consult learned men, and to be treated by Arab doctors.

In the tenth century Spain was certainly the coun- try which in all respects ranked first in Europe.

Cordova then contained a population of three hun- dred thousand souls. Her schools were a source of wealth. Her palaces, her mosques, her public buildings, all proclaimed her a metropolis of science and art. Her great mosque, built in 770 under the government of Abder-Rahman, was an immense structure supported by a forest of marble, granite, and porphyry columns. It had nineteen naves, leading to an equal number of bronze doors. The interior of the building was lighted by forty-seven hundred lamps. It was something marvellous and fairy-like.

Civilization was at its height in the Orient, when the Arab States were unexpectedly disturbed by the Crusades, and by the reaction which followed in all countries invaded by Christian warriors. And yet Syria, Persia, Spain, and even Egypt continued long after to cultivate science and art. In reading the works of Casiri, D'Herbelot, Leo Africanus, and various others, we are truly surprised that such huge quantities of literary and scientific works could have been amassed in that country, where printing did not exist. When we look over the catalogue still preserved in the Escurial library, we are amazed at the vast number of Arab writers who sprang up in Spain alone, and at the quantity of works due to their pen.

Thus, the revolution inaugurated in Arabia by Mahomet was not merely religious and military; it was, at the same time, literary and civilizing.

It now remains for us to give a brief statement of the principles of the Mussulman religion, or "Islamism," — the name given it by its followers, and which signifies "confidence in, absolute reliance on, the will of God."

Islamism is based on the maxims contained in the Koran, which are regarded as so many revelations from God. As we have stated, the first caliph, Abu-Bekr, collected them at the time of the prophet's death, without troubling himself to introduce any chronological order, or any methodical arrangement of subjects. Mahomet did not preach any religious doctrine having a determinate body; he confined himself to uttering, hap-hazard, and as circumstances required, religious dogmas, moral rules, or principles of equity, which he offered as so many divine revelations.

The Koran therefore is only a collection of sentences, without any connection, of the most heterogeneous description. Accordingly every Mussulman can quote, to suit the occasion, such or such a verse from the Koran to justify his ideas, and to give a religious air to the most diverse actions. This, too, is the reason why schisms are so frequent in this religion, truly without foundation.

Mahomet having appointed no form of worship and no order of clergy, the Mussulman religion has neither clergy nor ceremonial. The *Ulemas*, or *Imaums*, are jurists and professors; and their consultations (*fetwahs*) are not theological decisions, but mere legal memoranda. People often speak of a Turkish or Arab *mufti* as if he were a bishop or a pope; but the mufti is a wholly political and wholly secular character.

As for the form of worship which is usually supposed to be practised in the mosques, it may be reduced to prayers, which every man repeats in his own home at a fixed hour, and which merely consists in the repetition of certain verses of the Koran.

The repetition of verses from the Koran, therefore, is the only liturgy of the Mohammedans. Man prays through the medium of the Koran, and not from the emotions of his own heart.

Thus the idea of religious worship and a priesthood, dear to Christians, is completely unknown to Islamism. Mussulmans have neither priest nor altar, but only a book. God did not become incarnate in a prophet, as Christians claim for Jesus ; and the prophet, on leaving this world, did not leave his spirit to his disciples, who were to establish a church, a clergy, ceremonials, and rights. God merely revealed his thoughts to a man-prophet, and the man-prophet collected them ; then he died, and God entered upon His rest without revealing Himself further to mankind. Hence it follows that the Mussulman's only guide, whether religious or moral, is a single book, which it is his duty to study, criticise, and search, without looking for other light ; for God has spoken once, in the Koran, and He will not do so again.

The moral code of the Koran is the best side of Mahometanism, for it abounds in exhortations of the most pressing nature in regard to the practice of good works. Precepts of the purest morality illumine the pages of Mahomet's book.

From the religious point of view, Mahomet proclaimed himself as the reformer of the religion revealed by God to His prophet Abraham, but afterward disfigured by Christian and Jewish priests. He acknowledged all the characters in the Bible as prophets sent by God ; but he blamed

Christians for making a god of Jesus Christ. The
Koran denies the divinity of Christ and his death
upon the cross : [1] " The infidels," says the Koran,
" did not crucify the Messiah ; they put in his place
a man who strongly resembled him." [2]   Christ is
an apostle similar to those who came before him.[3]

The Koran asserts, in exact terms, the unity of
God and the immortality of the soul.

Mahomet was not the enemy of Jews or Christians, whom he considered as the brethren of the
Arabs.   All his anger was directed against idolaters.   He required them, on penalty of death, to
renounce their idols and worship one only God.
" Whoever," says the Koran, " utters blasphemy
against God, against His attributes, against His
holy prophet, against this celestial book ; whoever
denies the divine mission of Moses or of Jesus Christ,
shall be put to death without mercy or delay."

This passage is not tolerant, but it is only aimed
against idolaters.

Mahomet's religious doctrine is very simple.
Belief in one God, omnipotent, omniscient, full of
mercy and loving kindness, — this is his chief
dogma.   He believes, like the Christians, in the
resurrection of the body and the last judgment.
When the trumpet shall sound for the last judgment, the dead shall awake in their graves and

---

[1] Chap. lv. book i.
[2] Chap. iv. verse 166.
[3] Chap. v. verse 78 ; chap. vi. verse 100.

gather in one spot. There the eternal book of fate, wherein are written the deeds of every man, will be opened, and sentence will be pronounced. The good will be led to paradise, and the bad to hell.

Paradise and hell, with the Mussulmans, conform to the Christian idea of them : hell is a place of eternal torment; paradise a region of unspeakable delights. We know that the joys of Mahomet's paradise are all sensual. The Mussulman Eden is the most marvellous region of which Oriental imagination could conceive. It is a magnificent garden, watered by abundant streams and by rivers of milk. The air is loaded with sweet odors. The elect, gifted with immortality, are clad in silks and velvets, with bracelets of gold. Reclining on soft carpets, they are sheltered by enchanting shades formed by trees loaded with delicious fruits. Lovely children, who remain forever young, pour choice liquors to quench their thirst. Beyond fairy groves, enchanting landscapes are unfolded to their view. The men possess spotless virgins and houris of graceful shape. Their life passes in intoxicating feasts.

Hell, on the contrary, is the home of never-dying flames. In the lowest depths of this gloomy abode grows the tree *Zakkum*, whose fruits look like the heads of demons, and are intended to feed the damned, whose drink is boiling water.

God, however, may put an end to the torments of the damned. Less savage than Christian councils, the Koran foresees a limit to the sufferings of the inmates of the infernal regions.

Paradise is won by good works, humility, charity, fasting, prayer, chastity, patience, and pilgrimage to Mecca.

To explain the difficulty which the elect find in entering the kingdom of heaven, Mahometans represent, either literally or figuratively, the road that leads to paradise, as an iron bridge no wider than the blade of a sword. Those who by their good works deserve to cross this difficult viaduct, enter the abode of the blest; the others fall into the jaws of hell.

All this is clearly borrowed from the Christian legend of the last judgment, with its doctrine concerning punishment and reward. Having fully expressed our views on this head while writing of Christianity, we will not return to it. We think that we have shown the superiority of our theory of the rebirth and reincarnation of souls in the ethereal medium over Christian legend. Our criticism of the Christian last judgment, paradise, and hell will apply to Mussulman tenets, which are a mere copy of them.

Judaism.

In regard to Judaism, we can only repeat what we have just said of Mahometanism. Jews profess the same dogma concerning future punishment and reward, as Christians and Mahometans, — that is to say, they accept paradise and hell, preceded by God's judgment, a judgment itself delayed until the end of the world. As this is the only question in Judaism that interests us, we will not repeat, for that religion, the criticisms which we have already made of the legend of the last judgment, in speaking of Christianity, or the comparison which we established between that system and ours. The point has been treated at ample length. Only, as the Jewish question just now holds a certain place in public thought by reason of the wholesale exile of the Jews from Russia, and the persecutions to which they are subjected in Germany, our readers may be glad of a few particulars as to this cosmopolitan nation, and the importance which they attach to religious practices.

The following statistics are taken from the "Year-Book of Israelite Archives" for 1892.

The total number of Israelites in France is about one hundred and twenty-six thousand, divided as follows, in round numbers : —

Paris	50,000
Nancy	4,500
Bordeaux	3,000
Lyons	2,200
Marseilles	5,300
Bayonne	2,500
Vesoul	3,950
Lille	2,800
Besançon	2,600
Algiers	15,000
Constantine	9,000
Oran (10,000 foreigners)	25,000
Total	125,850

They are officially divided into twelve districts, managed by as many consistories, under the jurisdiction of a central consistory.

Israelites in Paris are divided between two forms of worship, — the German and the Portuguese. The former retain in their worship the pronunciation of Hebrew in use in Poland and Germany; the latter keep the pronunciation of Hebrew in accord with ancient customs in the South and East. There are also certain slight differences in their rituals.

As to the number of Israelites in the entire world, statisticians disagree. The "Israelite Year-Book" gives the following statistics, based on reliable data: —

Europe contains 5,400,000 Jews, distributed among the various countries in the following proportions: Germany, 562,000 (Alsace-Lorraine, 39,000); Austrian Hungary, 1,644,000 (Galicia, 688,000); Hungary, 638,000; Italy, 40,000; Netherlands, 82,000; Roumania, 265,000; Russia, 2,552,000 (Russian Poland, 768,000); Turkey, 105,000; other countries, 35,000 (Belgium, 3,000; Switzerland, 7,000; Bulgaria, 10,000; Denmark, 4,900; Spain, 1,900; Gibraltar, 1,500; Greece, 3,000; Servia, 3,500; Sweden, 3,000).

Asia contains 300,000 Jews. It is computed that there are 195,000 in Turkey in Asia (Palestine, 25,000); 4,700 in Asian Russia; 18,000 in Persia; 14,000 in Central Asia; 19,000 in India; and 1,000 in China.

Africa has 350,000 Jews (8,000 in Egypt; 55,000 in Tunis; 60,000 in Morocco; 6,000 in Tripoli; 200,000 in Abyssinia).

America contains 250,000, of whom 230,000 live in the United States.

Oceanica has but 12,000.

The sum total of the Israelite population throughout the entire world, accordingly, runs up to 6,300,000.

In Paris the Jews have four great temples, or synagogues : the temple in the Rue Nôtre Dame de Nazareth, which is the oldest in Paris, for it dates back to 1822, — it belongs exclusively to the Jewish community ; the temple in the Rue de la Victoire, opened in 1874, erected at the mutual expense of the city of Paris and the Jewish community, — it has now become the chief synagogue ; the temple in the Rue des Tournelles, built under the same conditions, two years later.

These three belong to the German ritual. The fourth is of the Portuguese ritual ; it was built without official participation, and was opened in 1877.

The Jews have also smaller oratories in various parts of Paris, notably in the Avenue de la Motte-Piquet and the Rue Legendre at Batignolles, and in their different charitable institutions and schools.

These temples and oratories are served by rabbis and public readers (chasan). There are about ten rabbis in Paris; among them Mr. Zadoc Kahn, lately elected, and the chief rabbi of Paris.

19

We know that the rabbi does not regard himself as having any sacerdotal character; the Jewish priesthood and sacrificial rites dying out at the fall of the temple of Jerusalem. The rabbi is the teacher of the law, the spiritual director, the minister of instruction and advice, rather than the special and necessary celebrant of worship; worship can be celebrated without his aid.

As for the reader, he is not a person invested with ecclesiastical character; he is a master of ceremonies, who looks after the details, directs the singing and the choir. There are two or three for each temple.

Nor have those persons usually called into families to perform the religious act of circumcision — the *mohelim* — any religious character. There are five of these in Paris.

Like the Mussulman, the Israelite is deeply attached to his religion, and religion acts powerfully in its turn upon social customs. It surprises some that the Jew never carries on any manual trade; that he is invariably engaged in commerce or in some profession not manual. The reason is to be found in the necessity under which he is of observing his religious rites. No Jew can be apprenticed; for he could not, if he were bound to a master, give himself up to prayer, observe Saturday, or eat the flesh of animals killed according to Hebrew usage. As he can never be apprenticed, he is never a workman. Hence he must needs devote himself exclusively to business, to finance, or follow one of the liberal professions.

When an Israelite is removed from his usual surroundings, — if he is put in prison, for instance, — the rabbi hastens to him. But what is his object? To take the necessary steps to insure the prisoner a supply of animal food killed by the sword. Nothing else troubles him half so much.

We may laugh at this constant care on the part of the Jews to follow out the precepts of their religion; we should rather admire them. Happy are the people who have a religion, who look upon it as good, and faithfully follow its commands!

CHAPTER XI.

I WOULD fain remove from the mind of my reader the idea that the considerations set forth in this work are mere dreams of my imagination, a sort of romance of nature, intended to connect, by a general theory, the phenomena of earthly life with astronomic worlds. I will therefore give the scientific facts which led me to the system wrought out here concerning the destiny of man after death.

The essential basis of all these views is clearly the principle of the existence of the soul and its immortality. Volumes have been written on this subject; and after all, the conclusion has been pretty generally reached that the existence of the soul is not capable of proof. Mere sentiment, personal conviction, aside from all logical proof, may, it is said, establish the fact of the presence within us of an immaterial, indestructible principle, which is, in all languages, called the soul, or the inner sense.

Such is not our opinion. The existence of the soul is, to our thinking, capable of proof. It can be proved oy various facts borrowed from the observation of every day.

The first of these facts to be cited relates to the impressions which man feels and expresses when he is subjected to the insensibility produced by the inhalation of ether, chloroform, or other agents now used in great numbers to cause insensibility in surgical operations.

Go into a hospital ward as the surgeon lulls to sleep with chloroform or sulphuric ether some sufferer about to undergo a serious operation. After a few moments' inhalation of the stupefying fumes, the patient becomes absolutely proof against pain, and the surgeon can hew his flesh and he know nothing of it, utter no cry, show no smallest sign of feeling, either general or local.

And while the steel divides, tears, cuts his muscles, wrings his nerves, removes a tumor, withdraws a sequestrum of bone, and sometimes amputates an entire limb, not only does the person operated on feel no pain, but he is most usually soothed by delicious dreams. He laughs, he sings, he sees smiling landscapes ; he is happy, and he expresses aloud his pleasure and content. The operation over, when he comes to his senses, he complains that he was too quickly snatched from his sweet dreams ; and it is with the utmost surprise that he sees the mutilation of his body. He was wholly unconscious of the operation ; he only knows that it was done by seeing the wound.

This is an every-day occurrence in the ordinary case of a surgical operation which occupies but eight or ten minutes. But within the last twenty years, surgery has made an immense advance. We no longer have operations of eight or ten minutes in length; we have an instrumental labor carried on in the centre of living tissues, lasting an hour, sometimes two hours, and even more. Ovariotomy, now forever won by surgical art, consists, as we all know, in opening the abdomen, and removing from a woman an ovary which is too large, diseased, or lacerated. The operation lasts at least an hour and a half; so that the chloroform or ether must be given several times to keep up insensibility.

During ovariotomy performed under the influence of ether or chloroform, the woman not only feels no pain from the division of the walls of her stomach, from the search for the tumor, its extraction, or the lengthy dressing of the wounds which close this dreadful scene; but she is usually lost in a perfect ecstasy of happiness. She sees her children, her nearest and dearest; she smiles upon them, and in a continual dream she expresses by her exalted language the joy that she feels.

The continued success of ovariotomy has led our surgeons to go on in the same way, and to-day laparotomy — that is to say, the opening of the walls of the abdomen at various heights — has become a common operation to facilitate the search for and extirpation of a tumor or an abscess, or the discovery of some internal obstruction. And not only is laparotomy used in the execution of an operation indicated in advance, but it also serves as a simple method of diagnostic. To open the stomach of a man or woman, to settle an uncertain symptom, to make sure whether or no the liver, spleen, pancreas, a part of the intestine, the bladder, or the kidneys are the seat of some disease, has now become a common surgical custom. The examination made, the walls of the stomach are sewed up again; a large antiseptic dressing is applied, and at the end of a few days the patient is as well as ever. This bloody operation is very seldom fatal, and it almost always makes the diagnosis a sure thing. Now, diagnosis, treatment, and cure go hand in hand.

The " Medical Union " reports, in May, 1892, the case of Dr. M—— of Paris, who, having long suffered from internal pains attributed to an intestinal cancer, and thinking himself doomed, nevertheless put himself in the hands of a friend who was a surgeon, begging him to locate the seat of his trouble by means of laparotomy. The surgeon opened his stomach, reached the liver, and grasping the small lobe of that organ in both hands, discovered that it was the seat of a large abcess. The skilful operator plunged a bistoury into the abscess, drew off nearly a quart of pus, and sewed up the walls of the stomach. So that to-day Dr. M—— enjoys the best of health, and attends his clients with perfect ease.

Again, a foreign body sometimes drops into the stomach and threatens the life of an individual; for instance, a fork is swallowed, a foreign body is introduced into the stomach by the œsophagus, and will certainly cause a fatal perforation. The surgeon does not hesitate an instant; he opens the walls of the abdomen corresponding to the part of the stomach occupied by the foreign body; he then makes an incision in the stomach, and takes out the fork or whatever it may be. He sews up the walls of the viscus, then the skin; and the patient is saved.

Such are the wonders of laparotomy, one of the most precious conquests of modern surgery, based on the use of antiseptic dressings.

Operations of so grave a nature are necessarily very long, especially if we include the time required for dressing the wound. Well, the mental state manifested during an operation of brief duration in a person under anæsthetics is continued during these masterly performances, which require considerable time, and necessitate the repeated applications of the anæsthetic. During the entire time the patient does not for an instant cease to enjoy agreeable dreams, to feel happy, quiet, and serene, and to testify his joy by his words to all about him.

What conclusion should we draw from this persistence of the manifestations of the soul, coincident with the annihilation of bodily sensations? We must conclude that the soul is independent of the body; that we are composed of a material substance, and an invisible, active, and sentient spirit, which has nothing in common with the body, and which we call the soul. The anæsthetic agent separates — as it were, severs — soul and body, whose union composes the human aggregate. It shows us the soul sentient, vibrant, expressive, while the body is deprived of all feeling.

The phenomenon of anæsthesia, which makes the existence of the soul and the double spiritual and material nature of man so obvious, serves to explain what must occur at the moment of death.

A man in a state of anæsthesia is, so far as mere feeling goes, a sort of corpse; he is as unconscious of all outward impressions as a dead man; he is a *temporary corpse.* When the end of life comes, the corpse state is final and positive; and as the *temporary corpse* retained and still held fast within it the spiritual principle, even enhanced in its manifestations, the *actual corpse* must also retain for a certain space the soul, or spiritual principle. Whether it be, indeed, the surgeon's knife which hews the body of a living man, lost in a state of anæsthesia, or whether it be the gnawing of earthworms, or of animalculæ destroying organic tissues, or of legions of microbes, which devour the actual corpse, both are equally insensible to outward agents; and the actual corpse, as well as the temporary one, retains the impressionable soul for some time.

Dreams are another proof of the existence of the soul. When we yield to sleep, the majority of our senses and physiological functions are abolished; life, taste, hearing, smell, touch are suspended; sensibility is dulled. Circulation, respiration, and absorption alone go on in a sleeping man. And yet, in that body stripped of most of its vital attributes, something endures, and often even manifests a vast activity: this is thought. In dreams our thoughts are multiplied, and follow in strangely rapid succession. The mind not only continues to act, but it is sometimes singularly vigorous. The body is torpid, motionless; while the intellect is stimulated, and works with matchless energy.

The surgeon Philip Ricord, mentioned in an earlier chapter, once told me an anecdote of himself, but little known and yet very interesting. He was nightly beset with awful dreams, which took possession of him the instant that he fell asleep. He would then utter loud shrieks, grow angry, and give way to every violence; so that his manservant was obliged to watch with him all night, to restrain and quiet him. When morning came, he would wake calm and cheerful. Nobody guessed, from seeing him busy at the hospital or in his office with his usual occupations, that his nights were disturbed by fearful nightmares. His health was not impaired by this singular nervous anomaly. He died at the age of eighty-nine, having always retained great bodily vigor, and the reputation of being one of the wittiest men of his time.

Natural somnambulism, which is an astonishing and inexplicable form of dreaming, shows us, even more amply, the intellectual faculties working with strange activity, when sleep has done away with most of the physiological functions. A natural somnambulist does not see, hear, or feel, since he is asleep. But all at once he speaks, hears, sees, walks, acts, writes, composes speeches, verses, music, mathematical calculations, dramas, architectural plans or sketches. He performs manual labor, and not unskilfully; he walks on the roofs of houses, without a misstep, all to the great amazement of those who follow him and watch his movements with equal surprise and anxiety. He does not hear with his ears; he does not see with his eyes, which are closed; and his sensations of touch do not come from the organ of touch, the skin. The mind alone is active.

Does not such a state show us with glaring obviousness the distinction between body and soul? The body is deprived of its senses, while the soul is in full enjoyment of itself.

The body therefore is merely the covering of the spirit, the transparent veil of the soul. By themselves, our senses would give us no perception, if the soul did not exist. It is the soul that feels, hears, sees, and acts. The retina of the eye, which receives an impression of images; the mucous membrane of the mouth and nose, which gives us impressions of taste and smell; the skin, which directs touch, — are only skilful anatomical arrangements meant to transmit a sense of outward things to the soul, the true sovereign of the human aggregate. When the senses are silenced as in a state of anæsthesia, in sleep and in natural somnambulism, the soul acts alone, and dispenses with the aid of the senses and the absent functions.

Hypnotism, which has been so much discussed for the last ten years, is nothing but a more marked degree of somnambulism, artificially produced and maintained. Under the influence of certain manœuvres, as practised by the magnetizers of earlier times, or more simply, by the fixed contemplation of a shining object, and particularly by an acquired habit, a person falls into that extraordinary state which we call *hypnotism* (from ὕπνος, sleep), to which modern physicians have given so much study. In this state sensibility is abolished. We may pierce the subject with needles, prick his skin with sharp instruments, burn him, and even perform upon him surgical operations, without his showing the least sign of pain, without a change in his expression. And not only he does not feel any pain, but, like a person under the influence of chloroform, one who has been hypnotized speaks, answers questions, and bears himself as in the waking state.

A person who is hypnotized often falls into a catalepsy. At the clinics of Charcot, at the Salpêtrière, we see men or women, at the mere sound of a tom-tom or a tuning-fork, become suddenly cataleptic, — that is to say, their limbs stiffen, they take the most singular, most painful attitudes, and keep them up a very long time without showing any fatigue. Wounds, pricks are a matter of utter indifference to them; their living bodies are like corpses. And yet these corpses speak, answer, express the thoughts that occupy their mind, or follow the bent which we choose to give them. Do you not plainly see here the separation of soul and body?

Suggestion is often manifested in the hypnotic state. We know how much thought modern physicians and physiologists, as well as magistrates, moralists, and students of nature, have devoted to this singular moral state.

What phenomenon, indeed, is stranger than that of *suggestion?* The person hypnotized, being questioned by the doctor or hypnotizer, obeys, with perfect passivity, whatever orders may be given him. He walks, talks, acts, according to the commands laid upon him. He is like a slave in the hands of a master.

We also know that *spoken suggestion* may give place to *mental suggestion;* that is, without uttering a word, the physician or the magnetizer may make his wishes known to the subject, and compel him to perform whatever acts he chooses. He is made to drink a glass of water, which he is told is champagne, and he swallows it with delight. He is shown fruit which he is told is poison, and he turns from it in horror; etc.

Let us add that certain operators have succeeded in issuing their orders to those they hypnotize without speaking a word to them. The magnetizer thinks; and the person magnetized, understanding his thought, executes the order which was given to him mentally. Neither the one nor the other has any means of communication except their mutual thought!

I do not know how hypnotism and suggestion, whether simple or mental, are to be explained; I even doubt whether the true explanation will ever be found, and consider that this secret will forever remain one of the mysteries of nature to be added to so many others; but it is most evident that this strange physiological state gives us the most complete proof possible of the existence of the soul. The bodily functions are suppressed; those of the soul continue to act; and in the case of mental suggestion, we have two souls in relation, without any intermediary means of communication.

The fact of the existence of the soul is, we hope, amply proved by all the foregoing considerations; and this point gained, we proceed with our argument.

In the material world nothing is destroyed, nothing perishes; everything is indestructible, eternal. Chemists, from the time of Lavoisier, have taught us that there is never any destruction, but a mere transposition of matter, in combinations and de-compositions of simple or compound substances. So, too, throughout Nature, living or dead, nothing is destroyed, nothing disappears ; matter changes its position, that is all. The sand of the desert is nothing but the result of the disintegration and division by water of the rocks round about ; their composition proves this. The sand that covers the seashore has the same origin ; it comes from the disintegration of the rocks along the coast. Here we have pebbles ; there, sand ; but pebbles and sand are of the same chemical composition as the rocks close by.

The air which we breathe is the same which was breathed by men when first they appeared upon this globe. Indeed, the oxygen of that air has served, in presence of the solar light, for hundreds of centuries, for the respiration of primitive man, of animals and plants, as well as for the alteration and destruction of rocks. But animals and plants have restored oxygen and carbonic acid to the air by their normal physiological functions, — that is, by their nutrition in darkness. The nitrogen of the air, which entered temporarily into the compo-sition of plants and animals, was set free later on in consequence of other vital actions. Thus the oxygen, carbonic acid, and nitrogen, of which the air is made up, are not destroyed, but merely change their places upon the earth.

When the body of a man, an animal, or a plant is abandoned to corruption, it gives out carbonic acid gas and nitrogen, compounds of hydrogen and sulphur. But these very combinations serve to compose other living bodies; and these latter after death will render back the same gases; so that the oxygen, carbonic acid, and nitrogen are never destroyed, and still make up the air that we breathe.

As for water, which covers three quarters of the surface of our earth, and which, reduced to vapor, floats in the air as clouds or mist, we can readily prove that the same permanence holds true of it. It is not difficult to show that the fresh water of rivers and lakes, as well as the salt water that fills the beds of seas, is indestructible, immutable; and that the water which we drink, that which makes up the clouds, that which flows in the bed of rivers or seas, is the same which our remote ancestors in primitive ages drank and used.

This fact is made obvious by what is known in meteorology as the " distribution of moisture " over the globe.

When moist air, driven by the wind, rises along the sides of a mountain, it is chilled, and at a certain height it becomes cloud or mist. Rising higher, this cloud melts into rain. If this rain falls at a very great height, it is frozen and covers the top of the mountain with snow. The cooling of the air which occurs in these high regions is due to the rarefaction which it necessarily undergoes in the higher strata of the atmosphere. A few hundred yards more suffice, at this elevation, to lower the temperature by one or more degrees. Thus we can understand what a vast quantity of snow must result from the condensation of the vapors contained in those great volumes of air laden with aqueous vapor which the winds bear from rivers and streams to the peaks of the Alps, Cordilleras, and Himalayas.

The water which falls on the heights is filtered through the earth ; it reappears later on and lower down in the form of springs, which descend into the valleys.

At the same time the annual melting of the snows which crown lofty peaks, abundantly feeds the little rivers running down from the mountains ; so that after the winter floods, which result from the rains of that season, come the summer floods caused by the melting of the snow.

Thus huge masses of water are constantly circulating between the atmosphere and the earth ; they fall continually as rain and snow, and incessantly ascend as mists. This eternal interchange produces the " distribution of moisture " over the globe, the essential instrument of its fertility.

The salt waters of oceans and inland seas are no exception to this general law of exchange between earth and air. The ocean, that huge liquid reservoir, swallows up in its vast maw the offerings brought to it by living streams which have bathed two continents; and it returns these same waters to the air in the form of vapors, which again descend to earth as rain, snow, or dew. These waters return to the ocean through the channel of rivers and streams; and thus we have that eternal cycle, that endless journey, which makes these same waters serve for the support and renovation of organic life on the earth.

Thus, water, whether fresh or salt, is no more susceptible of destruction than rocks and the elements of the air. Like them, it does but change its place, but travel from the earth to great heights; but it endures such as it was constituted at the creation of the world.

When a plant withers and is scattered by the wind, do you think that the chemical elements which once composed it are destroyed? No; the products of their natural decomposition — carbonic acid gas, nitrogen, sulphuretted hydrogen, carbonated hydrogen, water, and mineral substances — are borne away by the wind, and reuniting later elsewhere, form new plants. The vital spark which created the first plants by fecundating the germs of their seeds still endures and gives birth to new vegetable life from the old elements. Let but the spring sun warm it, and the living principle contained in the seed once more begins to exert its mysterious influence; other plants grow, and are covered with leaves, buds, and flowers. Whether they vegetate at one point or another on the earth's surface, the primitive elements of those plants remain, and nothing can destroy them. They travel from one plant to another, but do not disappear.

The same considerations may be applied to the body of men and animals.

Thus, nothing in Nature is wiped out of existence, nothing is destroyed. Upon the earth there is nothing old and nothing new; all is eternal and indestructible. That which we call new is a mere figure of speech which we have invented to aid the weakness of our understanding. But in the creation everything is permanent. A star may be dashed to pieces in the depth of space; a new star will be made of the fragments. The parts which compose a planet can no more be destroyed than those that form a flower. We make a distinction between a planet and a flower, because one is greater than the other; but to Nature and to God, both infinite, there is neither great nor small. Tree and insect, grain of sand and mountain, infusoria and whale, kernel of wheat and man, are all of equal importance in the sight of Nature and of God.

In short, nothing perishes in the organic world, any more than it does in the mineral world; but everything changes and is outwardly modified.

But if nothing perishes on our earth, the soul can no more perish than can the air, water, plants, animals, and rocks. It must endure like them.

The soul, having the conditions of being and a life opposite to that of the body, cannot decay after the manner of the body. The body perishes, restoring its elements to the earth; but the soul, whose forces are the opposite of those of matter, cannot be destroyed as is the body. A simple, immaterial entity, it must endure in its integrity. A spiritual entity, when it is set free from the body, it must reappear entire in the medium where it is released.

J. J. Rousseau says in "Émile" : —

" When the union of soul and body is broken, I conceive that the one may be dissolved and the other preserved. Why should the destruction of one entail the destruction of the other? On the contrary, being by nature so different, they are by their union in an unnatural state; and when that union ceases, they both return to their natural condition. The active substance recovers all the force which it used to move the passive and inert substance. Alas! my defects make me but too well aware of it; man but half lives during his life, and the life of the soul only begins with the death of the body."

Leibnitz, in his " System of Theology," indulges in the following argument : —

" The soul is a substance. Now, no substance can wholly perish without actual annihilation, which would be a miracle; and as the soul has no parts, it cannot even be divided into various substances. Therefore the soul is naturally immortal."

Thus the soul not only exists, but is endued with immortality and indestructibility, in its quality of spiritual being.

We have a right to grant the immortal soul the power of removal, of changing its residence in the universe; and we are not forbidden to suggest, as the Hindoo religion and the ancient Egyptian religion allow, that the human soul may pass through various incarnations, and thanks to a series of transmigrations enacted in celestial space, may constitute a train of higher beings, coming after humanity in the hierarchy of living bodies.

The system evolved in the " To-morrow of Death," as well as in the present work, is not therefore the product of idle reveries or a flight of the imagination, but it rests upon a succession and a chain of scientific facts.

We admit that it is in interplanetary space that the soul, on leaving its earthly abode, will be incarnated in fresh living types. This is the place to explain why we assign the vast interplanetary regions to the human soul for its dwelling.

Ancient physicists said that " Nature abhors a vacuum;" and perhaps this idea was not so ingenuous as we now hastily imagine. In fact, every medium is inhabited by living beings, and indeed it is often the abode of a superabundant population. The earth's surface feeds a vast quantity of animate beings of all sizes, — some visible, others only recognizable through a microscope, on account of their extraordinary smallness. There is not a single point of the surface of the globe, when covered by vegetation, which does not contain organic beings, animal or vegetable, visible to the naked eye or to the eye armed with a microscope.

The air, like the surface of the earth, is occupied by visible animals and invisible animalculæ; it is filled with vegetable spores and animal germs. Through the air are transmitted the infectious germs of epidemic diseases; in the air float the eggs of many inferior beings, as well as vegetal seeds to be developed later on the earth.

Fresh waters contain a quantity of visible beings, plants, fish, mollusks, articulates, zoophytes, and microscopic organisms, not to be distinguished by the naked eye, but recognizable with a magnifying-glass.

The seas, which occupy three quarters of the surface of the globe, have also their animal population, abundant and varied. Naturalists believed, but a short time since, that no living being existed in the lowermost depths of the sea, by reason of the enormous pressure from above and the absence of all light at such great depths. We accepted this theory, and it will be found stated as a fact in my works. Scientific progress now utterly contradicts naturalists upon this point; and they in turn loudly applaud, for a whole world of submarine beings of an order hitherto unsuspected is offered for their study.

We now know, thanks to the many submarine explorations and recent dredgings undertaken by different well-informed nations, that the bed of the sea contains an animal population as abundant as that which swims on higher levels. The fish, zoophytes, mollusks, etc., which occupy the lower regions of the sea, under fearful pressure, in absolute darkness, are blind, and possess a special organization which enables them to live in spite of the tremendous pressure which they endure.

Thus, all natural media, whether solid, liquid, or gaseous, are filled with living beings. Why should the ether — that is, the fluid which occupies interplanetary space — be destitute of them? Why should the vast spaces which divide the stars one from another be empty?

It is in virtue of this consideration that we take interplanetary ether to be the abode of re-arisen man. We might no doubt give him other planets than the earth for his home, and suppose that the superhuman being journeys from planet to planet, in the course of his successive metempsychoses. But in our opinion the number of planets in our solar system is too small to afford shelter to so many living phalanxes. We prefer to place them in ether, whose extent is limitless. Let us add that this it is that leads us to give the superhuman being the wings which Christian tradition attributes to angels and cherubim.

In our system, the superhuman being, dwelling

in interplanetary regions, is made up of a soul and a very airy body. This is the logical consequence of the organism peculiar to earth-born man : it is by analogy that we give to the superhuman being the physical constitution of earth-born man.

We next admit that the interplanetary individual dies and is born again, to pass into a new body, of yet more exquisite organization. This, again, is the logical sequence of what goes before.

As the final term of a long series of existences, we believe that the dweller in ethereal realms will end by falling into the sun, which absorbs him, and that he becomes a part of the radiant orb. We described at some length, in the " To-morrow of Death," the universal part which the sun plays in terrestrial phenomena. The source of light, heat, electricity, magnetism, and motion, the sun is probably also the cause of organic life and of the intelligence peculiar to living beings. Thus we admit that the central orb of our world is the seat of divine power, that which regulates the movement of the planets, as well as the evolution of life and of souls, in the beings inhabiting them. Having become a part of the " Divine Sun," the superhuman being, therefore, thus takes part in the government of the solar world to which he belongs.

We are guided in this thought by a consideration of the immensity of the part allotted to divine authority. It seems to us impossible that a single personality can suffice for the direction of the entire universe. Each sun, each star must be the seat of some divinity, who rules its existence ; and the supreme God, Jehovah, must reside at the central point of the combined orbits of all solar systems, at the mysterious point around which the stars, with their train of orbs and satellites, revolve. Emanations from the different stars, converging at this one point, in our opinion, compose the sovereign God. Indeed, unity cannot exist in the government of the worlds, by reason of the vast extent of space. Only a collectivity of divine powers can carry out the functions of the general government of the universe.

The reader will excuse the boldness of such views. In striving to explain the destiny of man after his death, we rely upon scientific reasoning and analogy. If we are mistaken, the blame rests with that moral instrument called logic, and with its consequence, philosophical analogy.

Such are the considerations, borrowed from natural and cosmic science, which have guided us in the conception of our system.

CHAPTER XII.

IT seems proper, in closing, to sum up the facts and ideas scattered through this volume, and to deduce their natural consequences.

From our review, in preceding chapters, we find that none of the religions now existing is fitted to banish from the heart of man the forbidding fears inspired by the idea of death. Neither Buddhism, with its distressing nihilism; nor Brahminism, with its hopeless fatality; nor Christianity, with its indefinitely delayed last judgment; nor Mahometanism, nor Judaism, which merely reproduce the old legend of heaven and hell, derived from antiquity and Christianity, — can inspire a man with courage to face with steadfast eye and quiet soul the moment of his end. Modern philosophy alone, based on science and reason, can dispel his fears. It shows him the reward instantly bestowed for a virtuous and honorable life. It asserts that he who has deserved it by his honesty, by upright practices, by the constant application of his free will to just and virtuous deeds, and by the cultivation of his mind and increase of his knowledge, shall enter, after his earthly end, into a new domain, where he shall assume the attributes of a superior being, — what we have called the " super-human being " and what the Church styles " angel ; " and that he shall pass the happiest of existences in the celestial abode, with the prospect of a continued growth of his intellectual and moral faculties.

As we have said, the intellect of man, born again in glory, will grow in proportions not suspected by him.   The universe will appear to him as it really is, with its radiant sun, with its planets and their satellites, composing each sidereal world.   He will plainly see the heavenly orbs moving in their orbits, and comets furrowing that harmonious whole, with their brilliant trains.   The exact sciences will have no secrets for him.   Physics will tell him the laws of the mutual action of bodies one upon the other; chemistry the reason of reactions and the mode of formation of new compounds by the direct vision of the architectural arrangement of molecules. Mechanics will be made plain to him, with the general mathematical cause of the movement and equipoise of solids, liquids, and gases.

Living nature will have no more mysteries for him   than   inanimate   nature.   Organic   life   in plants, animals, and man will be laid bare to him, in its mechanism, in its essential cause, and in its results.

Social iniquities, of which the earth affords us a sad picture, will be unknown in that happy home, where all will be love, peace, and fraternity. Hate, jealous dissension, which are the attributes of earthly society, will be banished thence. Justice, absolute equity will govern the actions of the inhabitants of planetary ether.

Our relatives, our friends, those whom we love, and whom death has snatched from us, will meet us in our second existence; and we shall renew the relations of affection, tenderness, sympathy, and devotion which we kept up with them here.

The natural faculties which society frequently condemns to lie idle in earth-born man will be given full play, and we shall be exempt from the torture which consists in busying ourselves with things which we dislike, and neglecting the occupations toward which we are strongly drawn.

Tasks begun on earth and interrupted by death will be resumed; so that efforts put forth here and results attained will not be lost, but will serve to carry on and complete the schemes which death cut short.

We shall enter into relations with the great men who have honored humanity, and whom we desire to know. The heroes who left a brilliant record in history will be ready to talk with us, and to tell us the secret of their triumphs and glory.

Finally, if we continue in our second life to practise good works, to keep our mind in a state of progress, to increase our knowledge, to bring our soul into a state of absolute perfection, we shall deserve to rise to a higher sphere in the heavenly domain, where beings have yet greater intellectual power and more numerous faculties.

By losing more and more of the material element which forms a part of their being, the inhabitants of those high spaces may ascend another round of the ladder in the hierarchy of the elect; just as a balloon rises higher and higher in the air as it throws out the ballast which delayed its ascent.

In the upper regions of the sky, which will be the scene of our third existence, the proportion of the material element in the superhuman being will be more and more reduced; his body will become more and more refined and aeriform, and his soul endued with more and more exquisite qualities.

After a new series of these celestial progressions and promotions, whose number and duration no one can possibly fix, our souls, attaining to a state of pure essence, will finally enter the central orb of our earth, the sun, whose inhabitants, possessed of immortality, will form a part of the divinity who rules over the government of this astronomic system.

Such is the career of light and glory reserved, in our opinion, for the beings who spring from earthly humanity and planetary humanity.

But to merit such sovereign joys, man should devote himself throughout his sojourn upon earth to improving himself without pause, to purifying his soul, to loving his fellow-men, to doing good in every direction, to increasing his knowledge and the compass of his mind. He who, on the contrary, perseveres in his state of immorality, vulgarity, injustice, or ignorance ; he who performs criminal or merely culpable acts will be condemned to begin his earthly career afresh, until he shall reach the perfection requisite to leave our imperfect globe.

We said, in the first chapter of this work, that to us man is the analogue of a certain class of animals ; namely, insects. We claimed that in life man represents the caterpillar stage of an insect ; his corpse is the chrysalis, and when re-arisen, he is the analogue of the airy butterfly. We have tried to define the higher faculties peculiar to a human being born again into perfection and glory, and we have traced the itinerary of his long journey through the vast extent of the heavens. We have shown that man, doomed on earth to inevitable suffering and constant misfortunes, will find, in the succession of new existences awaiting him on the other side of the tomb, infinite joys, and at the same time the reward of his virtues. Whence we must conclude that man should bear with resignation and courage the trials and sorrows of the present life, and that he should look forward without alarm or secret anguish, but rather with a steadfast heart, to the moment of his approaching end.

We have grouped, in a rapid synthesis, the philosophical considerations presented in this work. If the reader reject them, we must ask him to furnish another explanation of man's destiny and the cause of his presence upon earth.

Why, indeed, are we here on this sad planet, which is our forced abode? Did we ask to come hither? Why are we compelled to live here, subject to so many ills, weighed down by so much grief and toil, the victims of so much injustice and deception? Had we been consulted, we should have refused to pass through such a painful career; were we asked to begin it again, we should refuse with great emphasis. We came into life without our wish, and we leave it in spite of ourselves. Our presence on earth can only be explained by admitting that our sojourn here is merely a transient incident in the continuity of our existences, only a link in the chain of our successive lives; and that we are undergoing a season of trial and preparation before continuing our journey and ending it elsewhere.

If human existence were a final state, a day with no to-morrow, it would be the most flagrant injustice, the most cruel irony, an unending cause for despair and tears to the unhappy creatures doomed to such a fate. The doctrine which we offer is a perfect explanation of our presence on this globe, telling us, as it does, that our earthly life is but a transitory period, which prepares humanity for other destinies, and assures it a career of constant happiness, in the depths of eternal light, face to face with the marvels of creation, and in the immediate presence of God.

Let us say, in conclusion, that in so far as the doctrine of punishment and reward after death is concerned, none of the religions actually professed on the earth satisfy the heart or mind. They are pure legends, sometimes simple and artless, like those which sprang from the Oriental imagination, and which were exalted into dogmas by Buddhist, Brahmin, and Mahometan sages; sometimes terrible, like those forged by fierce theologians in the Middle Ages for the guidance of Christians. Conceived at a period of universal ignorance, these dogmas are absolutely opposed to the laws of Nature, and to sustain their worn-out scaffolding, we have nothing but a would-be *revelation* and *faith*, — that is to say, words very ingeniously invented to cut short all discussion, to deify absurdity, to sanctify an impossibility, to raise indifference upon a shield.

Hypothesis for hypothesis, I have seen fit to adopt another, which I did not, moreover, wholly imagine, but which I found in part in the writings of certain great thinkers of our age, — Jean Reynaud, Dupont (of Nemours), Charles Bonnet, and Pezzani. The theory of the transmigration of souls and of celestial resurrections has this advantage, — that it was conceived in an enlightened era, and is based on a knowledge of nature and the arrangement of the universe.

These ideas, which now seem strange and hazardous, will be the truths of the coming century ; for often last night's heresy is to-morrow's dogma. It is the dawn of the new day whence pure light shall come, in a future not far removed, to dispel the shadows of the superstitions of former ages.

THE END.

MESSRS. ROBERTS BROTHERS' PUBLICATIONS.

THE TO-MORROW OF DEATH;

OR,

THE FUTURE LIFE ACCORDING TO SCIENCE.

By *LOUIS FIGUIER.*

TRANSLATED FROM THE FRENCH, BY S. R. CROCKER. 1 vol. 16mo. $1.50.

From the Literary World.

As its striking, if somewhat sensational title indicates, the book deals with the question of the future life, and purports to present "a complete theory of Nature, a true philosophy of the Universe." It is based on the ascertained facts of science which the author marshals in such a multitude, and with such skill, as must command the admiration of those who dismiss his theory with a sneer. We doubt if the marvels of astronomy have ever had so impressive a presentation in popular form as they have here. . . .

The opening chapters of the book treat of the three elements which compose man, — body, soul, and life. The first is not destroyed by death, but simply changes its form; the last is a force, like light and heat, — a mere state of bodies; the soul is indestructible and immortal. After death, according to M. Figuier, the soul becomes incarnated in a new body, and makes part of a new being next superior to man in the scale of living existences, — the superhuman. This being lives in the ether which surrounds the earth and the other planets, where, endowed with senses and faculties like ours, infinitely improved, and many others that we know nothing of, he leads a life whose spiritual delights it is impossible for us to imagine. . . .

Those who enjoy speculations about the future life will find in this book fresh and pleasant food for their imaginations; and, to those who delight in the revelations of science as to the mysteries that obscure the origin and the destiny of man, these pages offer a gallery of novel and really marvellous views. We may, perhaps, express our opinion of "The To-Morrow of Death" at once comprehensively and concisely, by saying that to every mind that welcomes light on these grave questions, from whatever quarter and in whatever shape it may come, regardless of precedents and authorities, this work will yield exquisite pleasure. It will shock some readers, and amaze many; but it will fascinate and impress all.

Sold everywhere. Mailed, post-paid, by the Publishers,

ROBERTS BROTHERS, BOSTON

THE SOURCES OF CONSOLATION
IN HUMAN LIFE.

By Rev. WILLIAM R. ALGER,

Author of "The Genius of Solitude," "Friendships of Women," etc.

16mo. Cloth. Price, $1.50.

The writer of this volume, a well-known minister among the Unitarians of New England, having reached nearly threescore years and ten, fittingly takes in hand a topic of special interest to older people and not without attraction even to the young. He is able to speak from experience as well as observation, and to give additional force to what he has to say by having himself seen and known how continually human beings need consolation amid the troubles of life. His purpose here is to furnish a full discussion of the subject and a setting forth of the necessity, the ground, and the essential method of consolation. Nothing doubting that he has something to say which is worth saying, "he hopes to communicate his message in a winsome and effective way, free from the perfunctory quality and mawkish traits so prominent in most books dedicated to this subject."

Mr. Alger arranges the matter of his volume in ten chapters. First, the consolations in human life are classified and illustrated; next, the weeping of humanity in all ages, or "the history of tears," is given. Following this touching chapter comes appropriate and tolerably full considerations of the relation between the calamities of men and the providence of God; the mystery of early deaths, or the mission of the little child; "partings in human life, or the farewells of the world;" "our human need of faith in an all-pervasive and overruling God;" the "true lessons of grief;" the "tragedy of the sea, and its removal;" the "grounds for a cheerful trust in the perfection of divine providence;" "the consolation and true interpretation of the origin, office, and meaning of death;" and in a concluding essay his view of the "latest form of theology, the divine purpose in the universe a perfect consolation for every ill."

These are interesting passages, and they show with what thought and vigor the whole volume is written. The very title of the book will attract attention; and the reader who once opens it will read far into it and, finally, through it. Mr. Alger's style has a pervading charm, and his wide survey of a theme that appeals to the whole human race is made with freshness, force, and originality. — *New York Times.*

Sold by all Booksellers. Mailed, post-paid, by the Publishers,

ROBERTS BROTHERS, BOSTON.